FATAL FROST

Books by Nancy Mehl

From Bethany House Publishers

ROAD TO KINGDOM

Inescapable
Unbreakable
Unforeseeable

FINDING SANCTUARY

Gathering Shadows
Deadly Echoes
Rising Darkness

DEFENDERS OF JUSTICE

Fatal Frost

DEFENDERS OF JUSTICE | 01

FATAL FROST

NANCY MEHL

BETHANYHOUSE

a division of Baker Publishing Group
Minneapolis, Minnesota

Published by Bethany House Publishers
11400 Hampshire Avenue South
Bloomington, Minnesota 55438
www.bethanyhouse.com

Bethany House Publishers is a division of
Baker Publishing Group, Grand Rapids, Michigan

Printed in the United States of America

Library of Congress Control Number: 2016942747

ISBN 978-0-7642-1777-7

Scripture quotations are from the King James Version of the Bible or from the Holy Bible, New International Version®. NIV®. Copyright © 1973, 1978, 1984, 2011 by Biblica, Inc.™ Used by permission of Zondervan. All rights reserved worldwide. www.zondervan.com

The poem "To My Son, the Officer" by Shaen Layle has been used by permission of the author.

This is a work of fiction. Names, characters, incidents, and dialogues are products of the author's imagination and are not to be construed as real. Any resemblance to actual events or persons, living or dead, is entirely coincidental.

Cover design by Wes Youssi / M 80 Design
Cover photography by Steve Gardner, PixelWorks Studios, Inc.

Nancy Mehl is represented by The Steve Laube Agency.

16 17 18 19 20 21 22   7 6 5 4 3 2 1

This book is dedicated to the brave men and women of law enforcement. Thank you for your incredible commitment and sacrifice. You are true heroes, protectors of the people. I'm proud to bring you to life on these pages, and I pray that in some small way I've shone a light on your indomitable and courageous spirit.

God bless you.

TO MY SON, THE OFFICER

We started out so differently, you know:
you were the helpless one—suspended, unseen,
in the cradle of my ribs. My body, a shield for yours,
a galaxy of starry future. But years passed until

you were the helpless one (suspended, unseen)
no more. A protector yourself, shelter for others.
A galaxy of starry future. But years passed until
the scent of lilies hung thick in the air.

No more a protector yourself. Shelter for others
now only in the Redeemer, an embrace at your casket.
The scent of lilies hangs thick in the air,
as blue turns to eternal gold.

Shaen Layle

CHAPTER
ONE

The seemingly deserted street was lined with empty houses, their windows as blank and vacant as the eyes of those who had become casualties in St. Louis's war on heroin. Deputy U.S. Marshal Mercy Brennan gazed out the window of the black van as cold tendrils of rain slid down the darkened glass next to her, reminding her of tears. It was as if the tortured city of St. Louis wept because of the treacherous drug that had invaded her. The influx of cheap heroin had turned neighborhoods into war zones. The gangs that claimed ownership over their communities were killing men, women, and children for the right to rule. Crime was out of control, and many good people were trapped in their homes, praying they or their loved ones wouldn't become the next victims of the violence that raged around them.

In the background, her team leader barked out orders. Tonight, the U.S. Marshals, in conjunction with the police, were hitting a beehive—a house used for the distribution of the noxious poison. Normally the Marshals would leave an operation like this to the local police or the Drug Enforcement Administration, but this time there was a good chance they'd be able to get their hands on Darius Johnson, a notorious gang leader who had recently started calling himself D-Money. Just a few hours before the planned operation, the police received a tip that Johnson had been seen hanging around this house. It was possible he was hiding out here. The Marshals had been trying for months to apprehend him on a federal fugitive felon warrant, but Johnson had evaded them. He'd actually been in custody a year ago, arrested for the distribution of narcotics. Unfortunately the prosecutor's office had released him back out on the streets for reasons no one in law enforcement could understand. One week later, Johnson hunted down the officer who made the arrest and shot him. Thankfully, Officer Mike Galloway was still alive, but he'd never walk again.

Mercy's best friend, Lieutenant Tally Williams, looked at her and winked. The nervousness in her stomach quelled some. She and Tally were both worried about this raid. Just before they left the station, they were informed that Johnson may have been tipped off. That the gang knew they were coming. She could only hope it wasn't true. Bringing Johnson to justice had become more than a job. It was a mission.

Their team leader cleared his throat, the sound reverberating in the silence as the van slowed and turned off its lights. "Intel says our target was seen in the residence three doors down and to your right," he said in a low voice. "We're not sure where the players are positioned, so we're playing hide-and-seek tonight. As always, try to approach the residence without alerting any-one. Our main goal is to find Johnson, but we also need to shut down the beehive, arrest whoever's inside, and confiscate drugs, weapons, and money. Thankfully the weather is cooperating. There's a good chance our targets are holed up inside. Sergeant Morris will lead the search." He pointed to several officers, including Tally. "You'll go with me through the front door. Stay alert. There are definitely guns inside. We don't want anyone hurt if at all possible." He pointed at Mercy and two other deputy Marshals. "You set and hold the perimeter. Be on the lookout for runners. Don't let anyone get away." He paused for a moment. "Look, we're all hoping Johnson is here, yet we have to stick to normal procedure. If we get lucky, I want to make one thing very clear. I want him alive, folks. I mean it. We won't honor Mike by killing this scumbag. We need him to answer for his crimes. We can't allow this bust to get dirty. Got it?"

Everyone in the vehicle nodded or grunted their assent. Many times, raids were exciting. Adrenaline-charged. But tonight officers and deputies were quiet. They all wanted Darius Johnson off the streets. There was absolute silence in the van as they waited for the order to start the operation. Mercy clasped her AR-15 rifle against her vest. All LEOs had on their tactical gear. Underneath it, most of the cops wore uniforms. The Marshals and the police detectives were dressed in plain clothes. With their coats zipped up against the cold, the only way to tell the difference between the various law enforcement agencies represented were the words stamped on the back of their jackets. But tonight, departments, even rank, didn't matter. They were one unit with one goal.

Mercy's grip tightened on her rifle as the sound of the rain intensified. It was as if it were directly connected to the increased concentration surging through all the members of the unit. Seconds later, the commander yelled, "Go! Go! Go!"

The doors of the van burst open and everyone jumped out, intent on taking their assigned position. Mercy ran around to the back of the house, keeping as low to the ground as possible, thankful for the dark and the heavy showers. They were shields of protection until the residence was breached. She crouched down near the back door. Seeing another deputy take his place at the back of the yard, she signaled him with a wave of her hand to let him know she was in place. He signaled back. They were set. They both had to be ready to move quickly. If they had the right house, there would be runners. There were always runners.

Seconds later, she heard a shout. "Police! We have a warrant!" Several other voices echoed the same warning. Then came a loud bang, making it clear the front door had been broken down. Everyone inside the house was now aware of the raid. Mercy pulled the flashlight from her belt and trained it on the back door, her rifle held firmly with her other hand.

"Over there!"

Mercy swung her flashlight toward a lone figure running away from the house. He must have exited through a basement window. "Watch the door," she shouted to the other deputy. She sprinted after the runner, identifying herself as a police officer and commanding him to stop. Even though she was actually with the Marshals' office, calling herself a cop made it simpler for everyone to understand, especially the perps.

It was obvious this guy wasn't going to make it easy for either one of them. As she raced through an adjoining yard, a woman came out onto her back porch and began screaming obscenities at Mercy, ordering her to get off her property. Mercy swung her flashlight toward the woman and instructed her to get inside the house, but this seemed to incense her even more. Mercy had no choice but to ignore the irate resident and stay focused on the fleeing suspect. The icy rain not only made it hard to see, but the ground was also slick and Mercy slipped several times. Hopefully the suspect was having the same problem. As she rounded the backyard, she spotted someone in the alley. As she approached, the figure turned to face her. A streetlamp revealed a gun in his hand.

Mercy dropped her flashlight and took her stance. She raised her rifle to firing position. "Put it down now," she shouted. "Drop the gun or I'll fire." She was close enough to see fear on the man's face. Unfortunately it wasn't Darius Johnson.

She didn't want to shoot him, but if he didn't comply with her order, she might not have a choice. Instead of lowering his gun, he raised the barrel. In that instant, Mercy hesitated. For just a moment. That one second of uncertainty cost her. She felt the first bullet strike her vest. The second pierced her shoulder, and searing pain knocked the gun out of her hand, sending her to the ground. The shooter advanced slowly, the apprehension gone from his expression. It had been replaced with hate and victory. He pointed his gun at her, and Mercy prepared herself for the bullet that would end her life. She wanted to scream out that she was only twenty-six. Too young to die. But she knew the man with the gun wouldn't care.

As expected, she heard the sound of a shot, but surprisingly the expression on the suspect's face changed once again. This time he looked shocked. As he fell to the ground, Mercy heard Tally's voice calling her name.

Then there was only darkness.

CHAPTER
TWO

Angel Vargas pushed back the revulsion he felt as he looked into the face of a man he'd sooner shoot than speak to. Darius Johnson was a pathetic, dim-witted narcissist who saw himself as someone forceful—someone to be reckoned with. To Vargas he was nothing more than a cockroach. Something to be stepped on once his plan was successful. His father needed Johnson—for now. But once everything was under way, he'd squash him like the bug he really was. When the idiot shot a cop, the cartel almost took him out then. Thankfully their association with the gang leader wouldn't last much longer. Too bad the guy was so clueless he'd never see it coming. He was as good as dead already.

"I don't get it," Johnson huffed. "Why not just shoot this pig and be done with it? Ain't no reason to go to all this trouble."

"Because, Darius, shooting police officers will bring us the kind of notice we don't want. People are already up in arms about that crippled cop. Your stupidity brought a lot of heat down on all of us. Now isn't the time to go after more of them.

Not only will this work, no one will suspect us. And if the cops' attention is directed somewhere else, it'll make our lives much easier. I can bring in three times the stash you've been getting. It will open the door to everything we want. And the cops get the blame. Not you. Not me."

Darius frowned. "I ain't Darius no more."

Vargas shook his head. "Sorry." What was the ridiculous name the gang leader wanted to be called? He racked his brain for a few seconds before remembering. "I meant D-Money."

Darius offered him a self-satisfied smile. "But won't they know this ain't real, man? I mean, you and I know who hit this dude, and it sure wasn't no lady cop."

Vargas sighed inwardly. He needed Johnson and the other gang leaders in St. Louis to pull off the cartel's plan. They were coarse, mostly uneducated, and could act like rabid dogs when they were crossed. But they'd built a powerful kingdom based on fear, and fear worked to Vargas's advantage. In fact, the cartels thrived on it. Fear was power—and the gangs had power in several major cities. He and his father had hatched a plan that could ignite a time bomb capable of tearing the nation apart while strengthening the cartel and bringing in more money than they'd ever dreamed of.

"It will work," Vargas said, trying to hold on to his last shred of patience. "We'll be releasing these all over the country. It's easy. We shoot somebody, and then we fix the video to make it look like a cop did it. Show the video to the cop, threaten to release it, and we've got him dancing to our tune. If he resists, we send the video to the media. While the city burns, we take over. No one will care if it's real. A cop shooting an unarmed citizen will cause immediate chaos. Riot first, ask questions later. The truth gets lost in the mayhem."

Darius jumped to his feet. "Whaddaya mean it ain't real, man? The pigs are always stoppin' our cars. Throwin' us around. Tryin' to make us look like criminals. They're killers, and they gotta be stopped. Permanently."

Vargas heard this same song from every gang member he'd talked to. It was their mantra. Vargas could have pointed out that Darius and his thug pals were the actual criminals, as well as the real killers. But these guys had no use for common sense or reasoning. They were beyond it. Hopped up on drugs and violence, full of twisted logic, they could be easily manipulated if you knew which buttons to push. Drugs, money, power, and hatred for law enforcement. Appeal to those things and they were puppets dangling on strings that the cartel was holding. They were perfect for Vargas's purposes. Right now the gangs were a sure means to a lucrative end.

"Settle down. I have no love for the police." He pushed Darius's computer back toward him. "Don't let anyone else see this. In fact, delete it after you show it to the cop. Make sure he knows it will go viral if he betrays us. If that happens, his darling daughter's career will be ruined. After he leaves, delete everything. Do you understand me?"

Darius nodded. "I'm not stupid, man. I get it."

"Have you erased all our emails and the original video you shot on your phone?"

Darius sank back down into his chair as if he'd lost all his enthusiasm for the conversation. Vargas assumed his Swiss cheese brain had moved on to something else.

"Yeah, it's all gone. And after the cop sees his kid's future, I'll delete the new video you sent me. I promise. No one will never know nuthin' 'bout either one of them, aight?"

Vargas let his eyes travel up and down the gang leader's thin frame. Darius wore untied sneakers, blue jeans dropped low to show his blue boxers, and a white T-shirt. The uniform of the Crips. Vargas shook his head. If his son ever walked around with his pants hanging down like that, he'd beat him within an inch of his life. When Vargas was in school, kids who didn't know how to pull their pants up were sent to special schools.

"Give me your phone," Vargas said.

"Man, I told you I deleted the real shooting."

"I said, give me the phone." Vargas held his hand out. Darius swore and took the cellphone out of his pocket. He handed it to Vargas, who quickly ran through it, checking pictures and videos. Most of the things he found disgusted him, yet the original video wasn't there. Vargas gave Darius back his phone.

"Meet with the cop no later than tomorrow."

"You know he ain't caused us no trouble. Likes the money we give him. I don't know why you're worryin' about this dude, man. He's okay."

"He's important. We need him to achieve our goals here. I just want to make sure he stays 'okay.' This city is the perfect place to test our plan."

Vargas stood to his feet. Darius had been holed up for a long time in a house that belonged to another banger's mother. The place was dirty and smelled of sweat and hopelessness. Vargas couldn't take it another moment. Law enforcement might call him a criminal—just like Darius—but they weren't the same. Not at all. Vargas had a nice home. A family. Anyone looking in from the outside would think he was exactly what he purported to be: a successful businessman and church leader. In his mind, it was true. It's just that his business was drugs, and the bodies left behind were unfortunate casualties.

He shook the gang leader's hand and walked out of the house, wiping his fingers on his jacket. He could now assure his father that Darius would do what he was told. After that, Darius would die. Either by his hand or by some other gang leader's.

Either way, his fate didn't matter to Vargas.

And neither did the cop's.

CHAPTER
THREE

"You look good."

Mercy nodded at her father. Although she still kept him at arm's length, she'd agreed to meet him for an occasional lunch. After the shooting, he'd tried to see her, but she'd sent him away. Finally, after several weeks, Tally had convinced her that she should at least let him know she was on the mend.

"No matter what he did, he's still your father," he'd told her.

Tally had worshiped her father when they were kids. When Nick abandoned his family, Tally had been wounded as well. Tally had never known his dad, and Nick was the only older man in his life. The only man he respected anyway. Mercy was sure Tally's desire to be a cop came from his feelings for Nick. When Nick came back to St. Louis and rejoined the police department, he and Tally seemed to pick up where they left off. But Mercy wasn't able to do that. She would never forgive her father for leaving.

Nick cleared his throat and stared down at his plate. "I'm glad you're okay. I came by the hospital several times."

"I'm fine." Mercy took a bite of her burnt-ends sandwich, and the juicy smoked flavor of the meat exploded in her mouth. Pappy's Smokehouse in St. Louis was the best barbecue in town. She ignored the twinge in her shoulder. "Takes more than a couple of bullets to bring me down."

"Good." Nick picked up his brisket sandwich and stared at it. He hadn't eaten much since they'd sat down. Mercy wondered if something was bothering him, but she didn't care enough to ask.

"You two doing okay?"

Mercy looked up at the waitress, who stood next to their table. She was focused on Nick. If Mercy's hair caught on fire, the girl probably wouldn't notice. Nick was a handsome man. His dark hair framed a rugged face, and his steel-blue eyes and long dark lashes caught the attention of most women. The fact that he obviously worked out didn't hurt either.

"We're good," he said, smiling up at her. She blushed at his attention. "Do you need anything, Mercy?" he asked, turning to look at her.

Mercy shook her head and sighed.

When the waitress finally left, she seemed disappointed that she wasn't able to do anything else for her good-looking customer.

"So when do you go back to full duty?"

Mercy shrugged. "When the staff psychiatrist clears me. This woman won't be happy unless I have a complete nervous breakdown. I've told her I'm fine, but she acts like I'm lying. It's ridiculous. She seems to think all cops are two seconds away from going nuts and shooting up the mall."

"The same thing happened to me. When you're shot, they assume it will mess with your head. If it doesn't, they get concerned. If you tell her you've had some sleepless nights, and you occasionally relive the shooting in your dreams, she'll decide you're normal and release you."

"I . . . I didn't know you'd been shot," Mercy said. "You've never mentioned it."

Nick gave her a slow smile. "It happened about five years ago. We weren't in touch, and I didn't think you'd be interested."

Mercy didn't acknowledge that he was right. "What happened?"

"My partner and I were looking for a guy who'd been robbing banks in Richmond. We got a tip that he'd holed up in a house on the west side. We were going up to the front door when he flung the door open and fired on us." He shrugged. "One bullet hit my vest, but the other grazed my neck." Nick pulled his collar down and pointed to a deep scar on the side of his neck that Mercy hadn't noticed before. It appeared to be more than just a graze.

"Looks serious."

Nick grunted. "Bled a lot, but I got through it. My partner took the guy down before he had time to shoot me again. Department shrink wouldn't believe I was okay. You know, emotionally, so I made up some stories and convinced him I was traumatized. Eventually he bought it and I was put back on full duty." He chuckled. "Makes you wonder. If you say you're fine, they take you off duty, but if you convince them you're messed up, they stick you back out there. No wonder cops have so many problems."

Mercy marveled at how similar she was to her father, even though they'd been apart for so long. "Thanks for the tip. I'll give it a try."

"Happy to help." He stared down at his plate for a moment before clearing his throat. Obviously he had something on his mind.

"What's up?" Mercy said finally.

"I know it's not my business," Nick said, "but I just wondered how that guy got the drop on you. How did he get off the first shot?"

Mercy's spine stiffened. No one else had asked this question. Tally had assumed the punk who shot her got a round off so quickly that Mercy hadn't had time to respond. But she knew it wasn't the truth. Now her dad asked the same question she'd been asking herself over and over. Though he was the last person she wanted to talk to about it, she found herself answering him.

"I'm afraid I hesitated. It was my first shooting. I mean, he was young, in his twenties. I know we're trained to take down anyone who puts our lives at risk, but . . ."

"But it's not as easy as it sounds?" Nick said.

Mercy nodded. "I guess that makes me a bad cop."

"No." Nick looked deeply into Mercy's eyes. "It makes you human, and that's the hallmark of a great cop."

"Except I could have died. Shooting first and asking questions later is tough. Hard to do when some people think we enjoy taking lives."

Nick sighed. "No one's perfect. We can't be more than human. We're not diplomats, we're enforcers. Protectors. We have to make split-second life-and-death decisions. Most of us are trying to do the best we can. Sometimes we're going to get it wrong." He shrugged. "The important thing—the thing that will keep you sane—is knowing who you are. If you start seeing yourself through the eyes of our detractors, it will cripple you. You'll never be able to do your job."

"Easier said than done."

Nick nodded. "Yeah, it is. But it's the only way to come out of this life in one piece."

Mercy watched as her father finally took a bite of his sandwich. What he'd said made sense. It helped. More than anything the shrink had said so far. She was trying to find a way to thank him for his advice when his expression changed. He was staring past her, looking out one of the big windows in the front of the restaurant. His eyes widened, and his jaw became tight.

"Is something wrong?" she asked.

"No," he said too quickly. "Everything's fine."

It was obvious to Mercy that he wasn't "fine." The look on his face was one she'd never seen before. Although she wanted to turn around to see what he was looking at, she resisted the impulse. If he'd recognized a perp, it was the worst thing she could do. But why didn't he just tell her the truth? Maybe she could help.

Then as quickly as the change in Nick came, it left. He looked relaxed again, and Mercy decided to let it pass. If he wanted her assistance, he'd have to let her know. She couldn't read his mind.

He asked about Tally, and they spent the rest of their lunch talking about him and his family. Mercy wondered if Nick would bring up her mother, but he didn't. When he first came to town and asked to see her, Mercy made it clear that his leaving had driven his ex-wife to alcoholism and had exacerbated her mental illness. While he'd seemed remorseful about the effect he'd had on his children, he didn't have much to say about Mercy's mom.

"Gina was never emotionally strong," he'd said. "I'm sorry

I hurt her by leaving, but even when I was with her, nothing made her happy. She was determined to be miserable. I just couldn't take it anymore."

And that was it. His attitude had infuriated Mercy, and it had taken months before she'd agreed to see him again. If he felt living with Gina was too much to bear, how did he expect his young kids to do it? Unfortunately, what he'd said was true. Her mother seemed determined to live in self-pity. Starting at age ten, Mercy spent most of her young life taking care of her mom. Trying to find a way to make her happy until Mercy finally realized it was impossible. Eventually the responsibility took a heavy toll. Between dealing with her mother and trying to take care of her younger brother, she'd worn herself to a frazzle. If it hadn't been for Tally, she wasn't sure what would have happened to her. He gave her the courage to move out and join the police force.

Her mother had become distraught when Mercy told her she was leaving. She'd done everything she could think of to get Mercy to change her mind, including piling on the guilt. "Who will take care of me?" she asked, tears streaming down her cheeks. "Everyone leaves me. I'll be all alone." Upset by her reaction, Mercy almost relented, but in the end, and with Tally's encouragement, she decided she had a right to live her own life. Surprisingly, Gina found a way to cope. Mercy still stopped by her mom's house twice a week to make sure she was okay, but Mercy no longer took responsibility for her mother's actions. Dealing with her was still difficult, but at least now Mercy didn't allow herself to get dragged down by her mother's occasional outbursts of anger and self-pity.

"I need to run to the bathroom," Mercy said after she finished her lunch. "I'll be right back."

As she stood she noticed once again that her father's attention appeared to be riveted toward the front of the restaurant. He didn't say anything, just nodded at her.

When she returned to the table she carefully scanned the large windows near the entrance. There were people standing on the sidewalk—not unusual for Pappy's since it was always busy. A couple of large men caught Mercy's eye. They seemed out of place. They weren't talking to anyone else, and they looked stiff and uncomfortable. Were they the reason her father was so uptight?

She'd just sat down when Nick announced he was ready to leave. "I gotta get back to the station. Sorry."

"Not a problem." Mercy started to stand when Nick grabbed her arm and pulled her back down.

"Wait a minute," he said. His eyes searched hers, and Mercy felt uncomfortable. She pulled her arm away.

"I'm sorry, Mercy. Sorry I let you and your brother down."

"You've already said that—"

"Let me finish," he said sharply.

She fell silent and waited for him to continue, not really wanting to hear what he had to say.

"I need you to know that my leaving had nothing to do with you or your brother. It wasn't even your mother's fault. The fault was all mine. Every bit of it. The woman I left your mother for wasn't worth losing my family over. I thought she was, but down through the years I've learned that women who are willing to be involved with married men are selfish. Shallow. Destroying a family is a terrible thing to do. Only someone with a cold heart can even begin to consider it."

He rubbed his face with his hand and continued. "It sounds

like I'm blaming her, but I'm not. I'm the one responsible. My family should have been everything to me, and it wasn't. How I could have put her above you all is something I will never understand. I was blind. And stupid." He stared down at the table for a moment before looking up. Mercy was surprised to see tears in his eyes. "That's it. I just wanted you to know how much I regret what I did. I know I can never fix it." He took a deep breath and gave Mercy a smile tinged with sadness. "I also want you to know how proud I am of you. In spite of me, you grew up to be a fine young woman, and a great law-enforcement officer. I know you won't believe this, but I love you, Mercy. I've loved you every day since you were born, even though I've done a terrible job of showing it."

Although Mercy didn't want to be moved by his apology, she found she was. "Thank you for saying that," she said softly. "But as I told you before, it will take a long time for me to forgive you—if I ever do. Let's just take it one day at a time, okay?"

"I understand. I just needed to get those things off my chest. It's important to me." Nick's attention shifted back to the restaurant's front window.

"Look," Mercy said, "if you need backup . . ."

"No. I'm okay." He stood and grabbed his coat. "I'll call you later, Mercy. Keep your phone handy." For a moment, Mercy thought he was going to say something else, but he just stared at her for several seconds as if memorizing her face. Then he walked away, heading toward the back exit.

She waited until he left before pulling on her jacket and turning toward the front entrance again. The men in the window who'd seemed suspicious were gone now.

"You're losing it, Mercy," she said to herself. "You're seeing criminals around every corner." Even though she'd told the department shrink she had no lingering problems after the shooting, in truth, she was still jumpy. This wasn't the first time she'd thought some innocent person looked fishy. Angry at allowing herself to get pulled into her father's drama, she tried to push away the hard knot of concern in her stomach. But it wouldn't be so easily dismissed.

CHAPTER
FOUR

Mercy stared at her almost empty refrigerator. Some milk, left-over Chinese food that should have been thrown away a week ago, mustard, mayo, and a sad-looking wrinkled apple. She thought about picking something up from a nearby carryout, but in the end she grabbed a box of cereal off the counter, poured some in a bowl, and covered it with milk. Then she plopped down in front of the TV. At least she'd had a good lunch at Pappy's.

She'd been plagued all afternoon by a nagging sense of ap-prehension. Maybe it was just the aftereffects of spending time with her father. She tried to dismiss it, but her dad's face kept floating in front of her. He'd seemed . . . different. Introspective. She sighed and shook her head. It had been a long day, and she was too tired to think about Nick.

She'd just started watching a show she recorded a couple of days earlier when someone knocked on the door. She looked down at her sweatpants and old T-shirt covered with paint stains.

It certainly wasn't her best outfit, but anyone who thought it was okay to stop by without calling didn't deserve any better.

She put her cereal bowl down on the coffee table and went to the front door, first looking out the peephole. Mercy was surprised to see Tally standing there. Though he lived next door, he always called or texted before coming over. She pulled the door open.

"Your phone quit working?" she said teasingly. The look on his face stopped her cold. "What's wrong?"

"I need to come in, Mercy," he said, his expression frozen and unreadable.

She swung the door open and ushered him inside, out of the cold. Although she wanted to question him, she couldn't get any words out. They seemed to be stuck in her throat.

Tally walked over to her couch and sat down. He patted the place next to him. "Will you sit down, please?"

"No." Somewhere inside she knew what Tally was going to say, and she felt the need to stay on her feet.

Tally stared down at the coffee table for several seconds before meeting her eyes. "It's your dad, Mercy." He gulped several times, obviously emotional.

"He's dead," she said flatly. It was as if she'd known it for hours but hadn't wanted to acknowledge it.

Tally nodded slowly.

"How?"

"He got caught up in a gang fight. He was shot."

"When?"

"We found him a couple of hours ago. I . . . I asked the chief if I could be the one to tell you."

Mercy stared at Tally, unable to take her eyes off him. Her

father's last words to her echoed in her head, bouncing around as if they had a mind of their own.

"We had lunch today," she said quietly. "He was . . . strange. Apologized to me again. Told me he loved me and that he was proud of me. It was like he was saying good-bye."

Tally frowned at her. "I don't think he could have known, Merce. He was just in the wrong place at the wrong time."

Mercy shook her head. "No. He knew. I don't know how, but he did. I think I expected to hear something had happened to him."

Tally's skepticism showed on his face, but he didn't argue with her. "Please sit down," he said again. He pointed at her bowl of cereal on the coffee table. "Annie made the most amazing pot roast for dinner. I'll make you a plate. You need something better than this."

While she wasn't really hungry anymore, she didn't have the will to disagree. She finally came over and sat down on the couch. He put his arm out, and she leaned against his shoulder. They sat silently for a few minutes. Finally, Tally got up and left to get her food. Mercy stayed where she was, listening to a voice whisper in her head, *"I love you, Mercy. I've loved you every day since you were born, even though I've done a terrible job of showing it."*

Mercy's fingers trembled as she slid her key into the lock on her front door. Nick's funeral had shaken her. Unfortunately this wasn't her first cop funeral. Any officer killed while on duty was always treated to an almost military-like funeral with all the imaginable pomp and circumstance. City and state officials showed up in force, the chief of police presented a folded flag to the family, cops turned out in full dress uniform, and bagpipers played "Amazing Grace." At the entrance of the church two fire trucks were parked on each side of the sidewalk, a large flag draped between them for the mourners to pass under on their way into the sanctuary. Police helicopters flew overhead in tribute. On the way to the cemetery, the cold weather hadn't deterred citizens from lining the roads, many with their gloved hands on their hearts. Some waved small flags.

She was prepared for all of it, but what she couldn't prepare for were the people who had loved and respected her father. Their grief was real. She was bombarded by coworkers and friends from Virginia and St. Louis, who wanted her to know the kind of man they believed Nick was. She heard the same things repeated over and over: "A cop's cop. Honest. Brave. Selfless." As she forced herself to smile and thank them, she felt as if they were talking about someone she'd never met.

"Don't forget your flag."

After the lock clicked open, Mercy turned around. Annie held out the folded flag the chief of police had presented to Mercy during the funeral. Annie and Tally had driven her to the service, but before they left the cemetery, Tally had been called away. She wondered why. He'd looked upset after taking a call on his cellphone and had taken off without saying good-bye.

"Thanks for the ride," Mercy said. "It meant a lot to have you both there. I wish my brother could have made it, but . . ." Her voice trailed off. For some reason she didn't feel like making up an excuse for Jeremy. She understood why he hadn't come for Nick, but she wished he'd come for her.

Annie leaned over and gave her a hug. "I'm glad we could be here for you, Mercy," she said softly. "Do you have something to eat? Do you need anything?"

Mercy gently disengaged herself from Annie's arms and chuckled. "I have more food than I could eat in a year. Why is it people bring food when someone dies?"

Annie smiled. "They don't know what to do or what to say, but they want to let you know they're sorry for your loss. Dropping off food seems like a good way to do it."

"Well, if weighing five hundred pounds is supposed to make me feel better, then I guess it's a great idea. Seriously, you need to take some of this off my hands. Hope you like tuna casserole and chocolate cake."

"The kids will be happy about the cake. Not too sure about the tuna casserole. How 'bout I come over this afternoon and we'll go through everything? Maybe we can freeze some of it so you can eat it later."

"Sounds good," Mercy said. "Thanks again."

As Annie walked away, Mercy thought about how lucky Tally was to have found someone like her. Mercy was grateful for her too. Mercy and Tally spent a lot of time together, and after her shooting, Tally had visited Mercy every day she was in the hospital. Yet Annie never seemed threatened by Mercy's friendship with her husband. Once Mercy was released, Tally and Annie brought over food, did her shopping, took her to rehab, and picked up her prescriptions. Since Mercy lived in the other side of the duplex they owned, it might have been difficult for them to ignore her, but she knew their friendship was based on more than proximity. Mercy wondered if she'd ever find what Tally and Annie had together. Somehow she doubted it.

Mercy went inside, put the flag in the bedroom, and changed her clothes. She walked to her kitchen, planning to pour herself a glass of tea, when she noticed something was wrong. Just slightly off. It wasn't anything someone else would notice, but she did. Mercy had a place for everything, and it bugged her when someone moved her stuff. Tally had laughingly diagnosed her with OCD. Nevertheless, order was important to Mercy, and it was clear someone had been in her house. Whoever it was had tried to put things back where they belonged but hadn't quite gotten it right.

She went quickly to her bedroom and opened the drawer in her nightstand where she kept her gun. It was still there. After checking the house carefully and determining she was alone, she put the gun back and began to inventory every room. She couldn't find anything missing. She picked up her phone to call Tally. He could ask the crime-scene unit to check things out. Maybe their fingerprint techs could find something that would tell her who'd violated her home. She'd just started to select his number from her list when someone knocked on the door. Mercy frowned and glanced at her watch. She'd only said good-bye to Annie thirty minutes earlier. Surely taking care of her food situation could wait a little while.

Mercy pushed her irritation away. Annie was only trying to help. She pasted a smile on her face and put her phone down. When she looked through her peephole it wasn't Annie standing on her front porch. It was Mark St. Laurent. Mercy gasped and backed away from the door. What was he doing here? Since they'd quit seeing each other six months ago, their only contact was at work where their conversation was kept to what was absolutely necessary.

He knocked again, and Mercy realized she had to open the door. He probably wanted to convey his condolences. She wished he'd done that at the church, but there was no way out now. She slowly turned the doorknob and pulled.

"Hi, Mercy," Mark said when the door swung open. "I didn't get a chance to talk to you at the service."

"I—I know," she said. Could he hear her heart pounding? It seemed so loud.

"Can I come in?" he asked.

Mercy studied him for a moment. His wavy dark blond hair framed a face that would probably be described as ruggedly handsome. Gray-blue eyes under thick eyebrows and a perpetual five-o'clock shadow. Whenever they'd gone out together, women would turn to stare at him. While Mercy didn't care much about looks, she had to admit that being seen with him had been good for her ego. She was annoyed with herself for having such a shallow reaction. She detested shallow people.

"I'm kind of tired, Mark. This really isn't a good time."

"Please, Mercy. It's important."

Although facing Mark was the last thing she wanted to do at that moment, she stepped aside to let him in. "Can I get you something to drink?" she asked, hoping he wasn't planning to stay long enough to drink anything.

"Maybe some ice tea?"

"Sure," she said, swallowing her disappointment. She pointed to the couch. "Please, sit down."

As she poured tea into glasses, Mercy remembered her call to Tally. Hard to believe she'd momentarily forgotten about the break-in. Nick's funeral, finding someone had been in her house, and now Mark sitting in her living room—her brain was on overload, and it was getting harder and harder to stay focused.

"Look, Mark," she said as she carried the glasses into the living room. "When I got home I realized someone had been in here. I need to call Tally."

"Are you serious? Is anything missing?"

"Not that I can see. Of course, I may realize later that something's gone."

"Everything looks okay. Are you sure someone broke in?"

At first his question bothered her, but the look of concern on his face made it clear he was just worried.

"Yeah, I'm sure. Maybe the crime-scene unit can find something."

"You'd better change the locks."

Mercy nodded. "I'm sure Tally will do that immediately."

Mark stood and took the glass she extended toward him. "I wanted to tell you how sorry I am about Nick."

"Thanks."

Mark sat down again and sipped his tea. Mercy took the seat across from him. He looked nervous. Why was he really here? At work he basically ignored her. It could be because of Nick's death, only she had the odd feeling he had something else on his mind. Something he wasn't telling her.

CHAPTER
FIVE

"It's just not there. Getting angry with me doesn't make sense." Mayor Jacob Martin scowled at Darius Johnson. Darius was sprawled out on the couch, his Glock next to him. Stacks of cash and drugs were displayed on a large beat-up coffee table. It looked as if the gang leader was proud of his illegal bounty and wanted to flaunt it in front of the city leader. Jacob took his role seriously. The St. Louis area was made up of many smaller municipalities, and each one had its own government. Quite a few of them were run by people like him. Men and women looking for a way to use their position to benefit themselves.

"If I say it makes sense, it makes sense," Darius barked. "Whatever I say goes. You got that, J.J.?"

Jacob straightened up in his chair. He hated the egotistical gang leader with every fiber of his being. He felt like a fly caught in a web, the spider watching him from the corner, getting ready to pounce. Darius was a small man. Cowardly without a weapon in his hand, but dangerous with one. "Don't call me J.J.," Jacob said slowly. "You know I don't like it."

Darius pointed at him. "You ain't gonna do nuthin' about it, J.J. All you gonna do is exactly what I say."

"I sent some men to her apartment. Like I said, it wasn't there. She doesn't have it."

Darius shook his head, his blue bandanna slipping a bit, making him look like a drunken pirate.

Jacob stared at the gang leader. Darius wasn't attractive on a good day, but when he pouted, his looks were repellant. Stained and broken teeth, ruined by his addiction to heroin. Ears that stuck straight out. Sores on his face and needle tracks on his arms. Darius Johnson appeared to be balancing precariously on the edge of death. Jacob looked away, his stomach turning with disgust.

Frankly, he hated the gangs almost as much as he detested himself for consorting with them. He'd started out wanting to make a difference in his old neighborhood. Cleaning up crime, helping the people. But Darius and his gang ruled the area. They'd made it clear that if Jacob ever went up against them, his family would pay the price. Jacob took the threats seriously. Darius had spies in the police department and in the Marshals' office. He manipulated people through fear, intimidation, and money. If anyone understood how dangerous Darius could be, it was Jacob.

"I hope you were careful. Don't want her knowin' we was lookin' for somethin'."

"My people were very cautious. She won't know." Jacob sighed. "It wasn't easy. She's a U.S. Marshal, you know. And she's got that cop living right next door."

Darius banged his fist on the table, making the rickety structure tilt to the right. "It's my property, and I want it back. You got that? I bet you didn't look hard enough."

"Look, your guys went through the dead cop's apartment. You couldn't find anything either, and you probably tipped the police off. We did a thorough search and made sure everything was put back in place. It wasn't there. I'm sure of it."

"We didn't tip no one off. We took some stuff. Made it look like he was robbed. That's why I told you to get in and out of the lady cop's apartment without drawin' any attention. I can't let Vargas get suspicious. He'd kill me if he knew I downloaded that video onto my computer. How could I know Tink would copy it and give it to the cop? It ain't my fault."

Jacob had no idea what was on the video, and he had no intention of asking. But obviously it was something Angel Vargas didn't want ending up in the hands of the police. Jacob would alert Vargas in a heartbeat if it got Darius out of his life, only he was too afraid of retribution. Johnson now led one of the most notorious gangs in St. Louis, a recent promotion gained through the spilling of blood. He'd risen through the ranks by killing anyone in his way. He had no loyalties when it came to power. His newfound prestige stoked his ego, but behind the scenes most of the city's gangbangers still referred to him by his old gang name, Dumbo, on account of his big ears. However, to his face he wanted to be called D-Money. Calling him Dumbo could get you killed.

"We even went back to the restaurant and checked it out. Nuthin'."

"So now what?" Jacob asked, praying Darius's next step wouldn't involve him.

Darius shrugged. "We keep watchin' the lady cop. We'll get her alone before long. Then we'll make her tell us where it is."

"I can't understand why you're so convinced she's got it."

"Like I said, Tink said he downloaded the video and gave it to the cop. Obviously he was gonna turn it over to his pig bosses, but before he could, we took him out. There wasn't nuthin' on him. It wasn't at his place. You said it wasn't at the lady's cop's." Darius pointed at his head with his forefinger. "I ain't dumb. That means the lady cop still has it. Either she's got it on her or she's stashed it somewhere."

Tink had been a mild-mannered member of Darius's crew—someone no one paid much attention to—until the cops began to use him as a confidential informant. When Darius discovered Tink had been meeting with the police, Darius got all the information he could from him before he shot Tink in his car and then torched it.

Jacob formed his next words carefully. The last thing he wanted to do was antagonize Darius any more than he already was. "But why would he give it to her? She was his daughter, right? Wouldn't he want to keep her safe?"

"My boys said the cop was nervous at the restaurant," said Darius. "Kept lookin' around like he knew his time was up." He got up and walked over to Jacob, standing right in front of him, his ugly mug just inches away. "He had to get rid of it quick. Couldn't have given it to no one else. She's got it, man, I'm tellin' you. Either she don't know she's got it or she's hopin' to get paid for it."

"You're sure she didn't turn it in?"

Darius's face twisted into a sneer and he moved away. "I'm absolutely sure. Ain't nuthin' happens with the cops I don't know about."

Jacob could have pointed out that the U.S. Marshals weren't police officers, but Darius saw everyone in law enforcement as cops. His enemies.

Frankly, Jacob couldn't figure out what had happened to the flash drive. Why hadn't it turned up? Was Darius right? Did this female deputy Marshal have it? Was she waiting to see if someone would offer her money for it? That's what he would do if he had something that valuable.

"As far as Vargas knows, everything's okay?"

"Yeah. I showed Nick the fixed-up video like Vargas told me to. Told him what Vargas said about sending it to the TV stations. He was really shook. Promised to keep playing along." Darius shrugged again. "After I talked to him, I told Vargas everything was good. And it was good until Tink told Nick about the first video and Nick squeezed him into makin' a copy of it. I took care of both of them, but I still don't have the flash drive with the video on it."

"Won't Vargas get suspicious about the cop's death?"

"Hey, pigs die every day."

Darius tried to sound confident, yet Jacob could hear the apprehension in his voice.

"Man," Darius continued, "if Vargas ever finds out I didn't get rid of that first video like he told me to . . . well, it would be bad. Real bad."

"Maybe it won't turn up," Jacob said. "The important thing is that as far as Vargas is concerned, you followed orders, right?"

Darius nodded, and for just a second he almost looked vulnerable. He wasn't afraid of much, but he was definitely afraid of Angel Vargas. "The real video showed us poppin' someone for real. I guess if anyone saw it they'd know Vargas faked the other one."

Jacob felt the hairs on the back of his neck stand up. Darius had made a deadly mistake. The cop had gotten proof that could blow Vargas and his cartel to kingdom come. "What possessed you to disobey him?" Jacob asked, unable to keep the incredulity out his voice. This kid had most likely signed his own death warrant out of sheer stupidity.

Darius reeled around and stuck his finger in Jacob's face. "You ain't my mama. I'll keep whatever I want to. Don't you ever tell me what to do ever again, you got it, old man? I know what you've been up to. You don't do what I say and everyone finds out the truth about their *honorable mayor*." He laughed at his choice of words. Darius obviously thought he was much funnier than he actually was.

Jacob didn't answer. Darius Johnson was out of his mind, and trying to reason with him was an exercise in futility. Actually, Jacob was surprised the cartel hadn't killed him already. Why would they allow someone like Darius to put them at risk? All Jacob could figure was that at the time the plan was hatched, no one really thought ahead about the repercussions of working with a drug-addicted gang leader. Now Darius was panicking, and fear was making him reckless. Jacob didn't want to get caught in the crossfire. Did the fool plan to kidnap a deputy U.S. Marshal in an attempt to retrieve the flash drive? The girl was a trained law-enforcement officer. Snatching her wouldn't be a piece of cake. So far she was never in a place where she could be safely approached. She went to work and came home. Nothing else.

Now, if Darius could recruit her cop friend, he might have a chance. But Jacob knew Tally Williams. He was one of the good guys. A straight arrow that couldn't be flipped.

Jacob had good people working for him. People who wanted to stay in his good graces. He'd used them to break into the deputy's apartment, and now they were supposed to be watching her. However, without telling Darius, Jacob had begun pulling his people back. It was getting too dangerous and Jacob wanted out. There was no chance this was going to end well.

Being mayor, even of a small suburb, had its perks.

Jacob could do almost anything he wanted. He could even accept bids for city work from friends who slid him cash under the table. It was a good setup for everyone. And once he had someone under his thumb, he could manipulate them. Make them carry out his wishes. It was a sweet situation, and he had no intention of allowing Darius to ruin what he'd worked so hard to build. Besides, even though it might sound strange to anyone else, Jacob respected law enforcement. He didn't want to see the Marshal end up dead. If anyone needed to go, it was Darius. Perhaps it was too dangerous for Jacob to contact the cartel directly, but who said he couldn't tip them off anonymously?

He smiled at Darius, who scowled back. Maybe he could get rid of this punk for good. Before the day was out, Jacob was determined to come up with a plan that would get Darius Johnson out of his hair—forever.

CHAPTER
SIX

Tally waved at Mark when he came into the coffee shop later that day after the funeral. Mark stepped over to the counter and put in his order, then joined Tally at his table.

"How did it go?" Tally asked when Mark sat down.

"Well, let's just say she didn't welcome me with open arms. I hung around as long as I could, but it was . . . awkward."

"Sorry to put you on the spot, but you're the only person I know who's . . . who was close to Mercy. After what I learned from the chief, I didn't want her to be alone."

Tally and Mark weren't really friends, just acquaintances. While Mercy and Mark were dating, he and Annie had double-dated with the couple a few times. And he'd had lunch with Mark and Mercy on several occasions. Tally liked the deputy U.S. Marshal and thought he was a good fit for Mercy. When things went south in the relationship, he was sorry about it. Mercy hadn't said much, and Tally hadn't pushed her, but he could tell she still had strong feelings for Mark, although she'd never admit it.

"Who's watching her now?"

"There's an unmarked car across the street. But I have to be cautious. She's smart; she'll figure out something's wrong if we're not careful."

"Tell me again what happened."

Tally took a sip of his coffee. Ever since the call had come in, his nerves had been on edge. He hated leaving the cemetery before saying anything to Mercy, but he was told not to speak to her until he'd talked to the chief. "The gang unit in LA contacted Chief Kennedy. He said they'd uncovered a threat against Mercy. It has something to do with the Vargas cartel—and Darius Johnson. The chief called me since he knows I'm friends with her. I've reached out to one of my CIs. He says Darius Johnson is looking for something, and he thinks Mercy has it."

"What does that have to do with Vargas?"

Tally shrugged. "I have no idea . . . yet. And I don't know what Johnson is looking for. This is all the information we've gotten so far. We've got some CIs deeper inside the gangs. We'll get with them as soon as we can, but we can't just pull them in. If we move too quickly we might tip someone off. We need to keep these guys alive."

"Can LA tell us more?"

Tally nodded. "They've got someone deep undercover in the cartel, except that's even touchier. They have to wait until he contacts them. One wrong move . . ."

"I understand."

"So what did you tell her?" Tally asked.

Before Mark could answer, the girl at the front counter called out his name. Mark got up to fetch his coffee.

Tally's concern wasn't just for Mercy. She lived in the other half of the duplex he owned. If she was in danger, his family could get caught in the line of fire. His chief had promised to talk to Richard Batterson, the man in charge of the U.S. Marshals' office in St. Louis. Hopefully they would come up with a plan of action that would keep everyone safe.

Mark came back and sat down. "I just told her I was sorry about Nick. I'm hoping she'll chalk my visit up to that." He frowned at Tally. "She thinks someone broke into her place."

Tally's eyebrows shot up. "Is she right?"

Mark gave a little shrug. "It looked the same to me. Of course, I haven't been there in a long time. But you know Mercy. She knows where everything goes. If something's been moved half an inch, she can tell."

Tally snorted. "I found that out the hard way." He rubbed his hand over his eyes. He was exhausted. "If she's right, Johnson's already looking for whatever it is he wants so desperately. She could be in real trouble, Mark."

"I know. I'm worried about you and your family too. Maybe you should get your wife and kids out of town for a while. Can you send them to visit her mom or something?"

"I'm one step ahead of you," Tally said, nodding. "I plan to talk to Annie this evening when I get home." He sighed deeply. "Here's something else to add to the mix. Got a call before I left the station. Nick's place was hit. Whoever broke in tore it up pretty good."

"If someone really did break in to Mercy's, it could be related."

"It's very possible. You know, Nick was working undercover with the gang unit."

Mark blew out a quick breath of air. "I wasn't aware of that. If that's what got him killed . . ."

"Then Mercy's in even more danger than we thought." Tally stared down at the table for a moment. Then he looked up at Mark. "What's Mercy doing about her break-in?"

"She said she was going to call you. Ask you to send someone from the crime-scene unit, have them look for prints."

"She phoned earlier," said Tally, "but I didn't take it. I wanted to talk to you first. I can send the crime unit over there, but I bet they won't find anything. Anyone who took the time to be that careful probably made sure not to leave evidence behind." He shook his head. "When Mercy finds out about Nick's apartment she's going to get suspicious."

"You know how thieves hit empty houses during funerals. Maybe she'll think that's all it was."

Tally grunted. "She might have—if someone hadn't broken into her place."

Mark frowned. "You know Mercy better than anyone, don't you?"

"I think so. Why?"

Mark ran a finger around the rim of his cup. "She's supposed to be working with the shrink the department assigned to her, but I heard she's not cooperating. I've never known anyone so closed off emotionally." He looked carefully at Tally. "You know, we started to get close when we were together. I mean really close. Then the door slammed shut." He shrugged. "She says it's because I 'got religious.' But I think that was only part of it."

Tally was quiet for a moment, trying to decide what he could tell Mark without revealing something Mercy wouldn't want him to.

"I'm not asking you to betray your friendship," Mark said as if he'd just read Tally's mind. "You and I don't know each other all that well, but I still really care about her. If I'm not the guy for her, fine. But the way things ended . . . well, as soon as I told her I loved her, she began to change. Pull away from me. I don't know what to make of it."

Tally took a deep breath and let it out slowly. "Mercy and I have been best friends since grade school," he said finally. "I was a poor black kid from north St. Louis. Smart, skinny, and constantly bullied. I did everything I could to stay away from the gangs that cost my older brother his life, and I've worked hard to become a police lieutenant. I've got a wonderful wife and two children. The truth is, I owe a lot of my success to Mercy." He paused, took a sip of his coffee. "She was bullied too. That's why we bonded. After her father deserted his family, her mother started drinking and abusing prescription drugs. She'd show up at school, out of her head, and cause a scene in front of the other kids and the teachers. They had to ban her from the school. The school's principal called social services several times. Somehow Mercy's mom always managed to keep her kids. But just barely. Mercy had to build emotional walls to protect herself. Over the years they've only gotten stronger."

Tally shook his head. "She stopped crying, a fact some of the kids in school picked up on. They called her 'the girl who never cries.' And believe me, they tried everything they could to change that, but no one ever did. Through all the drama, Mercy and I gave each other strength. Encouraged each other. Her loyalty and friendship helped me to be brave. I knew she was on my side. So long as I had her in my life, I never worried about being alone. If she could believe in me, I could believe in me too. When Mercy found out I wanted to be a police officer,

she wouldn't let it go. Wouldn't let me back off from my dream."
Tally chuckled. "Funny thing is, I pulled her along with me.
She finally decided to join the force when I did."

"Then she transferred to the Marshals after her father moved
here from Virginia two years ago. Didn't want to work with
him, right?" Mark asked.

Tally nodded. "That's true, but to be honest, she loves the
Marshals. I really don't think she'd go back to the force."

Mark was quiet for a moment. "So you're telling me that her
father up and left her family, and then her mother deserted her
by diving into booze and drugs. Now she protects herself from
everyone so she won't get hurt again?"

"Yeah. I might be the only person in the world she trusts.
If she started to care too much for you—if you two got too
close—she must have felt the need to shut down the relationship. I suspect that's what happened, although she won't talk
to me about it . . . about you. Mark, she's the toughest person
I've ever known—on the outside. On the inside, though, she's
bruised. Tender."

"I wish she'd open up to Dr. Abbot. She's a good therapist.
I've talked with her."

Tally shook his head. "She won't. Trust me, something will
have to happen to Mercy to make her finally deal with her pain.
Something major." He drained the last of his coffee. "You said
you go to church?"

Mark nodded.

"Then pray for her. I worry she'll keep pushing her pain into
that deep, dark vault she's created until it finally spills out on
its own and buries her. If that happens, I don't know if anyone
can save her."

"Thanks," Mark said. "I know you didn't have to share any of that. I'll never let her know."

"Well, if we don't find a way to keep her alive, nothing I told you will matter." He pushed his coffee cup away and stared at Mark. "So, how do we protect her?"

"We wait to see what your boss and mine come up with. Then we pray it works."

Darius walked into the house with two of his boys close behind him. ManMan and Pretty Boy were enforcers. No one messed with D-Money when they had his back. Meeting with Crazy Tony from the Rollin' 60s was something he'd never do without firepower in evidence. Crazy Tony ran his Bloods gang with fear and intimidation, but today Darius was "the man." His partnership with the Vargas cartel made him invincible. No gang leader in St. Louis would take a chance on crossing him. Though Darius wasn't certain why Crazy Tony requested a meeting, he assumed he wanted to form an alliance. Darius and Angel Vargas had talked about the possibility several times.

"Once they know we're in town—and what we're offering— they'll jump on board," Vargas had told him in the beginning. "We can take over St. Louis when we're united. The cops won't stand a chance."

Darius believed he was watching the fulfillment of Vargas's prediction. The Crips and Bloods aligning. If he wasn't seeing it unfold before his eyes, he never would have believed it. This wouldn't be a slam dunk, however. There was a lot of bad blood between the groups, and Darius wasn't sure his boys would accept the new alliance. Of course, when it came down to it, you could go along—or you could die. The choice wasn't that hard.

Crazy Tony stood when Darius entered the room. "D-Money," Tony said with a smile. His grin reminded Darius of the look he'd seen on his father's face when he was eight. Right before he beat him or his mom senseless. The worst beatings came when he tried to protect his mother. One time his father broke Darius's jaw and pulled his shoulder out of joint. When that man was shot dead in front of him, it was one of the best moments of Darius's life. The police never caught the guy who did it. Too bad, because hardly a day went by when Darius didn't quietly thank him.

Darius grabbed Tony's outstretched hand, and they shook like old men, neither one willing to give into the other's gang handshake. That would never happen, no matter what kind of threat the cartel posed.

Darius noticed that Tony had brought his own protection. Four big men stood silently along the wall. They looked relaxed, but Darius knew their guns were close by. Probably stuck in the waistbands of their jeans. Most gang members kept their pistols in their pants, hidden under a long shirt so that the cops wouldn't see them.

On a nearby table, an AK-47 was within arm's reach. Obviously there as a threat. Again, Darius wasn't worried. His crew was armed and ready. They'd die before they allowed anyone to hurt him. They were his boys. His family.

Darius sat down at the table with Tony. "You called this meetin'," Darius said. "Whatcha want, Tony?"

"We know you been workin' with the Mexicans," Tony said, referring to the Vargas cartel. "They been bringin' in money to the hood. Lots of money. We want in."

Darius nodded slowly. "We might be able to make somethin' happen, but you gotta call off any wars. Any retribution. We gotta work together. I ain't sure you can do that."

Tony narrowed his eyes. "Ain't no big thing. You already done some of the work."

"Wasn't nuthin'. Just brought in the Bishops, the Brims, and the 92nd Street Devils." He rested his elbows on the table and leaned in. "You need to listen to me, Tony. When Vargas says somethin', I'll pass it along. But you gotta do it." He lightly slapped his chest. "It ain't me tellin' you, I'm just the messenger. Can you deal with that?"

Tony smiled again, and Darius started to feel a little nervous. This was too easy. It wasn't that long ago that Tony declared death to the Black Mafia, Darius's gang. Must be the money. Tony knew a good deal when he saw it, and this was an awesome opportunity. Before long, St. Louis would be drowning in heroin, and D-Money would be king of all the gangs. No one would be able to stop him. The entire town would bow at his feet.

"So you speak for Angel Vargas?" Tony said in a low voice. "You think you're his right-hand man, huh?"

His greasy grin spread even wider, and a warning bell went off in Darius's head. "I don't think it, I know it," he said, turning to catch ManMan's eye. He nodded, warning him to be ready for any confrontation that might break out. But ManMan just smiled at him.

"I bet you don't know I'm sendin' some of my crew after the deputy Marshal, who has somethin' you lost," Tony said. "We gonna kill her dead and get back the item Vargas wants."

Darius's brain locked up. What was Tony saying? How could he know about the Marshal? The muscles in his right hand tensed as he thought about grabbing the gun he had in his own waistband.

"Problem is," Tony continued, "Mr. Vargas is done with you, Dumbo. You messed up big-time. He found out what you did. He don't let anyone betray him and walk away alive."

Darius went cold inside. How did Angel find out about the video? It had to be Jacob, that dirty thief. He'd make sure Jacob paid dearly for his disloyalty.

Darius jumped to his feet and pulled out his weapon while he swung his head around to signal his crew, expecting them to grab their guns and take down Tony and his men. Their guns were drawn all right, but they were aimed at him.

Seconds before he took his very last breath, Darius realized he'd been played. And with his final words on this earth, Darius Johnson called out for his mother.

CHAPTER
SEVEN

Mark St. Laurent sat across from the Chief Deputy of the Eastern Division of Missouri's U.S. Marshals Service. Both men were silent as they contemplated what they were about to do.

"I don't think it's fair to her," Mark said quietly. "She's a deputy U.S. Marshal. She's earned her place here, and I think we need to show her more respect. We need to tell her the truth."

"I'm not saying I don't respect her," Richard Batterson said sharply. "I'm trying to protect her. Right now only you and I, Lieutenant Williams, and the chief of police know what's going on. We have a mole, and I can't take a chance this operation will fail."

"It's not her."

"Based on what?" Batterson scowled at Mark. "The fact that you dated her for a year? That hardly qualifies you to—"

"It qualifies me enough to tell you she would never betray us. Never. Besides, if the cartel is after her, why would she pass along information? It doesn't make sense."

"I know that. But maybe she hasn't worked with them

directly. Maybe she was working with Darius Johnson. A lot of money flowed through his hands. It wouldn't be the first time a law-enforcement officer was recruited by a gang, nor would it be the first time a cartel targeted someone working for them." He paused and let out a sigh. "Look, my gut tells me she's not the mole, but I can't go by my gut this time. For now, I have to assume she might be dirty, and you know why. So until we can figure out who's been selling us out, I don't want anyone beyond the three of us in on this deal." He leaned forward in his chair and rested his arms on his desk. "Someone tipped Darius Johnson off the night we raided that beehive. And there's been other things. Johnson was getting information from someone."

"Well, he's not getting anything from anyone anymore."

Johnson's body had been found in the middle of a vacant lot the night before. Shot in the head and abandoned like so much trash. While no one in law enforcement mourned him, it would have been better if they'd brought him in to face justice for shooting Mike, along with a long list of other crimes. But at least he was finally off the streets.

"We know now that the cartel is after Brennan," Batterson said. "It's been two weeks since Nick's funeral. We've done everything we can to protect her, but it's not enough. We've got to get her to safety, and we can't do it here. According to the gang unit in LA, Brennan is in extreme danger."

"Do you think the cartel has enlisted someone else? Another gang leader?"

Batterson nodded. "I do. Their plan is to use the gangs to do their dirty work. I don't know who they've recruited now that Johnson is out of the picture, but I do know they're ready and willing to do whatever it takes to get what they want. Being in bed with a huge cartel is like Christmas to these gangs."

Mark considered his boss's words. Batterson was right. After finding out that Mercy was in Darius's sights, their confidential informant was found dead. Shot while sitting in his car—a bullet through the back of his head. Then the car was set on fire. The gang's way of getting rid of evidence and sending a message. Now Darius was dead as well. They'd suspected the cartel was involved somehow, and the gang unit with the LAPD had confirmed it. The Vargas cartel was planning a big push into cities across the country. If St. Louis couldn't shut this down now, more people would die, and heroin would crash into the U.S. like a tsunami. Mark was determined that wouldn't happen.

"Vargas is pulling them in one by one," Batterson continued, "promising them some of the take from the drugs he's bringing in from Mexico."

"I've never seen this many gangs working together," Mark said. "He's building an empire—and God help anyone who gets in his way."

"According to an undercover cop on the task force, he's got the Nine Deuce Bishops now, as well as the Sixty-Two Brims."

Mark felt a chill run down his spine. Ephraim Vargas, head of the vast Vargas cartel, was building an army fueled by violent crime and hatred for the police. The fallout would be devastating. The cartel's plan would bring even more havoc and destruction to St. Louis.

"What about the Bloods?" Mark asked. Most people had no idea that the Crips and the Bloods were made up of many smaller splinter groups. And they didn't all get along, even though their roots were the same. Mark learned early on that when it came to terrorizing a city, gangs were experts. Although law enforcement considered the gangs to be nothing but low-life criminals, they respected their ability to tear a community to shreds. The police and the Marshals approached them with caution.

"I think they're headed for war," Batterson said, "unless we find a way to stop it. The Rollin' 60s don't like giving up any part of their territory. They may work together for a while—so long as the cartel's money is flowing their way. But long-term? I don't see it. I'm not sure Vargas understands that."

Mark knew quite a bit about the cartels. Next to overseas terrorist organizations like ISIS, they were the most cold-blooded groups on the planet. Gang leaders like Darius thought hooking up with them was smart, but it wasn't. One false move—a hint of anything that looked like betrayal—and the cartel would order hits as easily as Mark ordered fries at McDonald's. Darius had found that out the hard way.

"If Mercy has what they think she has, it could bring everything crashing down."

Mark breathed in deeply. "And if she found something like that, she'd have turned it in immediately."

Batterson rose from his desk, walked over to the window, and looked outside where snow was falling steadily. "Unless she's working both sides."

"Richard, you've known me a long time. When I tell you I'm certain Mercy Brennan isn't dirty, why can't you believe me?"

Batterson grew quiet for a minute, and Mark wondered if he was going to ignore the question. Finally, Batterson cleared his throat and stared at Mark with an almost hawklike expression. "Look, you and Brennan were a great team. I paired you because you're better together. But that was before . . . before you changed. When you got religion . . ." He waved his hand toward Mark. "I don't fault you that. Some of the best people I know have . . . faith. But after that, when you and Brennan broke up, you couldn't work together anymore." He shook his head. "I lost one of the best teams I ever had, and neither one of you is as effective as you used to be."

"What are you talking about?" Mark pushed down a surge of outrage that rose in his throat like bile. When Mercy ended their relationship, Mark had been devastated. He would never let her know just how much it hurt him. It had taken him months to get over it. Actually that was a lie. He still wasn't over her. Had it really affected his job performance? He always gave his best effort. Surely Batterson was mistaken.

"I'm still not sure you really loved her," Batterson said abruptly. "I think she was a challenge. An arctic queen with a frozen heart you were determined to melt. Did you know that when she worked for the PD, they nicknamed her 'Frosty the Snow Cop'? Here some of the deputies call her 'No Mercy Brennan.'"

"That's enough." Mark fired his words like bullets. He clenched his hands together, trying to choke back the rising anger.

Batterson seemed to realize he'd pushed the wrong button, because his expression softened. "I'm sorry, Mark. It's just that after Audrey . . . well, I don't want to see you go through something like that again."

Mark relaxed his fists but not before he noticed the impression of his nails on his palms. He had to calm down. He prided himself on being able to handle pressure, but this morning he felt like a kid whose favorite toy had been stolen. He had to get a handle on himself. "This is nothing like Audrey, Richard. She loved me, and I loved her. Leaving wasn't her choice."

"I know that. But you married her even though you knew she was dying. I'm just afraid you're looking for another . . . cause." He sighed, then said, "Look, Mark, I'm probably wrong, and I know I'm interfering. You're a smart man and you're still an exceptional deputy. Sorry to sound like a mother hen. Clearly I've stepped over the line."

"Maybe for my boss, but not for my friend." Mark managed a small smile. "Audrey wasn't a 'cause' for me. I truly loved her. I knew her chances of beating stage-four cancer were slim, but I really wanted to marry her. And she wanted to be married. I'm not sorry she died as my wife. I'm just sorry she died." He took a deep breath and tried to slow down his racing heart. "Now, let's get back to this new operation. I still think we're going about it all wrong."

Before Batterson could respond, there was a knock at the door. "Come in," he barked.

Batterson's administrative assistant, Carol Marchand, opened the door and stuck her head in. "Deputy Brennan is here, Chief."

"Thank you, Carol. Is the file ready for Deputy St. Laurent?"

"Yes, sir. It's on my desk." She nodded at Mark. "You can pick it up on your way out."

Batterson nodded. "You can show Deputy Brennan in now, Carol."

She nodded and closed the door. Seconds later, Mercy walked into the room. For a moment, Mark felt as if he couldn't catch his breath. He had the same reaction when he'd gone to her apartment. She still ignited a response in him he couldn't control. She certainly wasn't a classic beauty. Her nose was a little long, and her mouth was probably wider than what might be considered perfect, but he could get lost in her gray eyes. Her thick dark hair was pinned up today, but whenever she let it down, he saw a spark of vulnerability that usually stayed hidden. Mark was one of the few people who had ever been allowed to see beyond the professional façade she wore like a coat of armor.

He hoped he could handle what was ahead. This assignment was going to be tough. Almost impossible. But he couldn't allow anyone else to undertake it. He had to protect Mercy, even knowing that when she learned the truth, she'd be angry with him.

"You wanted to see me, Chief?"

"Yes, Deputy Brennan." Batterson gestured toward the chair next to Mark. "Sit down please."

She slid into the chair he'd indicated and nodded briefly at Mark. She looked surprised to see him.

Batterson picked up a file on his desk, opened it, and quietly perused it. Finally he put the file down and looked at Mercy, his forehead furrowed. "Dr. Abbot hasn't released you to full duty yet."

"Yes, sir. I'm aware of that."

No reaction, no irritation, no frustration. Just cold acknowledgment of the fact. As usual, she was unshakable.

"Do you know why?"

"Yes, sir. According to the doctor, I haven't dealt with my feelings about the shooting. Or about . . . my father's death."

This time Mark couldn't help but sneak a look at her. She'd hesitated before mentioning Nick. He noticed a muscle twitch in her jaw. An odd show of emotion for her. Mercy's eyes widened before she slipped back into her former emotionless expression.

"How do you feel about that?"

Mercy inhaled slowly. She was definitely bothered about Nick's shooting, even though she'd told Mark time and time again that her father meant nothing to her. Was there some truth behind Batterson's suspicions? Could she know more than she was saying? Mark hated himself for even a brief flash of doubt.

"She's entitled to her opinion, sir, but she's judging the situation with my father as if we'd had a normal relationship. We didn't. He left my family when I was ten. I barely remember him. As you know, two years ago he was transferred from the police department in Virginia to St. Louis. He did contact me several times, but our visits were few and far between. I'm sorry he's dead because he was a law-enforcement officer. We grieve over everyone lost in the line of duty. But his death didn't affect me any more than anyone else's."

Batterson closed the file and frowned at Mercy. "I'm not going to disregard Dr. Abbot's recommendation, Mercy, but I'm also not going to keep you behind a desk any longer. You're too valuable to me in the field."

"Thank you, sir."

Mark saw the relief on her face and steeled himself for what was coming.

"We have a witness in a small town about one hundred and thirty miles from here. Four years ago he testified against a crooked alderman who was rigging bids on city contracts for a group of corrupt businessmen. They were cutting deals with organized crime. He ended up in WITSEC." He reached over and picked up a sheet of paper. "His new name is Daniel Andrews. He's convinced someone's watching him. That he's in danger. I think he's wrong. Most of the people involved in the case are either out of business or in prison, including the alderman in question. None of them seem like much of a threat anymore." He peered at her over his thick black glasses, looking for all the world like a college professor rather than a trained law-enforcement professional. "But . . . as you know, our commitment to our witnesses makes them a priority. We can't take a chance he might be right. I want you and Mark to make a visit. Assess the situation. Let me know if there's any reason for concern. If there is, we may have to move him."

That got her attention. Mercy looked at Mark before she addressed Batterson. "I'm sorry, sir. You want both of us to check this out? That doesn't seem . . . necessary."

Batterson stood to his feet. "I don't remember asking you what you thought about this assignment, Deputy Brennan. Believe it or not, this isn't a democracy. When I say go, you go. Do you have a problem with that?"

Mark was amazed to see Mercy's cheeks flush pink. In all the time they'd been together, he'd never seen her blush.

"No, sir. I'm sorry. When do you want us to leave?"

"Right away. Go home and pack. Deputy St. Laurent will pick you up in"—he glanced at his watch—"three hours. You should reach your assignment by six this evening." He turned toward the window to check the snowstorm. It was coming down heavier than before. "Let's change that to two hours. We need to get you out of here before the city gets snowed in." He peered at her through narrowed eyes. "The St. Louis PD is graciously allowing us to send a friend of yours along as well.

Lieutenant Tally Williams was involved in the initial case. I want his expertise available to the both of you."

Mercy rose from her chair, her expression taut. Mark knew she hated being blindsided, and that had just happened in spades. "Yes, sir. I assume you've given all the pertinent information to Deputy St. Laurent?"

"You assume correctly. He'll brief you on the way."

She nodded and left the room.

"That was a little rough," Mark said when the door closed behind her.

Batterson shrugged. "Necessary. If we hesitate too long . . ."

"She could die," Mark finished for him, his voice soft.

"Yes," Batterson said, "she could most definitely die."

CHAPTER
EIGHT

"Did you have time to pack everything you wanted?"

Mercy glanced over at Mark. He was trying to make small talk, but she really wasn't in the mood. She realized, however, that the drive to Piedmont, Missouri, would be torturous unless they found a way to ease the tension between them.

"I have a packing list already made up. Keeps me from forgetting anything."

Mark sighed. "I should have known. You're so organized. Perfect. No room for messiness or spontaneity."

"You've got that right," Tally said from the backseat. "She was that way in school too. She used to chew me out because my desk was always disorganized."

"An attempt to control her environment," Mark said. "Makes her feel safer."

"Well, thank you, Dr. Freud," Mercy said, irritation evident in her voice. "You both need to concentrate on the job at hand. My personal life isn't applicable here."

"Sorry," Mark said. "It's going to be a long drive in this weather. Just trying to make the time go by a little faster."

Mercy bit her lip to hold back a snide retort. Mark was right. With the weather slowing them down, they would be in the car for a while. Even though she wasn't happy about being sent on this assignment with him, she needed to do her best to cope. After all, it wasn't his fault. "I still don't see why it takes all three of us to make sure this guy is okay," she said, changing the subject. "Seems like a waste of resources."

"The chief assigned it to me, and I asked for you," Mark said. "I knew you were probably miserable behind a desk, poring over those old warrants." He shrugged. "Sending Tally along was Batterson's idea, but I think he was right. Tally knows this case."

"But who cares about this witness now?" Mercy asked, trying to keep her frustration in check. "And how could anyone have found him out in the boonies? We do a good job of hiding our witnesses. The whole thing smells wrong."

"I have no idea, but Batterson isn't stupid. He wouldn't send us out here if he didn't think it was important."

"I guess you're right," she admitted grudgingly. Momentarily she turned her attention back to the world outside their car. It was really coming down now. The local news stations in St. Louis had certainly blown it this time. Their prediction was for nothing more than light snow. Hopefully it wouldn't last much longer. "I don't really mind going through old warrants, you know," she said. "In the past I've found several leads that way. I started my time with the Marshals reviewing warrants."

Mark grunted. "That's right, I forgot. Your first two months with the service you found information the police and the Mar-

shals missed. Reopened cases long forgotten, much to the cha-
grin of your colleagues."

"I didn't join the Marshals to be popular."

"Well, you've accomplished that," Mark said. He sighed
and shook his head. "Sorry, I don't mean to sound harsh, but
if you'd go out with us once in a while it would help. Accept
an invitation to get a drink after work. Let people get to know
you. They'd like you."

"I don't drink," she said evenly.

"I know that. I don't either, but I still go. I have a glass of
ice tea and talk to colleagues. You'd be surprised at how nice
they are. Besides, we all have a lot in common."

"Yeah, LEOs forever. I know the drill."

Mark was silent, and Mercy felt a twinge of regret. He was
just trying to help. "I know you're right," she said. "I'm just
not comfortable in groups. I guess I should try harder."

"Well, if I can help, let me know," Mark said.

"Maybe the three of us could get together once in a while,"
said Tally from the backseat. "We used to go out when you two
were . . . you know, a couple."

"Maybe," Mercy said, wishing the men would change the
subject. She had no desire to see Mark outside of work. Things
could get messy again, and she didn't want to take that chance.
Although she hated to admit it, she didn't trust herself around
him. He made her feel vulnerable, and vulnerability was nothing
more than weakness. Something she couldn't afford. "Batterson
said you'd brief me on the way." She needed to redirect the
conversation back to their assignment. "What can you tell me?"

"Not much," Mark said. "You know why our witness went
into protective custody. His real name is Samuel Murphy.

Twenty-six years old. Your age. Been in the program almost four years."

Mercy was surprised that Mark knew the witness's real name. Usually that information was never shared, even with the Marshals. "Wow, that's young to have already been in for four years. Most twenty-two-year-olds have connections they don't want to lose."

"Sam's parents are dead. No siblings. Bad breakup right around the time this happened. I guess he was ready for something new. We set him up in a house with some horses a few miles outside of Piedmont. He's done well. Originally he went to school to become a chiropractor. Now he's a rancher who breeds, sells, and boards horses."

"Impressive."

"Yeah, I guess he is."

Mercy watched as the snow began to blow sideways. It was obvious this storm was going to be much worse than predicted. She glanced at Tally in the rearview mirror. He hated cold weather. When he was a kid, his mother had a hard time paying the bills, and winters were tough. Tally had told her how he shivered beneath the covers most nights, making it hard to sleep. He'd always sworn that when he was an adult, his house would be warm in the winter. Even when they'd patrolled together, he hated calls that meant he'd have to spend long periods of time in the cold. She noticed a look on his face that concerned her. He'd been unusually quiet for the last few days, and she wondered why.

"You okay back there?" she asked him.

Tally, who rarely complained about anything, shook his head. "I . . . I'm concerned about Josh."

Mercy twisted in her seat so she could see Tally's face. "Josh? Is he okay?"

"Not really." He sighed deeply. "David Resnick's son is in Josh's class."

"Oh." About a month earlier, Officer Resnick had been shot and killed after stopping a car for a defective taillight. Unfortunately the guy driving the car had a trunkful of stolen items. He shot David as he approached the car. Thankfully, David's partner was able to phone it in quickly. The shooter was caught and arrested.

"He's terrified something's going to happen to me. I've done everything I can think of to reassure him, but it's not working."

Mercy frowned at him. "Why didn't you tell me about this?"

Tally shrugged. "You were dealing with your own stuff. Besides, I kept thinking he was okay. And he'd seem like it for a few days. But the nightmares keep coming back. He has them at least two or three times a week. He had a doozy last night."

"That's rough, Tally. I'm sorry to hear that," Mark said softly.

Tally was quiet for a moment. Finally he said, "I'm thinking seriously of leaving the force. Annie's dad owns a chain of car-repair shops in Georgia. He's offered me a job. Someday, when he retires, I'd run the business."

Tally's words were like a vise squeezing Mercy's heart. She wanted to say something, but it was as if the words were stuck in her throat. How could he think about walking away? He was a cop through-and-through. This wasn't the Tally she knew. He was the strongest person she'd ever met.

Her thoughts drifted back to the boy she'd met in grade school. His mother had named him after one of her heroes, Booker T. Washington. Unfortunately, Mr. Washington's middle name was

Taliaferro. Tally's real name was Booker Taliaferro Williams. Not a great name for a thin, geeky kid with a genius I.Q.

But now he was a police lieutenant, respected by his fellow officers, a true leader. With a wonderful wife and two children, he'd made his dreams come true, not allowing his environment to shape him like so many of the young people in his old neighborhood. How could he consider walking away from the only thing he'd ever wanted to do with his life?

"I don't want to hear this," she said, once she found a way past the lump in her throat. "You don't mean it. You're just having a bad day. You bleed blue. We both know that. You'll never quit. It's who you are."

"My blood is red, just like everyone else's," Tally said. "I can die. You can die. If something happens to me, what will become of my family? Annie is growing old before my eyes. Every time I leave the house, she's never sure I'll be back."

"It's always been that way, Tally. We all know what the risks are. Besides, you're not David Resnick." She then paused before asking, "Did my getting shot enter into this?"

"Of course it did," he said gruffly. "I almost lost you."

"But you didn't. You were there, and you saved my life. If it hadn't been for you, Tally, I would have died. Do you understand what I'm saying? If you'd been fixing cars in Georgia, I would be dead today."

Tally snorted. "I won't be *fixing cars*."

"Not my point," Mercy said, pushing back the emotion that threatened to overwhelm her. What would she do without Tally? He was the only friend she had. The only person she could count on. "I don't think you'd be happy working for your father-in-law. You were born to be in law enforcement."

"I was born to be Annie's husband and Josh and Gracie's father. They come first. Before the job."

"Sorry," she spit out. "I thought *I* was family too."

"Mercy . . ." Tally said, his voice low. "Don't make this tougher than it already is."

Mercy clamped her lips together and turned to stare out the windshield. The snow was coming down even heavier now, creating near whiteout conditions.

Frankly, the rotten weather matched her mood. The flakes were so thick she wondered how Mark could see where they were going. A perfect description of how she felt about losing Tally. She couldn't see a path that would allow her to survive without him—any more than she could see the road ahead in the middle of the storm.

CHAPTER
NINE

Mercy was silent for a while as Mark struggled to keep the car on the road. Even with the headlights on high beam, they could only see a few feet in front of them. He was only able to drive a little over twenty miles per hour.

"Do these shootings have something to do with why you've been following me around the past couple of weeks?" Mercy asked. Every time she'd stepped out the door of her house, Tally was there. It was really starting to annoy her, but she hadn't said anything because she figured he was just being overprotective.

"Maybe. I just want to make sure you're safe."

"Well, if you leave St. Louis, you certainly won't be able to keep me safe, will you?" she snapped. Immediately she was remorseful. "I'm sorry," she said with a sigh. "I know this is tough for you. Just please . . . don't make a hasty decision. Think about this carefully."

"Of course I will, Merce."

Tally was the best cop Mercy had ever known. St. Louis needed more officers like him. She was searching for another argument when she realized it was best to leave him alone. Tally would never walk away from his dream. He was just blowing off steam. Pushing him now would only make him more stubborn, and he might not be able to back down. He didn't like being challenged, even by her. The idea that he might leave St. Louis left her feeling more frightened than the night she was shot.

"How's your mom?" Mark asked, snapping Mercy back to the present.

"I don't know," Mercy said. "She started acting really strange after I was shot."

Mark laughed. "Strange? With your mom, I don't quite know what that means."

Mark had met her mom once while they were dating. Gina hadn't been friendly toward him. It wasn't personal. She hated men—all men. The meeting was more than awkward. It was embarrassing.

"You know my mother's never really gotten over my dad. Now that he's dead, I'd hoped she'd be able to move on. She's different . . . but I'm not sure what it means. Believe it or not, she's joined a church."

"A church? I thought you were going to tell me she was talking to ghosts or something."

"I guess she is—"

"The Holy Ghost," Mark finished for her. "Sorry. I knew where you were going."

Mercy couldn't hide a smile. When they were together, Mark had finished sentences for her more than once. No one had ever been able to read her thoughts the way he did. She missed that—and she missed him. The realization upset her. What was happening? She had to get it together.

"Maybe going to church, getting to know the people there, will help her," Mark said.

Mercy shrugged and wiped the condensation off the window, trying not to look at him. "Maybe. But not everyone who goes to church is like you."

"I'm sorry. I don't know what that means."

"You're not . . . I don't know, judgmental."

"Well, thank you. I appreciate that. So what church is she attending?"

"Some nondenominational place down the street from where she lives. She's getting involved in a kind of recovery group. Can't remember the name. I guess a bunch of sinners get together and share their terrible pasts." She shook her head. "Sounds awful. Nothing worse than a group of people sitting around feeling sorry for themselves. Of course, my mom's full of self-pity. She'll fit right in."

"Actually, I think I know the group you're talking about. A friend of mine is involved with them. They talk about their pasts, sure, but the idea is to deal with things and move on. Get stronger. Enjoy life."

Mercy snorted. "Oh, sure. The day my mother *enjoys life* is the day I crawl on my hands and knees down the aisle of that church and . . . become a nun!"

"It doesn't sound like a Catholic church, Mercy," Mark said, grinning. "I don't think they'd accept your request for nunship."

It was Mercy's turn to smile. "I've never heard the word *nunship*. I think you made it up."

"And you would be right."

"My uncle is involved with that group."

Mercy was momentarily startled when Tally spoke. She'd

almost forgotten he was in the backseat. "Which uncle?" she asked.

"Curtis. You remember him. The pharmacist?"

"Oh, yeah." She'd met Tally's uncle Curtis when she was in the fifth grade. He'd come to visit Tally's mom and ended up staying for several months. He slept on the floor in the living room, and many times when Mercy went over to Tally's house she'd find him there, snoring away. Even in the afternoons. He'd made Mercy uncomfortable. He always seemed strung out, not quite plugged into the world.

"How's he doing?" she asked.

"Pretty good. He's been drug-free for almost two years. Working again. My mom's over the moon about it." He cleared his throat. "My church just started a recovery group."

Mercy twisted around in her seat to stare at him. "What do you mean *your* church?"

Tally looked uncomfortable. "You know Annie and the kids go every Sunday."

"Yeah, I know. But you never do."

"I've gone."

"You've spent Sunday mornings at my house the past few weeks."

"I know. But after . . ." He cleared his throat again. Mercy could tell he was nervous.

"After what?"

"After . . . a while, I intend to start going with them."

Mercy turned back around to face the windshield again. *Great. First Mark decides to get religion, and now Tally falls for the hype?* She blamed it on Annie. Why did she have to shove her beliefs down Tally's throat? If he started trying to save her . . .

She felt Tally's hand on her shoulder. "Don't worry. It's not a disease. I'm not contagious. You can still be a glorious heathen if that's what you want."

Unnerved by his ability to read her mind, she spit out, "I'm not a heathen." Although she tried, she was unable to keep the annoyance she felt out of her voice.

"Sorry." Tally pulled his hand back.

"Why do you get so angry when people bring God up in the conversation?" Mark asked.

Mercy knew there was much more behind his seemingly innocent question. He'd asked her when they broke up why his new relationship with God threatened her so much. She didn't have an answer then, and she didn't have much of one now. "I . . . I don't know," she mumbled. But then a memory filtered into her mind. Something she'd totally forgotten. When her father walked out, she'd prayed. Prayed to a God she'd heard about but didn't know. Asked Him to bring her dad home. He hadn't answered that prayer. Her mother's emotional breakdown only added to Mercy's anger at this God who was supposed to be good and loving. Now she wanted nothing to do with Him. "I just don't believe He exists," she added, hoping that would end the uncomfortable conversation. "The idea of some heavenly puppet master pulling our strings is something I can't accept."

"And that's fine," Mark said. "You have the right to believe whatever you want."

He didn't seem upset at her response, and that puzzled Mercy. He'd been hurt when she ended their relationship, but he hadn't gotten mad then either. She couldn't quite figure out why.

"That's it?" she said. "Aren't you supposed to tell me I'm

a sinner and that I need Jesus? That I'm going to hell unless I ask Jesus into my heart? Isn't that the way you people say it?"

Mark glanced over and grinned at her. "Not while you're armed."

Tally's belly laugh from the backseat made Mercy smile. "Okay. I hear you. Now, can we put this subject to rest?"

"You got it." Mark held his hand up over the vents on the dashboard. "The windshield keeps frosting up. I don't know how much farther we can go. We may have to pull over until the storm passes."

Mercy checked the GPS. "That wouldn't make much sense. We're only a few miles away."

Mark gestured toward a motel on the side of the road. "That's our last chance until Piedmont, and I'm not sure what's available there. Are you guys certain you want to keep going?"

"Sure," Tally said. "We've got four-wheel drive. A little snow can't hurt us."

"Why does the phrase *famous last words* come to mind?"

Mercy reached over and switched on the radio. "Let's see if we can get an update on the weather. Will that make you feel better?"

"I guess so," Mark said. "I checked it before we left. Snow ending early. I'm not sure what qualifies as early. It's almost five o'clock."

Tally grunted. "Five? No wonder I'm hungry."

"You're always hungry," Mercy responded. Tally could eat anyone under the table, but he never seemed to gain weight. It was annoying.

"Sorry," Mark said. "We could have stopped earlier for something. I didn't think about it. Why didn't someone speak up?"

"I packed food," Mercy said. "After I find a weather report, I'll get out the sandwiches."

"*You* made sandwiches? I'm shocked."

"No," Tally said, "Annie made them. Sent them with us."

Mark nodded. "I should have known. Mercy's too cheap to buy food. About the only edible stuff I ever found in her apartment was out-of-date or had turned to penicillin."

"That's the truth," Tally said. "When I come over I've learned to bring something to eat with me. She buys enough to barely squeak by. I'd starve to death if I had to live at her place."

"When you're raised the way I was, you protect yourself," Mercy said sharply. "We never had two pennies to rub together. When my mother did get her hands on some money, she blew it on . . . stuff. Booze, restaurants, clothes, gifts. When it came to buying books for school, paying the electric bill or feeding her kids, there was never enough." She stared out the window. "I still tense up when I go to the store. Mom used to take food to the cash register and not have enough money to pay for everything. Usually the cashier or someone in the line offered to pick up the balance. It was humiliating. My mom counted on the kindness of strangers to get us through."

"I'm sorry, Mercy," Mark said softly.

Mercy couldn't understand why she'd shared that. Tally had gone through those times with her, but she'd never told Mark about it. Now she regretted saying anything. She hated feeling weak—especially around Mark.

She'd broken up with Mark after he started going to church, but that wasn't the real reason she'd ended the relationship. The truth was, she'd felt overwhelmed by Mark St. Laurent. As if she'd begun to disappear into him somehow, becoming only a shadow that followed after him. Fear of losing him—and of losing herself—drove her to do the only thing she could. Push him away before it was too late. When he'd told her about his newfound faith, Mercy realized she'd been handed the perfect excuse for calling it quits. She blamed it on that, and he appeared to believe her. At first she was relieved, but many nights, as she tried to drift off to sleep, those gray-blue eyes seemed to be staring into her soul, trying to pull her back. She glanced over at him. Being this close to him again left her feeling as if she were slipping back into an addiction. She wanted him—and she feared him. If only Batterson hadn't sent them both on this assignment. She forced herself to focus on the radio, scanning stations until she found a man giving the weather forecast.

"This storm has picked up moisture and power. When it hit a cold front moving through Missouri, snow began to turn to ice. This could be a very treacherous weather event. We're advising everyone in the affected areas to stay off the roads. Being caught out in this monster could prove dangerous. If you're already out, we hope you're prepared. If you get stuck, don't keep the car running. Turn off the engine for a while, then turn it back on occasionally for heat. Keep at least one window partly open when you're running your heater. You should have food, water, blankets, and flares. Please, folks, be safe out there."

Even though she didn't need to hear it, the forecaster mentioned the counties under the storm warning. They were right in the middle of it.

"Maybe we should have stopped after all," Mercy said.

Mark sighed. "You think?" He switched off the radio. "I can try to turn around, or we can keep going. We're about twenty minutes away from our destination. Hopefully this guy has a warm house, plenty of food, and someplace for us to sleep."

"Why can't we grab a motel in Piedmont before we get to his place?" Tally asked.

Mark shook his head. "He lives outside of town. We'll hit his ranch before we get to the town. I really think we need to stop before . . ."

He stopped talking as the sound of something hitting the car drowned out his voice.

"It starts icing?" Mercy said.

Mark didn't respond, just nodded and set his jaw. Mercy recognized that look. Now he was concentrated on one thing and one thing only. He was determined to get them to safety. When Mark set his mind on something, he was like a vicious dog with a bone. She kept quiet while he fought the car as it shimmied and skidded on the ice, but as the ice began to rain down with increased force, she became concerned.

"Mark, maybe we should pull over for a while. We have food and water. Shouldn't we try to wait it out?"

"I don't think that's a good idea," he said loudly, trying to be heard above the din of falling ice. Without warning their car began to spin wildly. "Hold on!" he shouted.

Mercy covered her face with one hand and grabbed the handle above the window with the other. She heard Mark praying as the car slid across the road, headed for a line of trees. A sudden jolt drove her forward in her seat. Then she heard something like an explosion, and everything went black.

CHAPTER
TEN

"Mercy? Mercy, can you hear me?"

As she struggled to open her eyes, for just a moment Mercy expected to find herself waking up in her own bed, warm and comfortable. But that idea vanished as the cold seeped in and she became aware of the pain that wracked her body.

"I . . . I'm hurt," she mumbled.

"I know. You'll be all right."

Mark's voice was comforting, but it seemed a long way off. She summoned all her strength to concentrate on his face, which was just a few inches from hers.

"Between your seat belt and the airbag, you've been beaten up pretty bad. I can't tell the extent of your injuries yet, although it doesn't look too serious."

Mercy reached up and touched her face. It was tender and she cried out.

"Sorry. We hit a tree, but you'll be okay."

"What about you? Are you all right? Where's Tally?"

She squinted at Mark in the low light. He looked okay, but as he leaned toward her, she saw him cringe.

"I'm fine. You know me. It takes a lot more than a tree to take me down."

"I'm okay too, Merce."

Mercy turned to see Tally leaning in through the open window. Thankfully he looked uninjured. She grabbed for his hand. "Where are we? What do we do now?"

"I don't know," Tally said. "I tried my cellphone, but I can't get anything. Is your phone in your purse?"

Mercy nodded. She tried to reach down for the purse she'd placed next to her on the floor, but it wasn't there. For the first time she realized she wasn't in the front seat any longer.

"The windshield shattered," Mark said. "I moved you to the back. I'll get your purse."

Mercy heard the car door open. It screeched as metal scraped against metal. A few seconds later, Mark was back. "I've got it. Do you care if I go through it?"

"Of course not," she replied, wondering why her words sounded so thick and muddy. She touched her mouth with her fingertips and came away with blood.

Tally squeezed her hand. "Don't worry. You just cut your lip."

Mark pulled Mercy's cellphone from her purse. "What's your code?" he asked.

Mercy rattled off the numbers before realizing what she'd done. She searched Mark's face, but he didn't seem to notice anything unusual. She breathed a sigh of relief. She was still using the date he'd first told her he loved her. She'd meant to change it many times but just hadn't gotten around to it. A voice inside her whispered *Liar!* She ignored it and steeled herself to concentrate on the situation at hand.

"Nothing," he said, scowling at her phone, exasperation in

his tone. "I can't tell if it's because of the storm or if we're just out of range."

"Can we drive out of here?" Mercy asked.

"No. The engine is toast. The inside light is working . . . for now, but I don't know how much longer we'll even have that." Mark cleared his throat. "Batterson knows we're on our way to the subject's house. He'll come looking for us when we don't check in."

"Maybe," she said. Her voice shook from the cold. "But if the cell towers in this area are affected, he may assume that's why we haven't contacted him."

"Seriously, Mercy. He'll send someone for us. We'll be okay."

How could he be so certain? Mercy didn't want to argue with him, yet they had to assume Batterson had no idea they were in trouble. They needed to formulate a plan to save themselves rather than wait for backup that might not reach them for hours. She was just about to say that when an odd sound cut through the noise made by the ice and wind. She could tell Mark and Tally heard it too.

"Stay here," Tally said, letting go of her hand. He pulled the hood of his parka up over his head. The car door creaked open again as Mark got out of the car to follow him.

"Not likely," Mercy muttered under her breath. When she moved, pain cut through her chest, but she kept going anyway.

Tally turned around and saw her struggling to get out of the car. Instead of protesting, he held out his hand to help her. Obviously he knew better than to argue with her. She covered her head with her parka hood, swung her feet out into the snow and ice, and carefully stood to her feet. She started to slip, but Tally caught her. She gently wrestled out of his arms, determined to make it without help. He nodded at her and then navigated his way to the back of the vehicle, holding on to the car for support. The ground was covered with about a foot of snow, but it was the ice layered over it that made walking so dangerous. Grabbing hold of anything she could to steady herself, Mercy struggled toward the front of the car. As Mark had said, it was totaled. The car had slammed into the tree so hard the engine had been pushed up toward the front seat. Another few inches and they probably wouldn't have walked away.

Mercy headed back toward the rear of the car, where Mark and Tally stood. As ice continued to fall, the three of them waited, peering out into the murky light, hoping the noise they'd heard was the whine of an engine. Was help on its way? Moments later a light cut through the darkness.

"It's a snowmobile," Mark said.

"I don't care if it's a sleigh with eight tiny reindeer," Tally said, "so long as we can get to someplace warm."

They waited until the snowmobile pulled up next to them. The man driving put the vehicle into idle and got off.

"You okay?" he asked through a ski mask. He wore a heavy all-weather coat with a hood. He was protected from the elements much better than they were.

"We're fine for now," Mark said, "but we need to get inside. My partner's hurt."

"Any chance you folks are from the Marshals' service?"

Mercy tensed. How did this man know who they were? She moved her hand close to her holster.

"Who are you?" Tally asked.

"I'm Daniel Andrews. I guess you're here to rescue me? You're certainly off to a great start."

"Yeah, sorry," Mark said. "This storm was a surprise. How did you find us?"

"When you didn't show, I began to wonder if you were stuck. Since this is the main road to Piedmont, I figured you might be here. Good thing I found you."

Mark nodded. "It sure is. Thanks for checking on us."

"Living in the middle of nowhere means you have to be prepared." He gestured toward the snowmobile. "I can only take one at a time."

Mark pointed at her. Usually, Mercy would argue with him. She didn't like being treated as if she were weaker or more vulnerable because she was a female agent, but this time she had no intention of quarreling with him. The pain in her chest made it hard to breathe, and the cold air wasn't helping.

"Okay," Daniel said. "You guys stay inside the car. It's your best protection. This will take some time. The ice makes it slowgoing. It might be an hour before I get back to you."

"We'll be fine."

"Don't forget the food and water in the tote bag," Mercy interjected. "Help yourself." She looked at Daniel. "I have a small bag in the trunk. Is there room for it?"

He nodded. "As long as you can hold on to it—and me—it's not a problem."

Mark took the car keys out of his pocket. Mercy held her breath, hoping the trunk would open. It did. He took her valise out and handed it to her, then slowly walked back to the car and got her purse.

"Can you handle both of them?" he asked.

Mercy put the strap of the valise over her shoulder and the purse strap around her neck, shifting it onto her back. It was all she'd brought with her except for the tote bag with food in it. Mercy knew how to pack. She brought clothes that could be mixed and matched, and she'd learned how to tightly roll everything so it didn't take up much room. At least now her hands were free to hold on to Daniel. So long as her purse didn't choke her to death, she'd be fine. Besides Tally's and Mark's suitcases, there was the gym bag with all their tactical gear in the back. One of the guys would have to bring it with him. She couldn't carry all three bags.

Mark moved to her right side while Tally held her other arm. They both helped her toward the snowmobile. First Daniel sat down, and then Mercy lowered herself gingerly behind him. She positioned the valise so it would be between them. That way it wouldn't fly off the snowmobile. As she moved closer, the bag pressed against her bruised chest. She almost cried out, but stopped herself. She fought back the pain and wrapped her arms around Daniel. At least she felt fairly secure. Tumbling off a snowmobile in the middle of an ice storm wasn't her idea of a good time.

"I'll be back as soon as I can," Daniel yelled. Growing in strength, the wind mixed with ice pellets swept furiously around them. "Lean against me," Daniel told her. "It will protect your face."

Mercy did as he suggested, burrowing her face into his thick jacket. When he put the snowmobile into gear, she jolted and it took every ounce of her strength not to cry out from the pain. As they took off, she turned around to see Mark and Tally making their way back to the car. If she were a praying person, she would have asked God to keep them safe. Leaving them behind felt wrong, but for now she had no choice. Her fate was in the hands of a stranger.

CHAPTER
ELEVEN

It seemed like hours had passed by the time they finally arrived at Daniel's house, yet it had only been twenty-five minutes. As he'd promised, Daniel had been very careful, albeit too slow for Mercy's liking. When they pulled up in front of the house, he leaped off the snowmobile and helped her to her feet. She was so stiff, not only was it hard to walk, it was distinctly painful.

"Let's get you inside and then I'll go back," he said loudly so as to be heard over the wind.

Mercy took the arm he offered. She was glad to see that he had cleaned off the sidewalk leading to the house. When they reached it, Mercy pulled her arm away. "I'm fine," she said. "Thanks."

He reached into his coat and pulled out a set of keys. Though she couldn't see much of the house due to the storm and the hood of her parka, it appeared to be a large cabin. After they stepped inside, the cabin feeling continued and stopped all at the same time. The walls were of polished wood, and the ceiling stretched to the second floor with its wooden rafters spanning the entire building. That was where the cabin feeling ceased. With modern and attractive furnishings perfectly arranged, the interior looked like something out of a magazine. Mercy couldn't stop looking around as she removed her parka. The room was actually very warm and inviting, and a crackling fire in the huge fireplace chased away the chill that seemed to have permeated every cell in her body.

"This is beautiful," she said.

Daniel held his hand out for her coat, and she gave it to him. He carried it to a coatrack near the door and hung it up.

"Thank you. I like it." He pointed to the wide kitchen that was part of the main room. "There's a coffee and espresso maker in there with lots of choices. Make yourself something hot." He swung his hand another way, toward the back of the room. "The bathroom is over there, and next to it is one of the guest rooms. You can put your things in there. I think you'll be comfortable. I'll be back as soon as I can." Without saying another word, he turned and walked out the door. Mercy still hadn't seen his face.

She carried her purse and her valise to the room Daniel had indicated. The knotty pine paneling continued on the walls and ceiling, the floor covered with thick gray carpeting. The king-size bed had a beautifully crafted quilt for a bedspread. The furniture was dark oak and looked antique. Mercy noticed a small fireplace in the corner. Hopefully she'd get to use it tonight to warm up. Her legs were blocks of ice, and she felt like she'd gone ten rounds with a heavyweight boxer—and lost.

She went to the bathroom and found a towel to dry her purse and valise. Afterward she carried them both back to the bedroom and slung them onto the bed. While the parka had kept her upper body dry, her pants were covered with snow and ice that was beginning to melt. Mercy needed to get out of them as quickly as possible. Thankfully she'd packed two pairs of jeans. She slowly removed her holster and gun, trying not to cause herself any more pain, and then she pulled off her pants. Even though her blouse was dry, she took it off as well, deciding to put on a sweater. She glanced at herself in the mirror and was shocked to see how bruised her chest was. It looked even worse than it did after the shooting. Her skin was mostly red now, but she could tell it would turn black and blue before long. She poked around a little and was relieved to find that nothing was broken. Bruises hurt, but in time they would heal.

Her face was still sore. Except for her cut lip, she hadn't sustained any damage that would show. All in all, she'd gotten off pretty easy.

After changing her clothes, she traded her leather pumps for sneakers. Feeling better, she grabbed her brush and went back to the bathroom to check on her hair. She'd pulled it up into a loose bun, but now of course it was a mess. She took it down, planning to pin it up again, but then decided against it. It was easier to leave it down. She brushed it out until it looked okay. Then she found some hydrogen peroxide and cleaned the cut on her lip. When she was finished, she gave the bathroom a closer look. A claw-foot tub sat in the corner with a shower head above it. A curtain on a rounded rod encircled the tub.

Although Mercy was used to quick showers, she longed to soak in the tub for a while. The hot water would help thaw her bones. It would also help to relieve the soreness from the crash. Hopefully she'd get the chance. The rest of the bathroom was comfortable and fully equipped. Lots of clean towels and washcloths, and a closet held several fluffy robes. It looked as if Daniel was used to company. It struck Mercy as odd for someone in witness protection. He must have really settled into his new identity and become comfortable with it. That didn't always happen. Most of the people in WITSEC came from big cities. The majority of them were criminals who'd turned on their associates. They were used to a very different kind of life than the small towns and out-of-the-way places where they were often relocated. Some of them didn't make it and left the program after a while. Daniel appeared to be the exception.

Before going to the kitchen, she went back to the bedroom and got her spare gun from her purse. It might seem silly to anyone else, but Mercy had a habit of hedging her bets when she was in a new place, faced with unknown circumstances. She went to the bathroom again and took steps to make sure her usual backup plan was in place in case she needed it. She'd never told anyone about it, not even Mark. Thankfully she'd never been forced to use it. However, knowing it was in place gave her a sense of security.

Once she was back in her room, she strapped on her primary weapon. Though she'd rather leave her holster off for a while, she was on assignment. No matter what, her gun would stay with her at all times. She gingerly fastened the shoulder strap. It reached across her chest and hooked onto her belt.

After attaching her holster, she decided to try her cellphone once more. Still nothing. As she put the cellphone back in her purse, she noticed the bottle of pain pills she'd been given for her shoulder. She'd barely taken any of them, not wanting to feel impaired in any way. But with the bruising on her chest, and her shoulder throbbing, she felt she needed the pills so she could function. Hopefully they wouldn't make her too fuzzy. She stuck a pill in her pocket and left the room.

In the attractive, modern kitchen she found the espresso machine Daniel had mentioned and selected a pumpkin spice latte. As it brewed, she poured herself a glass of water and swallowed the pain pill. A few minutes later, she was curled up on the couch with her latte. She checked her watch. Daniel had been gone a little less than thirty minutes. It would be at least another ten or fifteen minutes before he returned. After she'd finished her coffee, she decided to check out the rest of the house. She had no idea if Daniel's concerns were valid. This wasn't the first time someone in witness protection had felt unsafe, and it wouldn't be the last. In most cases, the threats weren't real.

A quick look around revealed three more bedrooms and a bathroom upstairs. The large loft area upstairs was obviously Daniel's domain. The rustic furniture was all made of pine, matching the walls, ceilings, and floors. The bedrooms downstairs were more like the guest room Mercy was in—classy but comfortable.

Mercy went over to the glass doors that led to the back deck. She opened one of them and peered out. Small ice pellets continued to fall. She remembered being in an ice storm years ago. It was bad, but this was much worse. How long would they be trapped here?

She could see a structure about two hundred yards from the house. It looked to be an old barn. She'd assumed someone who bred horses would have stables. Maybe the barn had been converted for that purpose. She wondered if there were horses inside. Would the cold harm them? A light from inside the structure made her think the area might be heated. She hoped so.

From what she could see through the storm and the dark, Daniel's house really did sit out in the middle of nowhere. There were no visible lights from neighboring houses. It would be easy to see anyone approaching if there really was somebody out there stalking him. Of course, even if Daniel were in danger, whoever wanted to harm him wasn't likely to try anything in weather like this.

They needed to find out why Daniel felt unsafe so they'd know what they were facing. She checked her watch again. He should have been back by now. Could something have gone wrong? As if in answer to her question, the sound of the snow-mobile's engine grew louder. He'd returned.

Mercy grabbed her parka from the coatrack and stepped outside. Daniel and Mark had just parked when a loud *pop* rang out and the glass in the door behind her shattered.

CHAPTER
TWELVE

Without hesitation, Mercy snatched up her gun and ran over to where Mark had pulled Daniel off the snowmobile, shielding him with his body.

"Get him inside," she yelled. "I'll cover you."

Mark grabbed Daniel and dragged him toward the house while Mercy walked backward, following them toward the front door while keeping her eyes and her weapon trained on a target she couldn't see. But no more shots were fired. After closing the door behind them, Mark secured Daniel several feet away from the front of the house. Then he turned off the front porch light.

"We need to reinforce that door," Mark barked. "Do you have any plywood? Anything that might work?"

"There's plywood in my workshop downstairs," Daniel said. "But before you get carried away, I think you need to look a little more closely at the *bullet* that hit the door." Daniel pulled away from Mark and opened the front door before Mark could stop him. "Look here," he said.

Mark and Mercy walked slowly toward him, their guns

drawn. In the middle of the shattered glass was a large chunk of ice.

Daniel pointed to a tree in the front yard. "That big branch broke off, and when it hit the ground, ice went everywhere. That's what hit the door. It wasn't a bullet."

Feeling foolish, Mercy holstered her weapon. "Sorry. It's just automatic. Protecting you is our top priority. It's in our DNA."

"Thanks," Daniel said. "Now I know I'm safe if we're attacked by ice."

Mark laughed, and Mercy forced a smile.

"I've got to go back and get your friend," Daniel said, walking out onto the porch.

"You shouldn't go out on your own," Mercy said. "We're here to protect you."

"Have you ever driven a snowmobile?" Daniel asked.

Mercy shook her head.

"How about you?" he asked Mark.

"No, sorry."

"And neither of you know how to get to the car from here. I'm afraid there's no other choice. The last thing we need is for you to run into another tree or go off the edge of an embankment and get stuck. If it makes you feel any better, if it's hard for us to get around, it's just as difficult for anyone else. I'll be fine, but your friend could die if we don't get him back here." Without another word, Daniel headed back outside.

Mark and Mercy watched him as he walked down the sidewalk and got onto the snowmobile. The engine started up and he took off.

"I don't like it," Mercy said. "If he really is in danger, sending him out alone isn't the best idea. Even under these conditions."

Mark nodded. "We'll talk to him when he gets back and make certain he stays close to home from now on. In the meantime, let's find that plywood and fix this door before he gets back. Otherwise we'll have a tough time staying warm."

About thirty minutes later they'd carried up several pieces of plywood from the basement. Although she was still sore, the pain pill had kicked in and Mercy was feeling much better. Mark found a drill and some screws and set about repairing the door.

Mercy watched as he worked. Once Mark finished, he came over and slumped down in a chair near the couch.

"I could really use some coffee," he said.

Mercy could see the weariness in his face. "Stay here. I'll get you a cup."

Mark's eyes widened with surprise. "Hey, thanks. That would be great. Usually you'd tell me to get off my rear end and get it myself."

"Unusual circumstances call for unusual measures," she said wryly. "Just don't count on this happening again anytime soon."

Mercy made herself another latte, then brewed a cup of regular coffee for Mark. That's the only way he'd drink it. Strong and black. She used to tease him about not having a taste for the finer things, and he'd come right back at her, claiming no real man should drink "froufrou coffee." As she stood in the kitchen, she found herself smiling at the memory. They'd had fun when they were together. In fact, Mark was the only person besides Tally who could make her laugh.

She was carrying the cups back into the living room when she heard the snowmobile approaching. She quickly sat the cups on the coffee table. Mark got up and followed her to the front door.

Daniel pulled the snowmobile up as close to the house as he

could. The ice had changed to snow again, and the wind had created drifts that pushed up against the porch. Mercy and Mark fought their way through the snow toward Tally, who seemed to be having trouble getting off the snowmobile.

"He's pretty cold," Daniel shouted. "We need to get him inside fast and warm him up."

Mark and Mercy helped get Tally onto the porch and through the front door. Mercy slipped twice and had a hard time getting back on her feet. The second time she accidentally used her right arm to break her fall. Pain sliced through her shoulder. She bit down on her lip to keep from moaning. The last thing she wanted was for the men to think she wasn't capable of doing her job.

Once they got inside, they took Tally over to the couch. Mark held on to him tightly as they lowered him down.

"I'm going to get you some hot coffee," Mercy told him.

Tally nodded. "Thanks. I . . . I'm fine. Jus . . . just cold."

"Let's get this coat off before the snow melts," Mark said. As he helped Tally off with his outer garments, Mercy brewed a large cup of coffee. After adding sugar and cream the way Tally liked it, Mercy carried the cup back into the living room.

Mark had wrapped a large blanket around the chilled police officer, who seemed to be much more comfortable. He was slowly taking off his gloves when Mercy put his coffee cup down on the table in front of him. She noticed Daniel standing by the front door, removing his coat and ski mask. She picked up her parka and held her hand out for Mark's. With a grunt he took it off and gave it to her. As she walked toward the coatrack, Daniel turned around. Mercy was surprised by how young he looked. She'd forgotten he was her age. At first she thought he looked familiar, but then she realized he was the spitting image of a young Hugh Jackman. Longer hair but with the same intense eyes.

He smiled at her and reached out for the coats she held in her hand. After they were all hung up, Daniel walked over to the couch where Tally and Mark sat.

"What now?" His question was addressed to Mark.

"Well, for now, we need to hunker down and survive," Mercy said, letting him know Mark wasn't the only Marshal in the room. She turned to Mark. "Have you tried your cell again?"

He nodded. "Nothing. The towers must be down or something."

"Not necessarily," Daniel said. "It's hard to get a signal way out here. That's why I have a landline." He went to the kitchen and pulled a phone out from beneath a counter. He picked up the receiver, listened, clicked the switch hook several times, and listened again. "Sorry, it's not working," he said. "The ice must have knocked down the line."

A loud crack sounded from outside, and the lights went out. Mark and Mercy jumped up, guns drawn.

"That wasn't a gunshot either," Daniel said firmly. "You guys have got to get used to that. Until this storm is over, it's probably going to happen a lot."

As if confirming his statement, there were several more loud crashes. Mercy moved to the back door to peer outside, but it was too dark to see much of anything. All she could see was a small area around the barn. The sound of frozen branches falling to the ground continued intermittently.

"We need to get some candles or—" The lights suddenly came back on.

"Backup generator," Daniel said. "We don't have as much power, but we'll be fine."

"Does this happen a lot out here?" Mercy asked.

Daniel nodded. "That's why there's a generator."

"I didn't see it when we rode up here. Where is it?"

Daniel hesitated and he glanced at Mark.

"It's on the west side of the house, isn't it?" Mark said quickly. "I noticed it when I looked out the windows."

"Yep. Great thing to have. Especially as cold as it is." His hazel eyes locked onto Mercy's. "You must be starving. Why don't I fix us something to eat?"

"Actually, I am hungry," Mercy said. "But before we eat, we need to make sure you're secure. I mean, that's why we're here, right?"

"Sure, but you can keep an eye on me while you're eating."

She studied him for a moment. "Can you explain to us why you think you're at risk?" she asked.

"A strange car driving by slowly," he said. "More than once. I'm pretty isolated out here. No one should be that interested in me."

"Maybe they want to buy your house." Mercy couldn't keep a note of frustration out of her voice. Why would Batterson send them out here unless he thought the threat had some merit?

Mark cleared his throat. "I believe the main problem was that someone in town asked about you—using your real name, right?"

That made more sense, though Mercy wondered why Daniel hadn't mentioned that first. Maybe she was reacting to the stress of the accident and the weather. Daniel was their witness, not a perp. Perhaps after she got a little food in her stomach, she'd feel better.

"Why don't I do a quick perimeter check before we eat?" Mark said. He pointed at Mercy. "You make sure the house is secure from the inside."

"What about the basement door and windows?" Mercy asked. "That would be the first entry site in my opinion."

"I wouldn't worry about it," Daniel said. "Metal door with locks and bolts, and the windows are barred."

Mercy looked carefully at him. "Were you expecting trouble?"

He shrugged. "The guy who owned this house before me put them up. I have no idea why."

"I can go with you," Tally said to Mark. "I'm fine now. Nice and warm."

"No, you stay here," Mark said. "I know you feel okay, but you've been in a car accident, and you've spent hours out in freezing temps. I need you to be one hundred percent. Rest up. And don't let Daniel out of your sight. I'll be fine." He gestured toward Daniel. "Are there any other outside lights on besides the front porch?"

"Not right now. There's a backyard light, but it's off. There's also a light in the barn, and it illuminates the back of the house some."

Mark nodded. "Okay. Why don't you scare up something for us to eat while I get a firsthand look at our surroundings?"

Mercy noticed the tension in his face and wondered about it. She'd worked with Mark many times, and she could tell he was worried about something. Since they seemed to be safe at the moment, she found his reaction a little unusual.

"Daniel, do you have a light-colored parka?" Mark asked. "Or anything warm that would make it hard for someone to see me out there?"

"I do. Follow me upstairs and I'll show you."

As the two men climbed the stairs, Mercy took the opportunity to check on Tally. She sat down next to him on the couch. "Are you okay?"

After taking a sip from his coffee cup, he nodded. "I told you I was fine. Can't figure out why Mark won't believe me."

"He's just being cautious." She glanced toward the stairs before lowering her voice. "Have you noticed that Mark seems distracted? Not quite himself. I can't figure out why. We haven't encountered any real threat."

"I haven't noticed anything," Tally said, frowning. "I mean, we wrecked our car, were stranded in the snow, and had to be carted through a major storm on a snowmobile. Not really the way we'd planned this assignment. I suspect we're all a little uptight."

Mercy sighed. "Maybe so. I don't like being in a situation where we can't get help if we need it."

"I don't either, but there's not much we can do about it, is there?"

Mercy agreed with him but found Tally rather dismissive, not the way he usually responded to her. Finally she decided she was just being paranoid. Besides the lack of outside contact, her chest was sore, and she wasn't happy about being snowed in with Mark. Maybe the stress she felt was making her overly sensitive.

They sat in silence as Tally finished his coffee. Mercy wanted to bring up his comments about leaving the police department, but she knew it wasn't the right time. It was probably her fear of losing him that was making her feel out of sorts. Still, the sense that something else was wrong just wouldn't go away. She rubbed her face with her hands. Some food and a good night's sleep would probably set her right again. Or as right as she could be under the circumstances.

A few minutes later, Mark and Daniel came downstairs. Mark was wearing khaki pants and a white hooded sweatshirt. He'd pulled it on over his coat, which made it a tight fit, but at least he would blend in with the snow a little better.

"Make it fast," she said. "It's freezing out there."

"I think the ice has finally stopped," Daniel said. "It's just snow."

Mercy shook her head. "Doesn't make much difference now. We're imprisoned in the stuff."

Mark arched an eyebrow. "If there really are any bad guys out there, hopefully it will be tougher on them than it is on us." He nodded at her before opening the front door. Then he slipped out into the night.

"I don't like him being out there alone," Daniel said. "The cold makes it hard to keep his head on a swivel." He walked toward the kitchen while Mercy watched him. She unbuckled her holster, put her hand on her gun and then started forward, following him.

"So someone in town asked about you? Using your real name?" she said to him. "Can I ask how you found out about it?"

Daniel frowned. "Why is that important? You sound as if you don't believe me."

"It's not my job to believe you or not believe you. It's my job to check out your situation and try to figure out if you're in danger. Asking about the threats against you is part of the job. What I can't figure out is why you seem to be bothered by my attempts to assess your situation. I thought you wanted our help."

"I do." He opened the cabinets and took out some cans. "Lots of chili." He then pulled the refrigerator open and scanned its contents. "Cheddar cheese, onions, sour cream. Looks like we've got it made."

"Chili will be fine," Mercy said. She walked closer to the kitchen. "So what do you expect us to do for you? Are you hoping to be relocated? That rarely happens a second time."

Daniel stared at her for a moment before clearing his throat. "I'm not sure. I guess that's why you're here. As you said, once you assess the threat, we can come up with a resolution."

She'd had enough and pulled her weapon, aiming it at Daniel's chest. He dropped a can of chili and made a quick move toward his waist.

"Well, that clinches it. But you're not armed, remember?" she said. "I want to know what's going on, and I want to know now."

"I have no idea what you're talking about. Are you nuts?"

"Keep his head on a swivel? Assess the threat? You've got training. You're not a witness. You're in law enforcement. Samuel Murphy, the person you used to be, was studying to be a chiropractor. There's no reason you should know the terms you do. And chiropractors don't automatically reach for a weapon when someone draws down on them."

"That's ridiculous. I watch shows on TV that—"

"Sorry, that won't work. Also, I don't think you've spent that much time in this house. Maybe enough to get a general idea of its layout, but not enough to know where your generator is—or even what's in your cabinets." Mercy glared at him. "Look, Daniel. If you don't explain yourself to my satisfaction, you'll be sorry. I'm not playing with you. My partner's exposed and I'll do whatever it takes to protect him. Do you have someone out there? Someone who can harm Mark?" She took a few steps closer, her gun trained on him. "I will shoot you in an extremity if you don't tell me what I want to know. You won't die, but you'll hurt more than you can imagine." Her voice rose. "Tell me who you are. Now!"

"Mercy, put your gun down," another voice called out before Daniel could respond to her.

She swung slowly around while backing up so she didn't turn her back on Daniel. Tally stood at the entrance to the kitchen, his gun aimed at her.

CHAPTER
THIRTEEN

Mark could tell something was wrong as soon as he came through the door. Daniel and Tally sat on the couch, and Mercy was across from them in a chair. None of them looked happy.

After he put his gloves in his pocket, he took off his coat, hung it up, then walked slowly toward them. "What's going on?"

"You tell me," Mercy said. She gestured toward Daniel. "This man isn't who he says he is, and I think you know it."

Mark hated seeing that look on her face. Betrayal. Confusion. He looked over at Tally whose expression made it clear he wasn't willing to push the deception any further.

Mark took a deep breath. "Mercy, do you trust me?" He stared into her eyes and didn't like what he saw there. "I know you have a hard time putting confidence in people, but I'm asking you to look into your heart of hearts. Do you trust *me*?" he asked again. He saw her mouth quiver. It was almost imperceptible, yet it was enough to tell him what he needed to know. "Okay," he said with a sigh. "We'll tell you everything. You won't like it, but I know you'll understand."

For a brief second he wondered if he'd made a mistake. He glanced at Daniel, hoping he wouldn't try to take over the operation. If he did, Mark could lose control. He intended to accomplish his mission and keep Mercy safe. Daniel looked like he was about to speak, but then he pressed his lips together and leaned back against the couch, as if waiting for Mark to resolve the situation.

Mark took a seat next to Mercy. "I'll tell you what you want to know, but it will take a while. Let's talk while we eat."

Actually, Mark wasn't all that hungry after downing two of the sandwiches Mercy left in the car, but he needed time to think. Should he tell her everything? What should he hold back? At that moment he just wasn't sure. Hopefully, Mercy would allow him some time to figure out his next move.

"I'm hungry, Merce," Tally said. "It won't take long to rustle up that chili."

Mark knew Tally was torn between his loyalty to his best friend and his commitment to protect her. Though they should be one and the same, at that moment it was hard to see it that way.

"No one's eating until I know who he is," Mercy said, pointing at Daniel.

"Okay," Mark said. "Mercy, meet Jess Medina. He's a detective with the gang unit out of LA."

"I . . . I don't understand."

"I'll tell you everything," Mark said, "but not right this minute. Please. As soon as the chili is ready, we'll tell you what's going on."

"But if we're not protecting *Daniel* from someone, what are we doing here?"

"Merce," Tally said in a low voice. "Please."

"Well, I don't seem to have a choice. But I don't appreciate being brought out here under false pretenses. I'm a federal agent. I should be treated as such." She glared at Tally. "Why wouldn't *you* tell me the truth? I can't believe you would lie to me."

"I haven't actually lied to you," he said. "I just didn't tell you everything." He reached over and grabbed Mercy's arm. "I couldn't, Merce. You'll understand once we explain . . ."

She forcefully pulled her arm out of his grip. "For most of my life, there's only been one person I trusted completely. Until now, that is."

Tally looked down at his hands. "That's not fair. You need to hear us out first. Then if you think I've betrayed you—I can live with that."

Mercy turned to Mark. "And you're supposed to be my partner on this assignment. Partners have to support each other. If you can't do that, you shouldn't have agreed to work with me." A sudden shadow crossed her face. "Does Batterson know? I mean, is he in on this?"

Mark took a deep breath. "Yes. It was his idea."

Mercy opened her mouth slowly, but then closed it. "Why keep me in the dark?" she asked.

Mark could hear the hurt in her voice. "Because there's a mole," he said. "We don't know who it is, and we couldn't take any chances."

"Surely, you don't think it's me?"

"No," Mark said emphatically. "No, I don't."

"But the chief does?"

Mark wanted to deny her suspicion, but he'd lied to her enough. Yet even though he didn't respond, it was clear Mercy wasn't fooled by his silence. Her wounded expression changed to stone. Mark had seen that look many times. It meant her defenses were up. The knowledge cut him to the quick, but he didn't have time to worry about her feelings. He had to make certain this operation was successful. Or at least looked like it was.

"Everything appears secure out there," Mark said, turning his attention to Jess and Tally. "I couldn't find signs of anyone near the house. No footprints. Nothing. For now, we seem to be all right. But it might not last long. They were very determined to get to us once we were isolated. We have to assume that plan hasn't changed."

"Seems to me the only way they could approach us is from the hill across the road." Jess gestured toward the front of the house. "The field behind the house is too exposed. They'd never come that way."

"Let's eat now, and then we'll set up surveillance. We can take turns." Mark absentmindedly ran his hand through his hair. "Even though you don't think we're vulnerable from behind, let's check the back of the house every so often. I've learned not to assume anything in this job."

"Don't you think one of us should be on the lookout now?" Tally asked.

"One of us can keep an eye out from inside while we eat. We won't take long. Right now I think our priority is to talk to Mercy. We can't move forward until we're all on board."

Tally grunted. "Hard to proceed with anything in the middle of a winter ice storm." He nodded at Jess. "I don't suppose you have any idea when we can get a signal out?"

Jess shrugged. "Not a clue. This storm turned into a monster before any of us had the chance to plan for it."

"Where are the people who own this house?" Mercy asked.

"They're friends of Batterson," Mark said. "Snowbirds who go to Arizona every winter. They told him we could use their house—so long as he fixes any damage." Mark cocked his head toward the front door. "The chief won't be happy about that."

"Not our fault," Tally said.

"You don't know our chief the way we do," Mark said, making a slicing motion with his finger across his neck.

Jess stood to his feet and smiled at Mercy. "I may be a fake witness, but I can prepare food from a can. Give me a few minutes to heat up the chili."

Tally got up too. "I'll do a quick check out back since Mark covered the front pretty well. Then I'll come back and see what we've got to drink besides coffee."

Once Tally had left, Mark got up from his chair and sat down on the edge of the coffee table so he'd be close to Mercy. "Look, if it was me, I'd be angry too," he said, keeping his voice down. "I want you to know that keeping you in the dark wasn't my idea. I told Batterson it was the wrong move, but he wouldn't listen. The shrink you've been talking to told him you were still *fragile*. Batterson translated that as weak."

Mercy's lips thinned. A sure sign she was angry. "I've worked for the chief for two years," she spit out. "He should know me better than that."

"He has a lot of deputies, and he's under pressure right now too."

Mercy got up and went over to the fireplace. The fire had died down so she added a few logs and stirred the embers with a poker. Within a couple of minutes the fire was blazing strong again. When she turned around, her expression was unreadable.

"We're stuck here, so there's nothing I can do about it right now," she said. "But if you think I'm going to just let this go, you're crazy. When we get back, I'm handing in my resignation. I'm sure the St. Louis PD will be happy to take me back. No one there ever treated me like a child."

"You should work wherever you want, but leaving the Marshals because your feelings are hurt *is* childish. It's not the reason to make such an important decision."

"My feelings aren't *hurt*. I hate being treated like some kid who has to be taken care of. And whether I stay with the Marshals or leave—that's not for you to decide."

"I know that, and I'm not telling you what to do. I'm just reminding you that losing your temper isn't the mature way to choose your career path."

She stared at him without comment. Mark finally glanced away. He'd never been able to stand up under her withering gaze. When she was like this, it was best to back off. She reminded him of an animal whose pupils dilated before it attacked. It wasn't that Mercy intimidated him, but once she made up her mind there usually wasn't any way to get her to listen to reason. It was one of her greatest weaknesses—yet he'd also watched her use it as a tremendous strength. When she was face-to-face with danger, she wouldn't back down. That's why he was so surprised when he learned she'd been shot by a frightened gangbanger. How had he managed to get one shot off, let alone two? Was she in trouble? Could the department shrink be right? She'd shouldered a lot of responsibility in her short life. Had she finally had too much? If she needed help, she'd never tell anyone. Especially him. It had taken time for him to make it past the carefully constructed walls she'd built around her heart, and then he betrayed her. Well, that's how she saw it anyway. And once you let Mercy down, there were no second chances. He'd lost her trust. Now all he could do was try to keep her alive.

He rose and walked toward the front of the house. He doubted they were in any real danger—yet. The problem they faced now was getting to safety before their adversaries were able to get through to them. Being unable to call anyone for help made them perfect targets.

"See anything?"

Mercy had come up behind him and was looking out one of the house's large windows.

"No, nothing. I could be wrong, but I think we'll have more to worry about when the weather starts to improve."

"You had no right to put me and Tally in danger."

He turned to look into her eyes. "It's just the opposite, Mercy. I'm trying to protect you. I . . ."

Before he could finish his sentence, Jess's voice rang out. "The chili's ready."

Dropping their conversation for now, Mercy and Mark joined Jess and Tally in the kitchen.

"Everything looks secure," Tally said. "I'll check again in a little while."

"Thanks," Mark said. There was a table near the doors that led to the back deck. As Mark sat down, he stared out the window. Thanks to the lights below the deck that Jess had turned on, and the light from the barn, they could see most of the backyard. It confirmed his belief that any threat would probably come from another direction.

"Are there horses in the barn?" he asked Jess.

"Nah. They're moved somewhere else every time the owners leave for Arizona. I checked it out when I first got here. There's nothing in there. Some feed, supplies for the horses, hay . . . not much else."

"Is it locked?"

Jess nodded. "I thought of that first thing. I made sure it was bolted and completely secure. I also nailed the windows shut. There were only two small ones, but I didn't want to take any chances. We don't need anyone hiding out there. That's why I turned on the light inside. I'm not saying it's as safe as I'd like it to be, but it's almost impossible for anyone to break in without our seeing them or hearing something."

"Good."

Jess brought four bowls of chili to the table, along with diced onions, shredded cheese, and sour cream. Then he took out a bag of corn chips from one of the cabinets. "That should do it."

Tally pointed at their glasses. "It's instant tea. I hope that's okay. If you'd rather have water . . ."

"It's fine, Tally," Mark said. "Thanks a lot."

"You're welcome."

After adding onions, cheese, and corn chips, Mark took a big bite of chili. Surprisingly it was delicious. The four of them ate in silence for a few minutes until Mark put his spoon down, making it clatter on the side of the bowl.

"Go ahead and eat," he told them. "I'm just going to talk for a while." He looked at Mercy. "What I'm going to tell you will be hard to hear," he said, "but you need to know the truth. Your life is at stake, Mercy." He cleared his throat and looked away for a moment. When he was ready, he peered deeply into her eyes, hoping to convey how serious the situation was. "The first thing I have to tell you is that your father wasn't shot by a random criminal. He died because he was targeted by one of the most powerful drug cartels in this country. He was murdered, Mercy. And now the cartel is after you."

CHAPTER
FOURTEEN

"What are you talking about?" Mercy couldn't comprehend Mark's words. Her father was killed during a dispute between two gangs. It was true the shooter had gotten away, but there was a witness. Someone who saw the whole thing unfold.

As if reading her mind, Mark said, "We're certain the so-called witness to your father's shooting was actually involved in the plot to kill him."

"I don't believe you."

Mark hesitated a moment, and Mercy could tell there was still something he was holding back.

"No more lies," Mercy said, trying to rein in her temper. "All of it. Now."

Mark looked at Tally, who slowly nodded at him. For some reason that made Mercy even angrier. She didn't like being out of the loop. It made her feel insecure.

"He was badly beaten before he was shot, Mercy. We kept that from you because . . . well, because we thought it was best."

"Thought it was best?" she repeated, each word sharp and emphatic. "He was *my* father. You had no right—"

"Mercy, Mark is telling you the truth," Tally said, interrupting her. He shook his head. "This isn't coming out right." He turned to Mark. "Start at the beginning. It's the only way it will make any sense."

"All right." Mark took a deep breath and pushed his chair back. Mercy could tell he was nervous, and Mark was rarely nervous. Her stomach was tied up in knots. She felt betrayed by the people she trusted most, and now her suspicions were working overtime.

"Everything started not long after your father came to town," Mark said, pronouncing each word carefully, as if every single syllable was invaluable. "As you know, he transferred from Virginia to St. Louis to be closer to you."

"So he said," Mercy shot back. "Let's leave my father's so-called good intentions out of this, okay?"

Mark frowned at her. "I'm not sure I can, but I'll try."

"You need to cut Mark some slack, Mercy," Tally said. "This situation had nothing to do with him. He was just following orders."

Mercy considered Tally's admonition. Maybe she *was* being unfair. She nodded at Mark, encouraging him to continue.

Mark rubbed his eyes before speaking. He was obviously tired. "Your dad worked with gangs in Virginia, so he was assigned to the gang unit in St. Louis. Since the gangs didn't know him, he was used in several undercover operations, alongside an undercover operative named Jose Alvarez. Your father's number one contact was Darius Johnson."

Mercy grunted. "Johnson again. You'd think he was the only

gang leader in St. Louis. It's like no other threat ever existed in the city except for this punk."

"It wasn't just his connection with the gangs," Jess said. "Johnson hooked up with Angel Vargas, the head of the Vargas cartel out of Mexico."

"The Vargas cartel is one of the most dangerous groups in this country," Mercy said. "Why would they mess with Johnson? They didn't need him."

"Except they did," Mark said. "The cartel's been moving heroin and other drugs into the city. Vargas came up with a plan to weaken law enforcement in St. Louis—and across the country. A way to take over major cities with heroin. They stand to make a financial killing."

"How?"

Jess got up and came over to her. He pulled up a chair next to her and sat down. "Vargas has deep, deep pockets, Mercy," he said, "but he has to have someone inside the gangs. Inside St. Louis. Darius Johnson was made to order. Before he died, he was the most powerful gang leader around—and he could give Vargas what he needed."

"And what's that?"

Jess looked over at Mark, and he nodded. Jess reached down and picked up a laptop he'd brought into the room earlier. He put it on the counter and flipped it open. Then he opened a link to a video and clicked Play. The video showed someone wearing a blue windbreaker with the words U.S. MARSHAL stamped in yellow on the back. The deputy's gun was drawn, and he approached a car pulled over to the side of the road. Although there wasn't any sound, it was obvious the deputy ordered the driver to show his hands. When the driver obeyed, the deputy looked around as if scoping out the area. Then, without warning, and with the driver's hands still visible, the deputy began firing shots into the car.

"I don't get it," Mercy said. "His hands were empty. Is there someone else in the car?"

"No one else in the car," Jess said softly. "According to the video, the Marshal shot an unarmed man. This happened a couple of months ago. The man in the car was William Smith."

"William Smith? You mean Dumb Willie? A Marshal did that? I don't believe it. Dumb Willie was a wasted drug addict. No threat to anyone."

"You need to look closer, Mercy," Tally said. "Watch it again. Look to see if you recognize the shooter."

Mercy let out a quick breath of air, upset by what she'd seen. Mark came over and sat down on her other side while Jess started the video again. This time, when the Marshal turned toward the camera, Mercy leaned in and looked closely at the image on the screen. What she saw caused her to gasp. She looked at Mark, her eyes wide with disbelief.

"It . . . it's me. But I didn't . . . I'd never . . ."

Mark reached over and held her arm as she swayed slightly. She felt as if all the blood had drained from her head.

"It's *not* you, Mercy," Mark said. "That's the point." He turned her toward him, taking hold of her other arm and forcing her to look at him. "The Mexican drug cartels are rich. I mean, incredibly rich. We found out a while back that they'd decided to use any bad blood toward the police for their own benefit. They plan to hook up with the most influential gang leaders in an area, pay them to kill someone, and then they film certain law-enforcement officers. They have an expert who turns the videos into this." He crooked his head toward the computer screen, still holding on to Mercy. "Is it perfect? Probably not. But all they have to do is release it to the news media. By the time anyone can prove this video isn't the real thing, the neighborhood will have already exploded with violence, looting, burning—all the ingredients necessary to direct police away from drug deliveries coming into the area. Violence is rampant right now for a lot of reasons, but most of it is coming from gangs killing each other for their piece of the action. It's only going to get worse when this plan swings into action. It'll be a bloodbath."

"But why would they use me in a video? I don't drive around the neighborhoods. I don't pull cars over. I'm not a cop anymore."

"They don't care about that. They have a reason for everything they do."

She pulled away from Mark but kept her eyes focused on him. She knew him well enough to see that he was being honest with her, and it made her feel cold inside. This was real. Her entire future in law enforcement teetered on the edge of an abyss. If this video ever got out . . . well, she couldn't even think about it. It was too awful.

"Okay, I get that," she said. "But again, why me?"

"I have to bring up your dad again, Mercy," Mark said gently. "Although his cover was never blown, as far as we know, he made himself appear invaluable to the gangs and the cartel. He got rid of evidence, warned them when the police were close by, and gave them information that would keep them one step ahead of authorities. Of course, this was all sanctioned by his superiors. His actions were part of their plan. And it seemed to work. The cartel grew to trust him. But Vargas was nervous, and he decided to make certain your dad would never turn on them. So they used you in a video and threatened your father with it."

Mercy shook her head, trying to understand what Mark was saying. "But why not put *him* in the video? Why would they think my dad would care what happened to me?"

"Vargas only had the original cellphone video to work with, and your dad was out of town on assignment at the time this murder occurred. So they looked for someone they thought he would care about. That was you." He looked deeply into her eyes. "Believe me, Mercy, many more people will lose their lives just so the cartel can make these videos. Some of them will be people the gangs want to get rid of. Rival gang members, CIs, anyone who is expendable. Once the gangs record the shootings, all they have to do is turn them over to the cartel. They'll do the rest. I hate to say it, but this plan will succeed. Evil and genius all at the same time. All law enforcement is at risk. No one's safe."

"And they won't just kill criminals to make these videos," Jess added. "Our CI told us everyone is a target. An innocent person coming home from work or going to the store. Anyone who fits the right time frame and can evoke empathy from the community."

"That's outrageous," Mercy said. "So they kill someone simply so they can make these fake videos? But their plan is doomed to fail. How many of them can they pull off before the public catches on?"

"That's the beauty of their concept, Merce," Tally said. "They don't have to release all of them to get the job done. They'll primarily use them as leverage. Law-enforcement officers know that truth doesn't necessarily matter in these situations. If the video gets out, their careers are over. Their lives, even their families, are at risk. Do you really think the people who hate cops will believe for one minute that these videos are doctored?" He shook his head. "They'll jump on anything they think shows us in a bad light. We'll never get the chance to prove the truth." He took a deep breath. "The cartel believes some cops will do anything to keep these from seeing the light of day. Including looking the other way so the cartel can accomplish their goals. It's a two-way threat. And don't think St. Louis is the only target. If it works here, it will spread all over the country. The Vargas cartel is a huge operation."

"But cops won't give in to that kind of extortion." Even as the words left her lips, the expression on her best friend's face made her stomach turn.

"Unfortunately, Mercy, some of them will. Out of fear. At least for a while. Long enough for the cartel to achieve their goals. Cleaning up the mess they make will cost untold lives and millions of dollars most cities don't have."

"So this attack is twofold," Mercy said quietly. The awful brilliance of the plan left her feeling almost breathless. "False videos stir up anger and distraction so the cartels can sneak heroin in, and at the same time they use these things to intimidate and manipulate the cops? It's a win-win for the cartels."

"And a lose-lose for citizens and law enforcement."

"But why can't we just expose it now? Before it starts?" Mercy asked. "Why not release the video? Get ahead of them?"

"The feds have some agents in deep cover with the Vargas cartel," Mark said. "Even we don't know who they are. They smuggled this out at great risk to their own safety. We can't go public with it. If it gets out, they could be exposed. The cartel will kill them. Except for the FBI and the higher-ups in the LAPD, no one outside of our agency has seen it."

"And Batterson knows all about it."

"Yeah. LA sent a copy of the video to him. He showed it to me and Tally. No one else."

"My chief hasn't seen it, although he knows you're in danger from the cartel," Tally said. "LA contacted him first when they found out about the threat, but they never shared anything about the video until yesterday."

"We had to be overly cautious, Mercy," Mark said. "Too much information has been getting out. Things no one else should know. In fact, this location was only given to me right as I was leaving Batterson's office. I'm the only one who's seen the file with the real information. Batterson wasn't taking any chances someone might find out where we'd be. Batterson and I only communicated through burner phones so no one could hack into our conversations. I tossed the one I had before I left and brought another one with me. Not that it's doing me any good now."

"We're the only ones who know where we are?" Mercy asked, shocked at how exposed they appeared to be. "Except for Batterson? What if something happens to him?"

"My boss knows," Jess said. "If anything happens to Batterson, my chief can find us. And we can trust him with our lives."

"Which is exactly what we're doing," Mercy said.

"But agents are following us, right?" Tally said.

Mark nodded. "That was the plan. They were only given our real location once they left headquarters. And they have people with them trained to watch over everyone carefully. No one will get a chance to release any information. I'm confident they'll be here soon."

"Well, that would be great planning—except for the major winter storm cutting us off from getting help," Tally said. He was obviously frustrated. Mercy completely understood how he felt.

Mark grunted. "Our window of time was extremely narrow. The threats to Mercy were growing, and we knew we had to get her to safety. Someplace where we could keep an eye on her. Letting her stay in St. Louis was too risky. Batterson decided to move her, knowing the cartel was watching. He wanted to draw them out—make them easier to catch. He and Jess's chief worked together on the plan. Chief Watson picked the detective he wanted here at the last minute to protect his identity. I didn't get Jess's name until I got the file after our meeting. Everything has worked out beautifully. But as Tally said, we didn't count on the weather. The forecast called for light snow. Not this. Might as well call it an act of God and move on."

"I don't think God had much to do with this," Tally mumbled.

Mark nodded. "Regardless, we're here, and we have to deal with the circumstances we've been given."

"So, as far as we know, we might not have any backup?" Mercy said.

Mark was quiet for a moment and stared past her. Finally he met her gaze. "As of right this moment, I have no way to answer that question. I think it's best we assume we're alone. We have to find a way to take care of ourselves."

CHAPTER
FIFTEEN

Mark's words seemed to hang in the air. Mercy looked around at the men with her, but no one had anything to add to his bleak pronouncement.

"Okay," Mercy said, "now the big question. Just why am I a threat now? Why does the cartel care anything about me? What is so important that you've put all of our lives at risk?"

Mark grew quiet as if searching for the right words. His expression made Mercy apprehensive.

"Although this plan was originally hatched in LA where the Vargas cartel is situated," Mark said slowly, "they chose St. Louis as the first location to implement their plan for two reasons. First, they were already there, even if they played a much more minor role than they are now. And because of past unrest, they felt our police department would be the most willing to capitulate to their demands."

"You mean because we're the most vulnerable?" Tally snapped. "That's not true. We have a top-notch department."

"The people who count know that, Tally," Jess reassured him. "Trust me. LA knows it too."

"Sure, everyone on the inside knows our true value," Tally said. "It's the outside forces that make it tough."

"Yeah," Jess said, "but the cartels and the gangs smell blood in the water." He shook his head. "I don't know how this is going to shake out, but one thing I do know. We just have to keep doing our jobs. Doing the right thing every day. Day in and day out."

Mercy reached over and put her hand on Tally's arm. "Jess is right, Tally. We'll be fine."

"I know. Sorry, Jess." He shrugged. "St. Louis PD has had a tough time lately. Besides other pressures, we lost a fine officer only a month ago. And when Darius Johnson shot Mike . . ."

"I completely understand." Jess offered him a smile, and Tally responded with one of his own.

Mercy couldn't help but find herself attracted to the handsome detective. She caught Mark staring at her and quickly looked away. Had he noticed? She silently scolded herself. Tally wasn't the only one being unprofessional. This was a job, and supposedly her life was on the line. What was she doing? She pushed thoughts about Jess out of her mind.

"You were going to tell me what the cartel is looking for," Mercy reminded Mark. "Why they're after me."

"Originally, the cartel contacted Darius Johnson to help them implement their plan," he said. "They sent Angel Vargas to St. Louis to manipulate Johnson into helping them."

"Angel is the son of Ephraim Vargas, the head of the Vargas cartel," Tally explained.

Jess nodded. "That's right. Angel told Johnson to shoot someone and make sure it was recorded on a cellphone. It was supposed to look as if the killer had no idea he was being filmed.

Johnson picked someone who just happened to be in the wrong place at the wrong time."

"Dumb Willie," Mercy said.

Mark nodded.

"Johnson sent one of his goons out to shoot Willie in his car," Jess continued. "Following Angel's instructions, the shooter approached him as if he were a cop. Told him to put his hands out the window . . . well, you saw that. Johnson filmed it. Once Willie was dead, Johnson was told to give the video to the cartel so it could be altered."

"It should have worked," Mercy said.

"It did," Jess said, "except Darius Johnson was an idiot."

"No argument there," Tally added.

"And he proved it. He gave the cartel a copy of the video and was told to delete the original. He erased it off his phone, but not before he downloaded it to his laptop. He wanted proof of what he'd done. He was proud of it. Unfortunately he couldn't keep his trap shut."

Mercy's mouth dropped open. "I take it the cartel had no idea he'd kept the original video?"

"Not until it was too late," Mark said. "Your dad found out about it and got a CI to download the video to a flash drive. The CI who was trying to stay out of jail on a drug charge did what your dad asked. But someone saw him and told Darius. He sent some of his thugs after the CI, but it was too late. He'd just handed the flash drive off to your father."

"Who's the CI?" Tally asked.

"You mean who *was* the CI?" Mark mentioned the name of a man recently found murdered.

Tally nodded. "We wondered about that. We try hard to

protect our confidential informants, but sometimes the gangs figure out what they're doing. We can't always pull them out in time."

"If my dad had that flash drive, he would have turned it in," Mercy said. "He wouldn't have given it to me."

"You're right," Mark said. "If there'd been time. The CI died the same day your dad did, Mercy. The day you had lunch with him, he was headed to the station—but the gang was already looking for him. Darius wanted that video back. Not only so the police wouldn't see it, but because he was afraid the cartel would kill him for doing something so stupid."

"And of course they did," Jess said. "D-Money was a dead man walking."

"There were some rough-looking guys outside the restaurant when we were eating," Mercy said. "My father seemed nervous about them. In fact, he cut our lunch short. He even left through a door in the back of the place." She frowned at Jess. "So Johnson thought my dad gave me the flash drive? But that's not true. He didn't give me anything. We ate. He left. About six hours later I was notified of his death."

"Batterson is certain those men you saw were sent by Darius," Mark said. "They probably grabbed your dad not long after he left the restaurant. They couldn't find the flash drive so they killed him. Made it look like he got in the way of a gang conflict. Even used someone to back up their story. Case closed."

"They're the ones who broke into my apartment during his service," Mercy said matter-of-factly.

"Yes," Tally said. "Right around that time Mark contacted me. He asked me to keep an eye on you. Make sure you stayed safe until they could figure out a way to protect you."

Tally sighed. "I stayed up most nights watching your place. Except for the nights Mark parked across the street to make sure you were okay."

Mercy looked over at Mark. "You did that for me?"

Mark colored a little. "Of course. You're a fellow Marshal."

Mercy studied him closely. Could he still have feelings for her? Surely not after the way she'd treated him.

"Then Batterson came up with the idea to draw out the cartel," Mark said. "He believed they'd be easier to capture out here in the country. They hide like rats in the city, making it almost impossible to find them. If we could arrest some of them, we could offer them a deal. Maybe we could take down the cartel and stop their heroin operations."

"Okay, I understand that," Mercy said. "But I still don't get why Batterson thinks I'm the mole. Why would the cartel try to incriminate me if I was helping them?"

Mark looked away and appeared to be staring into the fireplace. Once again her instinct told her Mark was hiding something from her.

"I know it doesn't make sense, but right now I think he suspects everyone," Mark said, still not meeting her eyes. "Knowing someone around him can't be trusted is driving him up the wall." He finally looked at her. "Don't worry about Batterson. Down deep he knows it's not you. He's cast a wide net because he has to."

"This operation was carefully calculated," Tally said. "As we said, only a few of us know about it. Hopefully we're safe. The idea is that when the bad guys are captured, Batterson will contact us and let us know it's safe to come out of hiding."

"We originally came up with this plan to keep you safe,"

Mark said. "Now we may have placed you in greater danger than you were in before."

"It's not anyone's fault," Mercy said. "If it wasn't for this storm, it might have worked."

"Batterson tried to cover all the bases. He even left a bogus file on his desk in case anyone tried to find out where we were. If our mole looked at it, they'd end up ten miles from our actual location. In the middle of a field. Our agents would be waiting there to scoop them up."

"And there was supposed to be a fake detour," Tally said. "A way to divert the cartel away from us. But I have no idea if it was implemented. It's possible Batterson never got the chance to use it."

"You have the correct file?" Mercy asked.

"Yeah, Carol gave it to me right before I left," Mark said. "No one has seen it except me. It has the right address—and info about Jess. His name, picture, bio . . . everything we needed to identify him."

"Let's get back to that flash drive," Jess said. "Here's what I can tell you, Mercy. According to our undercover guy, your dad had it when he left his meeting with the CI. He had it when he met you for lunch. And he didn't have it when they grabbed him right after he left the restaurant."

"Could he have left it at the restaurant? Hidden it somewhere?"

Tally shook his head. "We searched the place carefully. Even went through the dumpsters outside. Nothing."

"But I keep telling you my dad didn't give me anything."

"Did you leave the table at any time during lunch?" Mark said.

"Wow. I'm not sure I can remember." She frowned as she tried to recall that day.

"Did you make a phone call, try to find the waiter, use the bathroom?" Tally asked.

Mercy snapped her fingers. "Yes. I remember I had to wait on the bathroom because it was being cleaned."

"Did you have your purse at lunch with you?"

"Yes."

"Did you take it to the bathroom?"

"No," she said after thinking about it. "But there's nothing unusual in it. I would have noticed. I use it almost every day."

"Did you bring it with you?" Jess asked.

"It's in my room."

"Do you mind getting it?"

Mercy nodded and got up from the couch, though she was certain it was a waste of time. She carried a small purse. If there was a flash drive inside, she obviously would have discovered it by now.

When she reached the guest room, she looked out the window. "Great," she mumbled as the snow continued to fall steadily. Traveling would be almost impossible. They were so isolated. When someone could finally get through, would it be friend or foe? They needed to be prepared for every possibility.

She grabbed her purse and started toward the door when she remembered something. She pulled her leather jacket out of the closet and laid it on the bed. She'd worn it on the day she had lunch with her father and left it on her chair when she went to the bathroom. The jacket had lots of pockets. Some outside, and a couple of smaller ones inside. Pockets she never used.

A search through all the pockets didn't reveal anything except a wadded tissue, a pack of gum, and some lint. She was about to hang the jacket back up when she noticed a small tear in the inside lining. It was under the right sleeve.

"This is stupid," she whispered. But just to be certain, she felt the inside of the jacket, all along the lining. When her fingers touched something hard that had fallen down to the bottom, near the hem, she couldn't believe it. Not knowing what else to do, she ripped the lining open and reached inside. She pulled her hand out slowly and opened her fingers. In her palm was a small flash drive.

CHAPTER
SIXTEEN

Mercy stared at the thumbnail-size device in her hand, several emotions surging through her. The most powerful one was anger. How could her father have put her in this kind of danger? Didn't he know the cartel would come looking for her? She fought against the undercurrent of rage she felt inside. This was no time to think about her father's actions. She needed to figure out what to do next.

Her first instinct was to hand the flash drive over to the men in the other room. She trusted Tally with her life, and although she would have bet every penny she owned that Mark was on the up-and-up, Batterson was certain there was a mole in the Marshals' office. What if she was wrong about Mark? And what about Jess? She didn't really know him. Her father died over the information on this device. She made a quick decision to wait a while before telling the men what she'd found. Just until she was sure it was the right thing to do.

She looked around the room, trying to find a safe place to hide it. Putting it back in her coat was out since someone else might come to the same conclusion. Besides, now that she'd torn the lining even more, it could fall out. She settled on an old bookshelf in the corner. She pulled a book from the shelf and slid the flash drive inside it. She didn't think any of the tough law-enforcement officers in the other room would be borrowing Jane Austen's *Pride and Prejudice* anytime soon. It was a safe place for now, but later she'd have to find someplace more secure.

After replacing the book, she was starting back toward the living room when she remembered the reason she'd come here in the first place. She turned around and grabbed the purse she'd tossed onto the bed. Then she carried it out to where the men waited.

"What took you so long?" Mark asked when she came over and sat down.

"I went through the purse myself," she lied. "There's nothing there. No flash drive." She dropped the purse on the coffee table. "You can look if you want."

While she didn't really expect anyone to take her up on her offer, Jess snatched the purse up, opened it, and dumped out the contents. There wasn't much there. A small wallet with her driver's license, badge, and credit cards. Her brush and lipstick, a pack of breath mints, some tissues, her pain pills, and her keys. Mercy didn't carry much with her when she worked. She had a larger purse she used when she was off duty, but it was at home.

She realized that Jess was carefully checking the lining of the purse. "Don't tear that, please," she said. "There's nothing in the lining."

After looking it over one more time, Jess put all the contents back in the purse and handed it to Mercy. "I just don't get it," he said.

"Did anyone else come into the restaurant that day?" Mark asked. "Someone your father knew? Someone he could have passed it to?"

Mercy pretended to consider the question. Finally, she shook her head. "No. As I already told you, when he noticed the men outside, he cut our lunch short. He went out the back door and that's the last time I saw him alive." She looked at Mark. "Why didn't he just tell me the truth? We could have left together. Or at least I could have turned in the flash drive if he thought he was in danger."

"Because he knew you well enough to know you'd never let him walk into a dangerous situation without backup. I'm sure he was afraid you'd get hurt, Mercy. He gave you the evidence, but then he led the bad guys away from you."

Mercy's heart dropped. Her father did the only thing he could to protect her at that moment. He'd never intended to put her in danger.

"Well, we know for certain that whoever grabbed him didn't find the flash drive," Tally said, "or we wouldn't be having this discussion. Your father would still be dead, Mercy, but the plan the cartel created would be in full swing, and they wouldn't be looking for you. They believe you know where it is, and they're determined to make you give it to them."

Mercy tried to ignore the rush of fear that washed over her. She knew the cartel would do whatever it took to get the information they wanted. No matter what, she couldn't allow them to capture her. First they'd torture her—and then they'd kill her. When she didn't have what they wanted, her choices were simple. But now that she did, things were much more complicated. Three other lives were now at stake because of her.

"We're missing something," Mark said, "and I can't figure out what it is."

Mercy felt guilty for not telling him what she'd found. Yet many years on the police force had given Mercy a sixth sense—a feeling that she wouldn't ignore. That feeling had saved her life more than once. Those in law enforcement listened to their inner instinct. They respected it. And her instinct was shouting for her to keep quiet.

"Are you absolutely certain Nick had the flash drive?" Jess asked.

"He had it," Mark said. "According to our man undercover, our CI definitely downloaded the video of the shooting and gave it to him. Then he watched Nick walk away with the flash drive in his pocket."

"He should have gone straight to the station," Mercy said. "Having lunch with me first was a stupid move."

"Maybe he knew he was in danger and wanted to see you before something happened," Mark said.

"Or maybe he got lazy," Mercy said. "Something we can't afford to do in this business. What if Johnson had recovered the flash drive? This so-called plan the cartel cooked up would be putting lives at risk. Including cops. Having lunch with your daughter isn't a good enough excuse to jeopardize lives and ruin careers."

The men sat silently and stared at her. Finally, Tally said, "Merce, we'll never know what he was thinking. But he's gone now, so why not let him off the hook?"

Tally was right. Her feelings about her father weren't important right now. She needed to concentrate on doing her job. "Sorry. We need to deal with what is. Not what should have been."

Tally waited a few seconds and then said, "Let's go over it one more time. Nick has the flash drive. He has lunch with Mercy. Then he doesn't have the flash drive. It's not at the restaurant, not outside the restaurant, and Mercy doesn't have it." He shook his head. "It's not possible. Unless the stupid thing became invisible and hid itself, it has to be somewhere."

"What about his car?" Mercy asked.

Mark shook his head. "We searched it. Besides, he never made it back to his car after lunch. The gang grabbed him outside in the alley and took him away."

"When did you check the restaurant?" Jess asked. "How long was it after Nick's death before you found out about the flash drive?"

"Two days," Mark said.

"So it could have been taken by someone else?"

"We don't think so. First of all, the manager of the restaurant told us some guys came by saying they were with the police. They went through the place thoroughly. If it had been there, they would have found it."

"But they weren't really the police," Tally added.

"No, they weren't," Mark said. "They must have been Darius's men. They obviously didn't discover anything. Then we thoroughly went over everything again. Nothing."

"Maybe my father hid it and someone else found it," Mercy said. "Someone who didn't know what it was."

"Doubtful. Darius's men were there before anyone else had a chance to stumble across it. I mean, it's not impossible, but to be honest I can't see your dad tossing it where it could be picked up by just anyone. He knew how important it was, and he knew his life was at stake. He would have been very careful."

"You're right," Mercy said. She then remembered something her father had said before he left the restaurant: *"I'll call you later, Mercy. Keep your phone handy."* At the time she'd didn't think much about it. He probably planned to call her and tell her about the flash drive. Unfortunately he never got the chance.

Tally got up and walked over to the sliding glass door that led to the deck. He carefully pulled the blinds open a little so he could see outside. "So here we are, stuck in Piedmont, completely cut off from our backup, possibly being watched by the Vargas cartel, and we don't know where the flash drive is." He turned and looked at the group still on the couch. "What do we do now?"

Mark stood and said, "We do another perimeter check." He turned to Jess. "Shouldn't we check the barn?"

Jess shook his head. "Like I said, it's fine."

"We might want to turn the inside lights off. I don't want to give anyone ideas." Mark frowned. "Are there keys to the thing?"

"Yeah, on the key ring in the kitchen. My idea was to leave the lights on so we could see the barn. In the dark, it would be easier for someone to get in without our knowing about it."

Mark stared at him for a moment. "You might be right about that, but we also need to make sure the barn is still secure. We have to be certain Vargas's men aren't hiding out in there."

"I see your point," Jess said. "Listen, Mark, let Tally and I do the next check. We need to take turns and stay rested. Getting worn out won't help you . . . or any of us, including Mercy."

142

Mercy assumed Mark would argue with him, but he didn't.

"Okay," he said. "If you're sure. I'd appreciate that."

Jess grabbed his holster from the kitchen counter and strapped it on. Tally was already wearing his. He and Mercy kept their weapons near them at all times. It was like a part of their bodies.

After Jess was ready, the two men began gathering winter coats, hats, and gloves. Mark got them each a flashlight and walked them to the front door.

"Are we taking the snowmobile?" Tally asked.

Mark shook his head. "Too risky. The noise and the lights would make you easy targets. We just can't take the chance. We're lucky we got here from our car."

"We have to walk to the barn?" Tally said, his eyes wide. "You know how cold it is and how much snow is on the ground?"

"I know," Mark said. "Keep low. Be invisible."

"Thanks," Tally said, a hint of sarcasm in his voice. "It's going to take a while. The snow is deep and there's a thick layer of ice underneath."

"Yeah, treacherous. If it's too much, you'll just have to come back. I'm sorry about the snowmobile, but until we know if anyone's out there, it's too dangerous."

Tally looked at Jess. "I don't suppose you found any snowshoes or skis anywhere?"

"Sorry. Nothing like that. I was thrilled to find the snowmobile. My car is stuck out in a drift. It might be spring before I can thaw it out."

"Just make sure you don't get lost," Mercy said. "It's freezing out there, and the wind's blowing hard."

"The thermometer on the deck says ten degrees with the

wind chill," Tally said, his tone solemn. "I have a feeling I'm gonna feel like a Fudgsicle by the time we get back."

Mercy knew he wouldn't admit to his childhood fear of the cold in front of Mark. She thought about offering to go instead of him, but she couldn't come up with anything that wouldn't embarrass him.

"Be careful," Mark said. "And if something looks . . . wrong, get back right away."

"I don't think anyone's out there," Jess said. "Yet. But now it's a race. Who will get through the weather first? The bad guys or the good guys?"

"Maybe the cartel was better at forecasting the weather than we were and waited it out in St. Louis," Mercy said dryly.

"I honestly don't know," Mark replied. "If they sent anyone, it won't be more than two or three of their own people. They don't like to get their hands dirty. Especially if they have gang members doing their bidding. The cartels use them because they're brutal and willing to kill."

"True, but most of them are pretty undisciplined," Mercy said. "Would Vargas really trust them with something this important? I just can't see it."

"Maybe the gangs do the killing, but someone from the cartel oversees them," Tally said.

"Possibly," Mark said slowly. "They're extremely unreliable. I'm sure someone's controlling them. Either way, it's bad news. Both groups are full of bloodthirsty murderers."

No one responded to his remark. It was a fact. Cartels had slaughtered thousands of people as they tried to establish themselves and strengthen their foothold in America. They were ruthless and unfeeling. Mercy had once called them animals, but Tally corrected her. *"Animals don't kill just to kill, Mercy,"* he'd said.

The image of Tally's dog popped into her head. A year ago he'd rescued a small black-and-white fox terrier from inside a drug house in north St. Louis. His family already had a golden retriever, and although the dogs liked each other, two adults, two children, and two dogs made for rather crowded conditions. One day Tally announced to Mercy that Pippin, the name his son had picked for the dog, was now Mercy's. She'd refused to take Pippin in, though now everyone in Tally's family referred to Pippin as "Mercy's dog."

"You're afraid of falling in love with Pippin," Tally had scolded her, *"so you push him away. Just like you do people."*

Mercy argued with him, citing the time she spent away from home as the real reason she couldn't take the dog, but Tally wouldn't accept it. *"We told you we'd watch Pippin while you're at work. We already love him, so it's no problem."*

The truth was, Mercy felt drawn to the little dog. But loving him would mean that someday she'd have to say good-bye. She wasn't sure her heart could take any more good-byes, so she'd firmly but respectfully declined. She realized she'd drifted away and turned her attention back to the current situation.

"My money's on our people," Mark was saying. "They'll do everything they can to protect us."

"I hope you're right," Jess said. He cocked his head toward Tally. "Are you ready?"

He nodded. "As soon as we get outside, douse the lights, okay? Hopefully no one's watching, but if they are I don't want them to know we're outside."

"We'll take care of it." Mark grunted. "Wish we had walkie-talkies. I don't like being out of contact."

"Nothing we can do about that now," Jess said. "If we get in trouble, we'll wave our flashlights. At least we can communicate that way."

Mark nodded as he said, "Great idea if you want the guys with guns to see where you are."

"I'm talking about the kind of trouble where that no longer matters."

The serious tone in Jess's voice got Mercy's attention. She caught Tally's eye. "You be careful," she said, searching his face. "If something happened to you, your family would never forgive me."

Tally grinned and rolled his eyes. "Well, I see you have your priorities straight. You're more concerned about making Annie angry than my safety."

Mercy forced a laugh. "Hey, Annie can be pretty scary. Especially when it comes to making sure you come home in one piece."

She kept a smile pasted on her face as the two men slipped out the front door, even though she didn't really see any humor in their situation.

CHAPTER
SEVENTEEN

As soon as the men were outside, Mark turned off the exterior lights. "I really hate not being able to talk to them. If they get in trouble, how will we know?"

"I feel the same way, but they're smart and well-trained. They'll be fine."

Mark sighed deeply. "I need some coffee. How about you?"

"I could use a shot of caffeine." Mercy glanced at her watch. "It's almost midnight."

"When they get back we'll set up shifts. While one person keeps watch, the rest of us can get some sleep. We can't function if we're exhausted."

"Do you really think anyone's out there?"

Mark shrugged. "I honestly don't know."

"Could someone working undercover with the cartel have gotten word out that we might be in danger?"

"According to Batterson, the main guy is so deep undercover it's really hard for him to make contact. He's actually there to help shut down the entire operation. He just happened to hear about this new plan to move drugs into the city. That's about all he could leak. The FBI won't risk his real assignment for any reason. Even for us. Right now all the support we have is coming from St. Louis."

"And LA," Mercy said.

"Yeah, but Batterson's in charge of the operation since he's closer."

Mercy wrapped her arms around herself. She wasn't cold, but somehow it made her feel better. "So Batterson planned to send some agents after us? Seems to me it would have been smart to send them ahead of us. If we'd had people already in place, we'd be in a much better position."

"He might have, Mercy, but the truth is he didn't have much time. First we got information from our CI—then we heard from LA. At that point, we needed to move fast. The cartel was ready to make a major move against you. They planned to kidnap you, then force you to turn over the flash drive. We did the only thing we could do. Get you someplace where we could watch you 24/7. The idea about drawing out the cartel was secondary. If we'd had more time, this entire operation would be much smoother."

"You could have simply told me the truth and put me in protective custody," Mercy said.

"Look," Mark said, "we can go over this again if you want, but it is what it is. We made the best decision we could under the circumstances. I guess we could have offered to put you in WITSEC."

"You know better than that."

"Yes, I do." Mark studied her for a minute. "That's why we didn't do it. Believe me, I wanted to let you in on it from the beginning. So did Tally. It was Batterson's decision. Maybe I should have told you anyway, I don't know."

"No, you did the right thing," she said grudgingly. "I'm sorry. I shouldn't keep giving you such a hard time. I realize Batterson's in charge and what he says goes. You were only obeying orders. I would probably have done the same thing."

It was hard to admit that she would have followed the same path Mark had chosen, but following orders was something Marshals took seriously. Besides, there wasn't any sense in arguing about it now.

"I should have known something was up when Batterson assigned Tally to go with us," she said.

"Why? He works with the gang unit."

"Because Batterson doesn't like putting people together who have emotional connections. He says it makes them weak. He knows Tally and I are friends."

Mark stared at her, making her decidedly uncomfortable. "Then why do you think he put us together?"

She didn't respond because she couldn't answer his question.

Mark rose and went back to the kitchen, allowing his comment to hang in the air unaddressed.

Mercy followed him. "Okay, I give up. Why did he put us together?"

Mark pulled two clean coffee cups out of the cabinet and put them down next to the coffeemaker. "Batterson says we're better together. That for some reason we strengthen each other. And that it's the only time since he's been chief that he felt that strongly about two deputies."

Mercy hadn't worked for Batterson as long as Mark, yet she couldn't help being surprised. The chief was a by-the-book director and didn't seem willing to break protocol in any situation. It was true that she and Mark had done some good work together. Their last assignment was especially successful.

A hit had been planned on a local man who witnessed the murders of an elderly couple. Gang members had fired into their house, mistaking it for the residence of a rival drug dealer. The couple's neighbor saw the whole thing and was able to describe the car. He also saw the shooter and picked him out in a lineup. Usually in situations like this, witnesses were afraid to testify, but this man was determined to see justice done. Mark and Mercy were just as determined to keep him alive until he could appear in court. Not only did their witness walk away unscathed, the shooters were convicted of first-degree murder. That case was especially satisfying since in several parts of St. Louis gangs ran rampant, and fear often kept residents quiet. Retaliation was a real threat to the safety of innocent citizens, and very few residents were brave enough to incur the wrath of local thugs.

"I guess we've had some success," she conceded.

"I'd like to work together more," Mark said as he stuck a K-Cup into the coffeemaker. "That is, if you're game."

Mercy pondered this as he fixed their coffee. She really did like being partnered with Mark, but whenever she was near him, it seemed as if her emotions spiraled out of control. No matter how hard she tried to remain strictly professional, she found herself recalling those times they were together. His kisses, the words he'd whispered in her ear, his spontaneity, the times they laughed until she could hardly breathe. These memories tugged at her heart. But then he'd decided to get religious. After that, they had little in common except for their jobs. Mark's newfound passion seemed to seep into everything. Especially their love life. Though she had blamed him for the split, there was actually a sense of relief when it ended. He'd gotten too close. She felt vulnerable around him, a feeling she couldn't handle. Leaving herself that defenseless could never happen again. Never.

An image of his face flashed in her mind. His expression when she broke it off. He looked as if she'd slapped him across the face. The memory caused her chest to hurt, only these bruises were inside—deeper than the pain caused by her seat belt. Why couldn't she get him out of her head? And her heart?

"I guess we could do that," Mercy said at last, having a hard time getting the words out. "So long as you accept that nothing more can ever come of it. Nothing personal, I mean."

Mark was silent for a moment as he finished brewing their coffee. When he turned back around, he looked Mercy in the eyes and asked, "Is that really what you want?"

His question caught her off guard. She hadn't expected him to be so direct. "I . . . I don't know, Mark. We're just too different. We want different things."

He sat her cup down on the counter and scooted it toward her. He'd just opened his mouth to say something when a loud noise shattered the peaceful atmosphere. Mark grabbed her and threw her to the floor. He covered her with his body as several more bullets smashed into the kitchen, right above their heads.

CHAPTER
EIGHTEEN

Mark waited until he was certain the gunfire had ceased before rolling off Mercy. As soon as he braced his arm against the floor, pain shot through him. Involuntarily he cried out.

"I'm a U.S. Deputy Marshal," Mercy said angrily. "You don't need to protect me from . . ." Her expression then changed from resentment to concern. "Mark! Are you okay?" Still on her hands and knees, she began looking him over.

"I think so," Mark said thickly, "but I'm hit."

"You've been shot in the upper right arm," she said. "Looks like the bullet passed right through. We need to stop the bleeding." She crawled over to the refrigerator and pulled a dish towel from where it hung on the door handle. She wrapped the towel tightly around his arm just above the wound. "I'll wrap it as tight as I can for now—I'll do more as soon as I figure out what's going on. Stay here."

Mark tried to sit up, but immediately he felt himself start to black out. He couldn't protect Mercy if he was unconscious. He had no choice but to stay put. He watched as she slowly crawled across the floor. She needed to ascertain the shooter's position so they'd know how to protect themselves. Mark prayed that the house hadn't already been breached. He reached across his chest to his holster and pulled his gun out with his left hand. He wasn't much of a shot with his weaker hand, but he could still shoot someone who got too close to them.

He scooted around the corner of the kitchen cabinets so he wouldn't lose sight of her. After getting to the couch, she waited a moment before coming around the side and putting herself out in the open. Though they'd turned off the main light in the living room, there was a lamp on a nearby table that gave off enough illumination to make it easy to see if someone was watching the room. There were no more gunshots as she approached the table and switched off the light. At least now she wasn't such an obvious target.

She got up and crept toward the front of the house, keeping her head down. The plywood they'd placed on the side of the door earlier was shredded now by bullets, the glass on both sides shattered. If anyone wanted to gain access to the house, it wouldn't be difficult. Mercy glanced back at him. He'd pulled himself up to a sitting position, leaning back against one of the kitchen cabinets. His head swam, yet he was able to stay conscious. He had to be awake to help her. Nothing else mattered.

"Stay there," she called out. "If you move around, you'll lose more blood."

He nodded while keeping a tight grip on the gun in his left hand.

Mercy peeked outside through the broken windows, her gun in front of her ready to fire. She turned back toward Mark. "These shots came from a distance," she said. "I doubt the shooter knows he hit anyone. We have some time. First we need to take care of you, and then we need to fortify the front entrance."

"Tally and Jess must have heard the shots," Mark said. "Turn the porch lights on so they can see who might be out there. If the shooter approaches the house, they can take him out."

"I hope you're right. I don't want to make them targets."

"We don't have a choice. They know how to protect themselves."

Mercy found the light switch to the outside lights and flipped it on. She put her gun in its holster, pulled up the larger pieces of plywood, and tried to insert them into the open holes next to the door.

"If I ever buy a house, remind me not to get one with glass next to the front door."

"I will." It was a terrible design that made it easy for criminals to gain access to a home. Or, in this case, law-enforcement officials trying their best to stay alive.

Once again Mercy crouched down and crawled back to Mark. As she approached him, he noticed blood seeping through her jeans. She'd cut her knees. When she reached out to him, he saw her hands were bleeding as well.

"You're hurt," he said softly.

"Well, you're hurt too, so I guess we're even." She stared at him for a moment before saying, "Mark, I need to leave you for a while. I've got to check on Tally and Jess. Give them backup."

He shook his head. "No, Mercy. Stay here. They can take care of themselves."

She checked his arm. "You know better than that. You'd go out there if you could. I have to help them. And if they're okay, we all need to be together. Separating us makes us easier targets."

He nodded, recognizing she was right. Even so, he was worried. "I don't think I can go with you."

She put her hand on his cheek. "I'm aware of that. I've got some pain pills in my purse. I'm going to get them for you."

"No, I need to stay sharp."

"It's up to you. I've taken them, and I don't think they impaired me. I'm going to leave them here anyway. You take some if you need to." Staying as close to the floor as she could, she made her way to the coffee table where her purse was. She grabbed the bottle of pills and hurried back to Mark. "Here they are," she said, putting the bottle on the floor next to him. "Keep them nearby. I'll be back as soon as I can. Why don't you pray to that God of yours? We could sure use some help."

Maybe it was the pain, or maybe it was his concern for her, but Mark couldn't stop his eyes from filling with tears. He put his gun down on his lap and covered her small hand with his. "Please be careful, Mercy. If anything happened to you . . ."

She shook her head. "I know." She leaned toward him and kissed his forehead. "I'm sorry. Sorry for hurting you. I'm just . . . messed up, Mark. But never doubt that I care for you." She moved her hand and checked his wound again, then stood to her feet. "Keep your gun close. I'll be back."

"Do you promise?"

"Yes, I promise."

She gave him a small smile, and even though it wasn't an appropriate time for him to be moved by her beauty, he found that he was. In that moment he felt overwhelmed by love. It was stronger than the fear of losing her, stronger than the pain in his body. He'd never stopped loving Mercy. Was this the last moment they'd spend together? Was she going to her death? If someone entered the house, would he be able to defend himself? Realizing this might be the last chance he'd ever get, he took a deep breath. "I love you, Mercy," he said quietly. "I always will. If we get another chance . . ." As he looked into her eyes, Mark saw the conflict there.

"Just stay still, and don't do anything stupid," she said.

He watched as she started to walk away. But then she hesitated and turned back toward him. "I love you too," she whispered.

A few seconds later, he heard the shattered front door open and shut. Mark slumped against the counter, his gun in his hand and a prayer on his lips. A prayer for the safety of his friends, and a prayer for the love of his life.

Mercy had covered herself the best she could, but the cold struck her like a slap in the face. The snow had finally stopped falling, and now the wind whipped up what was already on the ground with intense fury. She could barely see where she was going. The shots had come from somewhere in front of the house. The shooter had to be across the road, hidden behind a high ridge of trees. Problem was, she couldn't see the trees now—or even the road. But that meant he couldn't see her either. It probably explained why his shots were so wild, and why there were so many. He'd been shooting blindly. For a moment the thought crossed her mind that perhaps he was close by, that he'd crossed the road. Pushing away panic, she hurried around to the side of the house and hid herself in a small alcove where she hoped she couldn't be seen.

Her first concern was to find Tally and Jess. Were they in trouble? Why hadn't they come back? She waited for a couple of minutes, trying to watch for any movement in the blowing snow, but there was nothing. Finally she crept out of her hiding spot and continued around the side of the house, sweeping the area around her with her gun drawn. The quiet was disconcerting. All she could hear were gusts of wind. She wished she had something to cover her face. It stung every time the small crystals struck her exposed skin. She was already trying to ignore the pain in her knees and hands—now she had to disregard the discomfort from the raw skin on her face. Physically she'd never been so uncomfortable, but for now she had to overlook all of that and concentrate on her job.

While she needed to stay focused on her goal—finding Tally and Jess—she couldn't stop thinking about Mark. About the first time he'd said the words "I love you." They'd attended a musical at the Muny, an outdoor theater in St. Louis's Forest Park. Then they'd walked through the park to the Boathouse Restaurant and sat at an outdoor table near the water. It was the perfect evening. The sky was clear, and the moon full. Mark took her hand in his and said, *"I've had a hole in my heart ever since Audrey died. But I realized this evening that it's gone. You've not only filled it, you've healed it completely. I love you, Mercy."*

She'd wanted to tell him she loved him too. In fact, she tried, but the words just wouldn't come. Somehow he seemed to understand, and her reticence hadn't ruined the moment. She realized that after that night, things began to change. She started to find fault with him—little things. Things that meant nothing. And now she might lose him forever. What was wrong with her? Why had she ruined the best thing she'd ever had? "Stop it!"

she said out loud, as if her mind was something she couldn't control. Feeling attacked on all fronts, she paused to gather her mental resources. She had to work through this. People she cared about were counting on her. Giving in to her emotions right now could make her unfocused. Unreliable. Love was making her indecisive. It was time to finish her mission and rescue her team. Summoning every bit of stamina she could, she redirected her thoughts to the task at hand, forcing everything else out of her head as she committed herself to saving her friends.

Mercy kept moving around the large house, crouching behind bushes or corners of the building that offered protection. Eventually she made it to the backyard. Even with the lights on, it was hard to see anything. The blowing snow kept her surroundings hidden behind a curtain of white.

She wanted to call out to Tally, but the wind would just cast her words back at her. Even if she could make herself heard, she would risk drawing unwanted attention.

At that moment she wished the outside lights were off. Even with the snow cover, she felt exposed. She kept bracing herself for another round of bullets, but none came. It took a few minutes for her to reach the area under the deck. She collapsed behind a built-in storage unit and slid herself back as far as she could, trying to catch her breath and figure out her next move.

Through the drifting snow she could see a faint light. It had to be coming from the barn. Could Tally and Jess have made it that far? While it wasn't impossible, she doubted it. The snow was too deep for them to have gotten there so quickly.

A sickening thought popped into her head. What if they were hurt and couldn't get back to the house? She took several deep breaths to steady her nerves. Different scenarios ran through her mind as she plotted how to locate Tally and Jess. Whatever she did, she needed to be quick so she could get back to Mark.

"Concentrate, Mercy," she said out loud, reining in her racing thoughts. If God really existed, she sure could use some assistance. "If you're real, God, help me," she whispered. "Or at least help Mark. He's one of yours." She shook her head. She was really starting to lose it. She was talking to a nonexistent being, hoping for some kind of divine help.

She decided to finish her trek around the house. It took a while to check the other side, but afterward she was confident that Tally and Jess weren't anywhere near the house. That left the barn. She checked her watch. She'd been outside for almost an hour. Before trying to reach the barn and putting herself out where she might be seen, she needed to find out if the men had returned. She fought her way through the snow to the walkout basement door. It was locked. She glanced up at the deck. If she climbed the stairs, she could knock on the glass sliding door. Mark should be able to hear her and let her in. So long as he was still conscious, that is. But if she climbed those stairs, she could become a target. Making that move was a gamble. A big gamble.

She stood there for a moment, weighing the risks.

Get inside, a voice whispered. *I'll keep you safe.*

Mercy held her gun out in front of her and swung it around in an arc. Who was out there? Where were they? When she was certain she was alone, she laughed and shook her head. "Man, I really am losing it." Chalking the odd experience up to stress, she decided to make the climb. With the snow blowing around her, she hoped she wouldn't be visible to anyone who might be watching. If Tally and Jess weren't back, she'd have to go out again. She'd have no choice but to try to reach the barn. Even though she had confidence in her training and ability, at that moment she wished Mark was at full strength. She could really use his help.

"Okay, God, I need some cover," she muttered. "If you want to keep me safe, I won't turn it down. If not, we may soon be meeting face-to-face." It occurred to her that this was the second time she'd addressed a being she didn't believe in. She shook her head. Mark was starting to get to her, and it was causing her to lose concentration, even hallucinate.

She cleared her mind of everything except the stairs ahead. Stay down, scramble up as quickly as possible, lay flat on the deck when she reached the top—and hope Mark heard her knocking. She took a deep breath and started her ascent, but before she could reach the second step, someone grabbed her from behind.

CHAPTER
NINETEEN

"Stop! It's me!"

Mercy's first reaction after letting out a yelp was to fight her way free and train her gun on her attacker. But when she turned, she saw Jess's stunned expression. She immediately felt silly. She should have seen him and she shouldn't have screamed. It was a feeble response. Embarrassing.

"I've been looking for you," she said loudly to be heard over the wind's roar. She glanced around. "Where's Tally?"

Jess didn't answer, but instead pointed to the top of the deck. At first she refused to move, but when he started climbing the steps, she followed him. He kept himself as low as possible, his actions mirroring her previous intentions. When they reached the sliding door, Jess knocked on the glass. Just as she'd hoped, Mark came to the door. When he saw it was them, he quickly pulled on the handle and slid it open. Jess and Mercy tumbled in. When they were safely inside, Jess closed and locked the door, then pulled the drapes.

Mercy removed her coat. "Where's Tally?" she demanded.

Jess winced in pain, and Mercy realized he was hurt.

"What happened?" she asked as she helped him to a chair at the kitchen table. "Are you all right?"

He tried to unzip his coat but didn't seem to be able to raise his arm without considerable pain.

Thankfully, Mark appeared to be doing a little better, although he was still weak. He'd changed into a clean T-shirt, and she could see that his gunshot wound had been redressed and bandaged. The bleeding had stopped.

Mark and Mercy both helped Jess get out of his coat.

"I . . . I need something hot," he said, his voice faint. "Please."

Mark went over to the coffeemaker and turned it on. "We'll get you whatever you need, but you've got to tell us what happened out there. Where's Tally?"

Jess slumped forward and dropped his head into his hands. Then he looked up and said, "We circled the house. Everything was fine. So we decided to go to the barn. The wind started picking up and it got harder to see. We were about halfway there when . . ."

Mercy waited impatiently for him to finish. It felt as if her heart were in a vise that was getting tighter and tighter. The coffeemaker made a gurgling noise behind them. There wasn't another sound except for the howling wind buffeting the house.

"When *what*?" Mark asked.

"When we were attacked," Jess finally replied. "I wouldn't have gotten away if it wasn't for Tally. He fought them like a crazy man, giving me a chance to run the other way. The men disappeared into the storm with him. That's all I know." He gazed into Mercy's eyes. "I started to go after them, but then I realized I'd either lost my gun or one of them had taken it.

Since I couldn't help Tally, I decided to come back here, pick up another gun, and get your assistance."

Mercy felt as if the ice outside had seeped into her body. She couldn't move. Couldn't seem to speak.

For the first time, Jess noticed Mark's arm. "What happened to you?"

"We were shot at," Mark said. "I guess by the same people you ran into outside."

"Was Tally all right when you saw him last?" Mercy could barely get the words out. They felt like rocks in her mouth.

"They beat him up pretty good . . . like they did me. But he was conscious. I got the impression they didn't want to kill us. They wanted us alive."

Mark brought a cup of hot coffee over and sat it in front of Jess. "It's clear the cartel has found us. But they won't kill us until they get what they want." He turned to Mercy, and she saw the concern in his eyes, though he tried to appear calm. "I'm beginning to think they were here when we arrived."

"But that doesn't make sense," Mercy said, her mind struggling to put the pieces of a confusing puzzle together. "How would they know where we were going? You said Batterson put this together at the last minute. How would the cartel know about this place ahead of time?"

Mark looked grim. "It had to be the mole," he said. "Someone told them about our operation. It's the only thing that makes sense. No one could have followed us in this weather. They were waiting for us."

"But our people aren't here? Batterson knew our location. Where is our backup?"

Mark just stared at her. Mercy could tell her question had

hit home. Even if there wasn't much time to put their plan into action, Batterson was nothing if not prepared. It wasn't like him to take so many chances.

"There *was* time, Mark," she said. "Time to send someone out ahead of our arrival. Maybe I don't know Batterson as well as you do, but he's smart. And careful. I can't believe he'd get us in a situation that could spiral out of control like this. I mean, we didn't know a major storm was coming, but everyone knew the weather could be rough. He would have taken that into consideration . . . and then taken proactive steps. Isn't that what he's always telling us to do?"

Mark appeared to roll this over in his mind. "Yeah, that makes sense. To be honest, something about this operation hasn't felt right from the beginning."

Jess, who had been quietly sipping his coffee, looked up at them. "I hate to ask this question, but"—he put his cup down on the table in front of him but kept his hands wrapped around it—"is it possible Batterson is the mole? Could he have sent us out here knowing the cartel would find us?"

Slowly, Mark went over and sat down at the table. "I . . . I don't think so. I've known him a long time. He wouldn't betray his people. Not for anything."

"Mark, did you talk to anyone else about this?" Mercy asked. "Do you know who he sent after us?"

The look on his face answered Mercy's question. She didn't even need to hear his response. "He told me to keep it quiet. Not to say anything to anyone about it."

Jess grunted. "I think Batterson is working for the cartel. This entire scenario was a setup designed to lure Mercy out here where the cartel could get to her."

"But why go to all this trouble?" Mercy asked. "Why not grab me in St. Louis?"

"That would be really risky," Mark said. "People knew about the video." He gestured toward Jess. "LAPD for one."

"Once we told Batterson about it," Jess said, "if something happened to you, it could lead them right back to him. He knew that. So he sends you out of town with the idea of catching the cartel when they follow you. He says he will protect us and help us shut down the cartel. But the truth is, he just sent us out like sheep for the slaughter."

"But Tally . . ."

"Tally was the only other person who knew about the video, Mercy," Mark said. "Maybe that's why he sent Tally with us. To get everyone out here who knew the truth."

"Like you said," Jess said, "LA knows. He can't fool them."

Mark shrugged. "Unless Batterson's working with someone there. The Vargas cartel operates out of LA. Who knows? They might already be blackmailing your people with this cellphone-video scheme. One thing I've learned about Vargas—he never leaves loose ends."

"But how can you suspect the chief?" Mercy asked Mark. "I thought you were friends. You've always respected him."

"I don't want to, Mercy," he said. "I mean, I don't really . . ." Mark sighed. "Give me another explanation that makes sense. Batterson kept this quiet. He gave us the file with this address. He's orchestrated everything . . . except the storm."

"He couldn't have predicted that we wouldn't be able to contact anyone."

"But why would that worry him? If we were in trouble, he's the person we'd call. It's the perfect plan."

"Look, you two," Jess said, "I know you're upset, but we need to come up with some kind of strategy to get us out of here alive. I'm not sure how many people are after us, but I'm fairly sure we're outnumbered."

"Our first priority is to find Tally," Mercy said, trying to keep her voice steady. Fear of losing him made her feel almost paralyzed.

"We can't help Tally if we're dead, Merce," Mark said. "Jess is right." He got up and walked over to the sliding glass door. "When the wind dies down, we'll have an advantage. We should be able to spot them before they get here. We need to guard our perimeter. It's our only chance to stay safe." He glanced at a large clock on the living room wall. "It's a little after two in the morning. In four or five hours we'll have some daylight. If we can hold them off until then, that should give us time to figure something out."

"If we get much light," Jess said. "With all the cloud cover and blowing snow, it will be tough going even with the sun up."

"What about Tally?" Mercy asked. "You can't just abandon him."

Mark shook his head. "We're not abandoning him, but we have no idea where he is. Going out to look for him now is too dangerous, plus we have almost no hope of finding him. They could have moved him miles away by now. And none of us is one hundred percent. Instead of forging ahead without thinking it out first, we need a solid plan. We've got to figure out the best way to save Tally—and ourselves."

"We need that flash drive," Jess said.

"If I did know where it was, I'd never give it to them," Mercy said angrily. "I'd die before I'd turn it over."

Jess was silent for a moment. Then he clasped his hands together and stared at her. "Mercy, you need to think about that very carefully."

"What do you mean?"

"I think that's why they took Tally. They're planning to use him as a bargaining chip."

The sickening truth sank in then as Mercy slowly nodded. "They're going to kill him unless I give them the flash drive, aren't they?"

Neither man answered her. They didn't need to.

CHAPTER
TWENTY

After opening his eyes, it took several painful moments for Tally's vision to clear. He hurt from having the butt of a gun slammed into the side of his head. He was sitting on something soft, his hands tied together behind him, wrapped tightly around some kind of pole. As he attempted to get his bearings, he realized he was inside a barn. Was he still on the property? He tried to chase the cobwebs of confusion from his brain. What was it Jess said about the barn? Horses had been kept here. Something about the owners moving the horses while they were in Arizona. But there was no sign horses had ever been inside this building. No feed. No stalls. Maybe he was somewhere else. If so, that would make it almost impossible for his team to find him.

"You finally awake, man?"

Tally looked to his left and found a young man staring down at him. "Who . . . who are you? Where am I?"

The guy sneered at him. "Sit still and don't cause no trouble. I'll tell 'em you back with us."

With that he turned and walked away. The guy looked like a gang member. Tally could tell more about him if he could see his tats, but he had on a large lined sports jacket associated with the Bloods in St. Louis. What was someone like him doing out here? Had he been sent by the cartel?

Tally wriggled around until he could sit up straighter. Besides a severe headache, his side hurt. He had a fuzzy memory of being kicked before he was hit with the gun. He tried to remember what happened, but the last thing he could recall was walking through the snow with Jess. He tried to concentrate even harder, but it hurt to think. When were they attacked? How could they have been overcome by gangbangers? They were trained law-enforcement officers. He tried to move his head around to see if Jess was with him, but no one else was near.

"Hello, Officer." A big man walked around from behind a partial wall. Dressed in black, he looked as if he were ready to venture out onto the ski slopes. Obviously he was prepared for the cold. It was certainly warmer inside the barn than it had been outside. Tally's ears and nose felt frozen. His hood had been pulled off, leaving his head exposed. Thankfully he still had on his coat and gloves.

"You wanna tell me what's going on?" Tally demanded.

The man pulled up a wooden chair that sat against the wall. He didn't look familiar. His face was badly pockmarked, and his teeth—which he displayed as he gave Tally a mocking smile—were stained from nicotine. Tally could smell cigarette smoke on his clothes even from several feet away. With all the hay scattered on the ground, Tally prayed he wouldn't accidentally set the barn on fire.

"You are not in a position to ask questions, my friend," the man said.

Tally could hear an accent. Hispanic. Was this guy connected with the Vargas cartel?

Tally tried to shift a little to get more comfortable, the effort causing him to want to groan from the pain. But he forced himself to keep quiet—he wouldn't want to give his captor the satisfaction. "Where's my partner?"

"Not to worry. He made it back to your other friends. He's telling them that we have you. And just about now they're probably figuring out that if they want to see you alive, they will give us what we want."

"The flash drive? You guys have it all wrong. Mercy Brennan doesn't have it. She never did. You're wasting your time."

The man leaned back in his chair and crossed his legs. Tally noticed he had on black boots with pointed toes. Not fit for skiing after all, although Tally had been right about the outfit being geared for warmth. The man sported a messy Fu Manchu mustache, and his eyes were black and soulless, reminding Tally of a shark.

"You're wrong—she has it. We know she does."

"And how could you know that? I'm telling you she doesn't."

The man licked his lips as if preparing for a meal. "She has to. She's the only one her father saw before he was . . . dealt with. She is the only person he could have passed it to."

"Before he was killed, you mean. Has it occurred to you geniuses that she already turned it in? That the authorities have it?"

"No. They do not have it. We are sure of this."

Tally made a sound of disgust. "Oh, yeah. Your *mole*. Maybe

Mercy knew about the mole and gave it to someone else. Someone who has help on the way."

The man laughed harshly. "I am afraid you are suffering under a delusion, my friend. No one is coming. You are quite alone. And before this day is over, we will have what we need from Marshal Brennan."

"I don't think you will. There are two U.S. Marshals in that house and an LA detective. Not people to mess around with. They know what they're doing, and they won't be easily overcome."

"It has been handled," the man said.

If it were physically possible for Tally to be any colder than he already was, a chill would have run through him at the criminal's words. Had they already breached the house? Were his friends in danger? He tried to shift his weight again. "You're underestimating them. And me."

The man didn't answer, just continued to stare at him.

Realizing he wasn't gaining any ground, Tally decided to take another approach. He needed to know what they were up against. "Who are you?" he asked. "And who's with you? Your friend looks like a gangbanger. Hardly reliable backup. Is he all you have?"

After a hoarse laugh, the man made a sweeping motion with his arm and nodded his head. "I am Elias Vargas. My brother is Ephraim Vargas, the head of the Vargas cartel. I have several men with me. Yes, some are gang members." He grunted and looked behind him to see if anyone was listening. "Necessary evil if we are to get our . . . products distributed throughout your city." He shrugged. "You're right. They are certainly unreliable, but they will kill without hesitation. And if we decide we don't need them anymore, not many people will mourn their loss." He laughed again. "Cheap labor."

Tally kept silent as he considered the information Vargas had given him. He wasn't naïve; he and his team were in danger. He also noticed that Vargas wasn't trying to hide the truth, and there was only one explanation for that. He had no plans to keep any of them alive.

CHAPTER
TWENTY-ONE

Mercy took a quick, hot shower and changed into dry clothes, strapped on her holster, checked her gun, and made sure she had plenty of ammunition. She grabbed the book off the shelf where she'd hidden the flash drive. After sliding the device into a plastic sandwich bag she'd found in the kitchen, she stuffed it into her jeans pocket. It wasn't a good hiding place, but she wanted it with her until she could figure out something better. It was a little after six in the morning and she'd gone over twenty-four hours without sleep. She was operating on pure adrenaline.

Mark wouldn't be happy with what she was about to do, but she didn't care. At that moment she had one purpose, and no one would keep her from carrying it out.

When she came out into the living room, she found the men sitting on the couch. There were plates of cheese, crackers, and some kind of meat on the coffee table, along with fresh coffee.

"Not the most nutritious breakfast," Jess said when he saw her, "but it will do in a pinch."

He looked better than he had before his shower, yet she could tell he was tired. And while Mark was strong, losing all that blood had weakened him. He looked pale, and there were dark circles under his eyes. It was clear neither man was at full strength. She would have to count on herself to get them through the next few hours.

"What do you think you're doing?" Mark asked when he noticed the coat she held in her right arm.

"I'm going after Tally." She said it firmly, hoping he knew her well enough to realize she had no plans to debate her decision.

Mark jumped to his feet, then swayed a bit before he regained his equilibrium. "No, you're not. I won't allow it."

Mercy pulled on her coat and zipped it. "I don't care whether or not you *allow* it. I'm not asking permission. I won't leave Tally out there without help. No way."

Jess stood slowly. "I'll go with you, Mercy."

She gave him a small smile. "No, Jess, but thanks for offering. Even though I know you want to help, in the end you'd just slow me down. Besides, you need to protect the house. Once I get Tally, we'll need a safe place to come back to."

"You seem to forget that I'm in charge of this operation," Mark said through clenched teeth. "And I'm ordering you to stand down. We have no idea what's out there. You could be walking into an ambush."

"Mark, I'm going. The only way you can stop me is to shoot me. And I don't think you'll do that."

"I have to agree with Mark," Jess said. "It's a bad idea, Mercy."

Mercy didn't bother to respond. There was no way she could turn her back on Tally. She knew he would do the same thing for her. She also knew what Batterson would tell her—what her training told her—but some things superseded her directives. And Tally was one of them.

"I won't let you go." Mark walked around the table and stood in front of her. "I won't shoot you, but Jess and I can keep you from leaving, no matter how bad off we are."

"I can handle myself, and I can deal with these scumbags," Mercy said, trying to keep her voice steady. Of course she was afraid, but there was no other choice. The faces of Annie, Joshua, and Gracie were front and center in her thoughts. Tally's family needed him, and if things went wrong, Mercy had to know she'd done everything she could to save him.

"They're after that flash drive," Mark said harshly. "They will torture you until you tell them where it is. Since you don't know, eventually they'll kill you, but not before you beg to die." His eyes searched her face. "I won't allow that to happen to you." He grabbed her arm. "If you leave this house, I'll follow you."

Mercy sighed. He wasn't strong enough to protect himself—or her. He'd only get himself killed. But she could tell he'd meant every word he said. He would follow her until he dropped.

Jess clutched his side, trying to act as if he weren't in pain. "And I'll go too. You can't go out there alone."

"So we all head out into the snow, you two collapse, the bad guys take our house, and we're left outside. Then we freeze to death." Mercy looked back and forth between them. "Great strategy. If you're trying to get us all killed, that is."

"We know that," Mark snapped. "But just like you can't leave Tally without assistance, we can't let you go out there alone. Instead of acting like the Lone Ranger, why can't the three of us come up with a plan to rescue Tally? Don't you think that would be a lot more effective?"

A voice inside Mercy's head argued against Mark's suggestion. Of course, it made sense, but there was an overwhelming sense of alarm that kept pushing her forward, trying to force her into charging ahead without caution. Was it her stubbornness or was it instinct? At that moment, she couldn't tell. If she waited too long, and Tally died, she would blame herself for the rest of her life. And to be honest, she wasn't sure what the remainder of her life would look like without him. If it would even be worth living.

She glanced at the clock on the wall. Seven in the morning. A new day. She walked over to a window and looked outside. The sky was still overcast and it remained windy, yet it didn't seem as strong as the day before. Maybe the weather was finally improving and help was getting nearer. Could she spare the time to talk to Mark and Jess and attempt to hatch some kind of plan? Should she tell them about the flash drive? She stared at the two men, who were ready to risk their lives for her and for Tally. Perhaps it was time to take a chance, to trust them with the truth.

"All right," she said, "let's try to come up with some way to rescue Tally. But I can't give this a lot of time. I'm convinced he doesn't have any to spare." She took a deep breath and let it out. "I have something to tell you that could change everything. First, I need another cup of coffee."

Mark waited as Mercy went to the kitchen to grab a mug. What was she planning to share? There was a part of him that wanted to tell her to be quiet. He couldn't vanquish the fear that she was getting ready to make them vulnerable. And that could be a huge mistake. The last thing he wanted was for Mercy to stop trusting people, but he was fairly certain they were in immediate danger. He wanted to let it play out so he could be certain. He worried he might be making a mistake, yet if he put a stop to things too early he might not get all the information he needed to keep them all safe. Right now, he desperately needed Mercy to trust him.

As he waited he couldn't stop thinking about how much he wanted to tell her again that he loved her. He'd slipped once, but he couldn't do it again. Not just because of the situation they were in. There was more to it than that. He was still keeping secrets from her, which left him feeling guilty. Was it better for her not to know everything, or was honesty more important? He wasn't sure anymore.

For some reason he thought back to the day he discovered God. Another deputy Marshal had asked him to church, and for some reason Mark said yes. To this day he wasn't sure why. When he walked into the building, he felt something he'd never experienced before. And when the people began to worship, Mark encountered a real, living God. A God who loved him. Who had a plan for his life. He was never the same after that. Slowly but surely, he was beginning to find himself. To like himself. He might not be the smartest person in the world, but he knew one thing. If he sold his soul for anyone or anything, he would slip back into the abyss he'd found himself in after Audrey died—and he'd never be the man Mercy needed. Or the human being he was destined to be. He prayed for Mercy every night, still hoping that God would work a miracle and bring her back to him. But so far, that prayer had gone unanswered.

Just then she came back into the room and sat down in a chair across from him. As he looked at her, he realized he could never make her more important than God. If there was any chance they could be together someday, he'd have to keep his priorities straight. Only God could bind their hearts together.

"There's something I have to tell you," Mercy said matter-of-factly. She went on to explain how she'd found the flash drive in the lining of her jacket. "I'm sorry I didn't let you know right away," she said, "but I just wasn't sure what to do. I didn't really know you, Jess, and I needed time to think. So now what do we do?" she asked when she finished.

Mark's hand went to his gun. He was ready for what he was almost certain was coming. And he wasn't disappointed.

"Now you hand that flash drive over to me," Jess said, pulling out his gun and pointing it at Mercy. His face was twisted into a cruel smile.

CHAPTER
TWENTY-TWO

"I don't think so," Mark said, raising his gun and aiming it at Jess.

Mercy couldn't believe what was happening. "Mark?" she said.

"It's okay, Mercy." Struggling to his feet, Mark faced Jess. The two of them stood pointing their weapons at each other as if they were in some kind of Old West showdown. It was obvious to Mercy that Jess's *injury* had miraculously healed.

"I don't think it's okay, Mark," Jess said. "I really don't want to hurt you, but I will if I have to. My father will insist on it unless I give him that flash drive."

"And just who is your father?" Mercy asked.

"Ephraim Vargas," Mark said. "I'm guessing you're his son, Angel. Am I right?"

For the first time since he'd pulled his gun, the man Mercy had come to know as Jess looked a little unsure of himself. "How do you know that?"

"Just a lucky guess," Mark said. "As we said earlier, gangbangers are incredibly unreliable. No self-respecting cartel would send them out alone on an important assignment. I had to ask myself how I would handle this situation. If I were them, I'd use someone I trusted to oversee the operation. We know Ephraim won't get his hands dirty, so who else would he send? I could only come up with one answer. His next in command. His son, Angel. We already knew you were working with Darius Johnson."

Angel laughed. His demeanor had changed dramatically, and Mercy couldn't understand how she'd ever thought him attractive. "Why didn't you tell me?" she asked Mark.

"It wasn't until he came back without Tally that I began to put two and two together. If I'd told you then what I suspected—"

"You were afraid I'd give it away."

Mark nodded. "I know how much Tally means to you. I felt I needed to let things play out until I was certain—and until we had the truth. I was concerned your love for Tally would make it impossible for you to wait for the answers we needed. I hope you understand."

Mercy didn't want to admit it, but Mark was probably right. She wasn't sure she could have held it together. She might have decided to beat the truth out of Angel Vargas.

"I'm so glad you cleared that up," Angel said, his tone dripping with sarcasm. "Now take off your holster and gun, Mercy, and kick it over here."

The last thing she wanted to do was remove her gun, but she was afraid he'd shoot Mark so she followed his instructions. Angel scooted her holster closer to him and then shoved it under the couch.

"So is Batterson really behind all this?" she asked. "He's the only one who could have pulled it off."

"Not that I owe you an explanation," Angel said, "but no, Batterson had nothing to do with it. We made an offer to someone close to him, and they got us the information we needed."

"But the file . . . I mean, Batterson told us to meet you here."

"Actually, Batterson told you to meet Jess Medina at a location two miles from here. My friend in Batterson's office changed the address, and I became Mr. Medina. You were supposed to trust me enough to tell me where the flash drive was. But now things have changed."

"But your reactions," Mercy said with a frown, "they were exactly right. Just the way someone in law enforcement would respond."

"I had a cousin in the LAPD," he said.

"Sounds like he turned out better than you," Mark said sharply.

Mercy saw Angel's eyes widen and his free hand clench in anger. Mark had hit a nerve. Maybe there was still a way to reason with Vargas's son.

"Depends on which side of the family you ask," he said bitterly.

"What about the real detective from LA?" Mark said. "Where is he?"

Angel spit out a derisive laugh. "Let's just say he's on ice, okay?"

"You killed him?" Mercy asked.

"It was for the greater good. A sad fact of life, but there it is." Then, looking at Mark, Angel said, "By the way, I don't believe in lucky guesses. Explain to me how you figured out who I am or . . ." He moved his gun until it was pointed at Mercy's head.

Mercy frowned at Mark. Why hadn't he taken the shot? He could have easily taken Angel out, but if he fired now, Angel's finger might twitch enough to get off a round, and she'd be dead. Yet Mark didn't look concerned.

"You said a couple of things that didn't make sense," Mark began. "They didn't register at first. You called Darius Johnson *D-Money*."

"So?"

"Darius is the only one who called himself that—besides a few of the people in his posse. He just recently started using it. It's not a well-known nickname. No one from LA would know it."

"Maybe you mentioned it."

Mark shook his head. "No, we didn't. And then there's this place. It's close to the description, but anyone who raises horses would have stables and a corral. I know Batterson was probably scrambling for a location, only he wouldn't have used this place—or he would have described it differently. And one other thing. Maybe you know all the right lingo, but you're not comfortable carrying a gun. I noticed you're not used to a holster, and you don't keep your piece near you at all times. For those of us in law enforcement, our weapons are like part of our bodies."

"Too bad you didn't figure all this out when it could have helped you."

A slow smile spread across Mark's face. "Who says I didn't?" He winked at Mercy. "You're not the only one who has a backup plan."

Mercy stared at Mark as confusion washed across Angel's face. Hope leapt inside her when she realized Mark wasn't the least bit worried.

"I don't need either one of you," Angel said. "I only need the video." He quickly swung the gun around and aimed it at Mark. "This conversation is over."

Mercy dove for Angel's arm, trying to keep him from firing, but she was too late. He pushed her away just as he pulled the trigger. But instead of hearing a shot, the only sound was a click. Angel looked surprised and pulled the trigger again. Another click.

It only took a few seconds for Mark to rush over to Angel, grab him, and push him to the floor. He stood over the stunned man, his gun pointed at Angel's head. "I removed all the ammunition from your weapons while you were in the shower," he said. "You won't be shooting anyone today. And I'll kill you without a second thought if you ever point a gun at this woman again."

"There's no way you can win. My people are out there. They've got Lieutenant Williams, and nothing will stop them from getting that flash drive. Trust me, if you want to see your friend alive, you'll give them what they want."

"You're wrong. We'll stop them."

Angel shook his head. "You can't save Tally. Not without their help."

Mark nodded at Mercy. "We need to secure him. I put the bag with our gear in your bedroom earlier. Can you get some handcuffs?"

Mercy hurried off to her room, found the bag, and pulled out a set of handcuffs. She also rounded up a belt and two scarves. When she got back to the living room she found Mark and Angel still in the same position.

"Cuff him," Mark said. He noticed the scarves and belt in

her hands. "I think we need something stronger than that to hold him. There's some rope downstairs."

"Right." Mercy strapped on her holster, went over and took Angel's empty gun from his hand, then stuffed it in her belt. She started to handcuff him, but then had an idea. "Mark, let's secure him to the stair rail. It's sturdy enough to hold him so he won't get away."

Mark walked to the stairway that led down to the basement. After checking the handrail, he nodded. "Right here," he said, pointing to a spot where the banister was bolted firmly to the wall. "I don't think he can loosen this."

Mercy pulled out her gun. "Over there," she said, gesturing toward Mark. "And hurry up." Angel swore under his breath, but he didn't fight her. Once he reached the stairs, Mark pushed him down.

"Right here," Mark commanded. Angel sat on the step Mark indicated. "Don't go until I've got him secured," he told Mercy.

She gave Mark the handcuffs with one hand while she pointed her gun at Angel with her other.

Mark put a handcuff around one of Angel's wrists, threaded the other cuff through the banister and secured his other wrist with it. Now there was no way for Angel to escape unless he was able to pull the banister from the wall—and that wasn't likely.

"Let's get the rope anyway," he told Mercy. "I want to make absolutely sure he can't get loose."

"Before you go," Angel said, "you should know your partner is keeping secrets from you. You really shouldn't trust him."

Mercy looked at Mark. "What's he talking about?"

"He's just trying to rattle you," Mark said, his voice low.

"Don't pay attention to him. Just get the rope. We need to find Tally."

"Okay." She ran downstairs and found several lengths of rope. Unsure of what Mark wanted, she gathered them all together.

As she worked she couldn't help but think about what Angel had said. Was Mark really keeping secrets? She felt ashamed for even allowing the question into her mind. Mark was right—Angel wanted to divide them. Get her to question her partner. It was his way of trying to weaken them. But as she carried the rope upstairs, she wondered if there might be a nugget of truth in what Angel had said.

"I don't believe it."

Richard Batterson had served as director of the Eastern District of Missouri's U.S. Marshals for eleven years. In that time he'd seen a lot of things. He'd had to deal with problems people wouldn't believe. But until recently he'd trusted the people he worked with. In fact, he had more confidence in them than in all three of his ex-wives. Of course, there had been a few problems. People who had to be disciplined. Even a couple who had to be removed. All in all, though, his deputies were loyal. Dedicated to the service—and to him. A few months ago it became clear they had a mole in their midst. He'd hoped it was someone outside his office. Not anyone close to him. So the information that was handed to him from Deputy Marshal Liz Dent left him dumbfounded.

"I'm sorry, Chief. I found this in the dumpster outside. It's real."

"Why in the world would you crawl into a dumpster, Dent? I don't understand."

Her eyes widened as if surprised by his question. "We heard there was a mole. Several of us have been searching for the leak."

"No one was supposed to know. How did word get out?"

He noticed the edges of her mouth quiver. "I guess you trained us too well, Chief. It's hard to keep secrets from your deputies."

He rolled his eyes and let an exaggerated sigh escape his lips. He actually appreciated her comment, even though some secrets were actually meant to be kept. If this information had gotten to the wrong person, it could have been disastrous. "So something made you suspicious and you decided to jump into the trash?"

"I wouldn't say I *jumped* in," Dent said, this time allowing herself a small smile. "Derek helped me climb inside. I offered him the honor, but for some reason he declined."

"I imagine he would." Batterson shook his head as he stared down at the crumpled documents lying on his desk. "If these had been shredded the way they were supposed to be—"

"We'd never have discovered the truth. I think our mole began to suspect someone was watching. She decided to get rid of the evidence as quickly as possible."

Batterson groaned. This betrayal felt incredibly personal. How could someone so close to him—someone he'd done so much for—do such a thing? He racked his brain for an answer, but nothing about it made any sense.

"Okay. I'm going to the conference room. I want to talk to her. Give me about fifteen minutes to prepare." He pointed at Dent. "And be cool. Don't tip her off before she's secured.

Running after perps is something I don't do anymore. I'm too old for it."

Dent nodded. "Got it, Chief. Fifteen minutes." She walked out of his office, leaving him alone with his bruised feelings and deflated ego.

How could someone on his own team help the cartel? Their partnership with local gangs was destroying major parts of the St. Louis community. People were dying right and left. The Marshals were dedicated to protecting the public. Knowing that someone he was close to had aided their destructive attack on his city made him want to throw up.

Batterson made several copies of the papers on his desk and then locked up the originals in one of his desk drawers. No one could get in there. He had the only key, and he kept it with him at all times.

He squared his shoulders and tried to prepare himself for what lay ahead. After taking a few moments to gather his thoughts, he left his office and walked down to the conference room. Dent and another deputy stood outside, guarding the door. He nodded at them and went inside where he found the person responsible for throwing away the recovered papers slouched in a chair. Her head hung down, and she didn't look up when he came in. Obviously she knew why she'd been rounded up and taken to the conference room. He stood for a moment and stared at her, then slowly closed the door.

"I'm praying you have an explanation for this. Something that will make sense to me."

Carol raised her head and met his eyes. It was clear she'd been crying.

"I don't think you'll be able to understand," she said softly.

Batterson pulled out the chair on the other side of the table and sat down. "Try me, Carol. I really want to understand. Is Marlon all right? Did someone threaten him?"

Carol was a single mother, raising her son, Marlon, who was only thirteen. Batterson couldn't remember her ever mentioning any other family. It had always been her and Marlon, and for as long as he could remember.

"Marlon's fine. He has nothing to do with this."

"Then why? Was it the money?"

A tear traced down her cheek. "Marlon is a good kid. His grades are almost perfect. He deserves to go to college. He deserves a chance to be . . . someone."

"But being *someone* isn't all about money or education, Carol. It's about character and ethics. It's about being the kind of person who can be admired. A person who stands up for what's right. Who helps people. Like I do. Like you did."

"I've been here for ten years," she said, venom in her tone. "I can barely pay my bills. All that *helping people* certainly hasn't helped me—or my son."

Batterson fought to control the resentment that rose up inside him. "Explain to me what's going on. This information was supposed to go to Mark St. Laurent. I'm assuming the file you gave him is different from this?"

She rubbed her eyes with the hand that wasn't cuffed to the table. "Yes."

"Carol, did you change the address?" He pointed at a spot on one of the papers.

She nodded.

Dread filled him as he slid the other paper over in front of her. "Is there anything else?"

The silence was awful as he waited for her answer. Finally she pulled the piece of paper next to her and pointed to a picture. "This," she said.

Batterson swore loudly. "You've betrayed the Marshals. You've aided and abetted known criminals, and you've put the lives of two Marshals and a police officer in danger. If they die—"

"Don't try to put that on me," she snapped. "I'm not holding a gun on them."

"No. You just handed them to the cartel on a silver platter. That makes you an accessory. If I have my way, you'll never see the light of day outside of prison again."

Her previously impudent expression melted and was replaced with apprehension. "But what about Marlon?"

"I guess you should have thought about that before you engaged in criminal activity and put our friends in harm's way."

Batterson didn't bother to hide his disgust for the woman. He hurried over to the door, swung it open, and ordered the two deputies waiting outside to take her away. He didn't bother to look back as they led her down the hall, but he heard her call out to him.

"Please, Chief. Please take care of Marlon."

When he got back to his office, he picked up the phone and made a couple of calls. Within minutes two of his top deputies sat in front of his desk.

He handed them each copies of the papers Carol had altered. "She took the file I gave her and changed the information before giving it to St. Laurent and Brennan."

Deputy Thomas's thick eyebrows shot up. "What does that mean?"

By the way he asked the question, Batterson was aware he knew exactly what it meant, but someone needed to say it.

"It means we have no idea where our people are. And the team I sent after them won't be able to locate them. The only thing we can be sure of is that they're in great danger—and not only from the outside. Frankly the threat from within is even worse." He pointed at the paper that contained a picture of LA Detective Jess Medina, along with his bio and professional information. "Carol sent them right into a trap set by the Vargas cartel. Unless we get our deputies and Lieutenant Williams out of there right away, they're dead."

CHAPTER
TWENTY-THREE

Mercy went over and grabbed her coat.

"That won't be enough," Mark said. "You need to put on all the clothing you can. Double or triple your socks, put on your boots—wear anything you can to protect yourself from the cold."

"How long do you think we'll be out there?" Mercy asked.

Mark, who had grabbed his own outerwear while Mercy was in the basement, pulled on his third sweater. If the situation wasn't so serious, Mercy would have laughed at him. Mark looked like the bundled-up boy in *A Christmas Story* who complained to his mother that he couldn't put his arms down.

"Like you said, we may not be able to come back at all. Once we vacate this house, whoever's out there just might take it over."

"I hope that doesn't happen," Mercy said, shaking her head. "We may need to get Tally somewhere warm, and fast."

"We've got to take the snowmobile. I know it makes us a target, but at this point I don't think we have a choice. We're running out of time. I didn't see many other houses out here, but we passed a couple of farms on the way to this place. Maybe we can reach one of them. We need help finding Tally. If we can get a call out to law enforcement, we'll have a much better chance."

"But if our phones are out, what makes you think everyone else's isn't?"

"You might be right. Still, we've got to try. One of the farms may have a snowplow, or some other way of getting help. If nothing else, at least we can stay warm."

"And put an innocent family in danger."

Mark paused in his efforts and glared at her. "If you have a better idea, I'm happy to hear it."

"Maybe one of us should go for Tally, and the other one should guard the house."

"Absolutely not. If we split up it will make it that much easier for the cartel to take us out. Our greatest strength is to remain together." He shook his head. "Look, either we stay here and protect ourselves until help comes, or we search for Tally. We can't do both." He took a deep breath, then blew it out forcefully. "If everything goes our way, maybe we can rescue Tally and get back to the house before the cartel finds us."

Mercy knew he didn't actually believe that. And he was right. In the St. Louis PD, cops told each other that they "had their six"—had their back. Right now, rescuing Tally and watching out for each other was their most important job. Keeping the house secure came last.

"Let's just get out there. Tally needs us."

Mark finished pulling on his coat. "I found these in the closet," he said, grabbing some large rubber boots. "I don't know if they belong to Angel or the homeowner, but I'm taking them."

"If this isn't the place we were supposed to be," Mercy said, "then what happened to the people who own this house?"

"I think Angel told the truth about the homeowner being gone. I saw some brochures for a resort in Florida in a kitchen drawer. Who knows? Maybe the guy who lives here is a friend of the cartel. My guess is the cartel picked this place because it was the closest thing they could find to fit the original description. I wondered why horses would be kept in a barn instead of in stables, but it was the lack of a corral that really made me suspicious."

Mercy stopped pulling on another pair of boots she'd found in the closet. "Maybe there are horses. We need to check—just in case. They might need help."

Mercy had a soft spot in her heart for horses. When she was little, she used to take riding lessons at a local stable. It was the one thing her dad did with her. When he left, her mother stopped the lessons since they couldn't afford them. Mercy not only lost her father, she lost something else she loved—her horses.

"I'm as sure as I can be that they're not there, Mercy, but we'll check on it when we can. It's clear we've got to see inside that barn for a variety of reasons. Hopefully we won't get an unpleasant surprise. I've been wondering if Vargas's people are hiding out there."

"Which means Tally might be with them."

"It's possible."

They were both silent as they finished preparing for their trek outside. Mercy couldn't help glancing at the man handcuffed to the banister. It was still hard to believe *Jess* had turned out to be Angel Vargas. Why hadn't she sensed something was wrong sooner? Where was that gut instinct she thought she could trust? It seemed to be failing her. "Which way out?" she asked when she was ready to go.

Mark hesitated for a moment. "The snowmobile is still in the front yard, but we can't just walk out there since we've already been fired on once from that direction. Let's go out the basement door and around the side of the house. If we stay down and keep ourselves behind the bushes, we might be able to pull the snowmobile out of sight before we start it up."

"Okay. Whatever you think."

Mark turned toward her. "Could you repeat that? I'm not sure I heard you right."

"Very funny. Trust me, if I think you're wrong, I'll tell you."

"I don't doubt that."

He walked toward the stairs. Angel didn't say anything, just glared at Mark as he approached

"Hey, what if our guys get here while we're gone?" Mercy asked. "Shouldn't we leave a note to let them know this is Angel Vargas? He could tell them anything. The last thing we need is for him to talk his way out of those handcuffs."

Mark stopped in his tracks. "Good point."

Mercy grabbed a notebook on the kitchen counter and wrote a quick note explaining who Jess really was.

"Don't mention why we're not here or where we're going," Mark said. "No point giving the cartel a way to find us."

"I agree." She left the notebook open to the page she'd used for her message. "That's all we can do." She then remembered something. "What about his gun and ammo?"

"I hid them. I don't think he'll find them if he manages to free himself, which would be almost impossible."

"Okay. Let's get out of here."

Once again they headed for the stairs. Mark was already downstairs and out of sight before Mercy started down. As she stepped around Angel, his hand grabbed her ankle. She yelped in surprise as she tumbled down the stairs.

"Mercy!" Mark called out. "Are you all right?"

"I'm . . . fine." But she didn't feel fine. She'd slammed her head on the hard floor when she got to the bottom and for the first time in her life understood what it meant to see stars. She pulled herself up into a sitting position. Through the strange lights and images that floated in front of her eyes, she saw Mark run past her and slug Angel.

"Stop it, Mark. I said I'm fine." She grasped the stair railing and shakily pulled herself up.

Mark hit Angel one more time before backing away from him. Mercy could see the anger on Mark's face, but hitting Angel wouldn't help anything. He ran back down the stairs to Mercy. "Are you sure you're not hurt?"

She nodded, even though the movement made her feel as if she might pass out. "I need to stop by the bathroom for just a minute," she said, trying to paste a smile on her face. "Don't know why falling down the stairs makes you have to use the bathroom, but I do."

Mark stared closely at her, but Mercy kept her expression steady.

"There's a bathroom down here," he said, pointing to his right. He reached out and grabbed her arm. "Please don't lie to me. If you're in trouble, tell me the truth."

"I told you I'm all right. Quit interrogating me. I'm not some delicate flower you have to protect." Mercy was barely holding on to consciousness. Maybe she should tell Mark the truth, but he needed her help, and so did Tally. She had no intention of letting either one of them down.

"Okay," he said, "I'll meet you at the basement door."

When he was far enough away, she staggered to the bathroom, opened the door, and fell in front of the toilet, heaving. When she finished, she cleaned up the best she could and stared at herself in the mirror. Her pupils were too big, and she was unnaturally pale. Gingerly she untied the string under her hood and pulled it down. She slowly removed the wool hat that covered her ears and used her fingers to feel her scalp. There was a large bump on the back of her head. When she touched it, she became nauseated again and dry-heaved a couple of times. She pulled her wool hat back on, being careful not to touch the bump again. She probably had a concussion, something she would take seriously if she were back home in St. Louis, but she couldn't deal with it now. She had no intention of telling Mark that she was hurt.

She left the bathroom and hurried toward the basement door. As she walked past the stairs, Angel called out, "I'm sorry, Mercy. I didn't mean to make you fall."

Mercy stopped and looked at him. "It doesn't matter whether you did or not. I'm okay. You're not going to control me—or this situation."

Angel shook his head, his face bruised by Mark's fists. "They'll kill you for that flash drive. You don't stand a chance. Just give them what they want. I'll ask them to let you live. I'm the only one who can get you out of this in one piece."

"Shut up," she said. "As far as I'm concerned, you can drop dead."

"If that's how you feel, why did you tell Mark to stop hitting me?"

"Because we might need information from you later. You're nothing more than a resource to me."

"I don't believe you. You're a good person." He took a long, shuddering sigh. "Mark isn't telling you everything, Mercy. You need to be careful."

"Save it. I don't believe a word out of your mouth. Your family is the epitome of evil. You use people for your own greedy gain, and you don't care about anyone."

"No one is completely evil, Mercy. Maybe I work for my father, but I'm still a human being. Can you really leave me like this? What if you don't make it back? I could die here."

"I don't have a choice. Besides, you caused this. Not me. Not Mark. And certainly not Tally."

Without another word she walked away. The room swam around her, and she stopped for a moment to steady herself. When she felt stable, she started forward again.

"Are you ready?" Mark asked when she approached.

Instead of answering his question, Mercy reached out and put her hand on his arm. "Before we go out there, I need to say something." She took a deep breath and tried to ignore the voice that screamed in her head, telling her to shut up. "I know I'm messed up, Mark. I've been this way for a long time. I know when it started, and I think I know why, but I just don't know how to fix it." She gazed up into his bluish-gray eyes. "When my dad walked out I blamed myself. And my mother blamed me and my brother. According to her, if we hadn't been born he wouldn't have taken off. We spent our childhoods feeling guilty—and also responsible. For everything. For my parents' breakup and my mom's emotional problems. Since my brother was younger than me, I felt it was my job to fill in for my mother.

I may not have done a great job, but he turned out okay and I'm grateful for that."

She looked away for a moment, summoning the courage to say something that frightened her. But this might be her only chance. "There's a part of me that's terrified of being left behind again. Afraid that if I care too much about you, you'll leave, and I'll get hurt. Just like when my dad left. Like the way my mom deserted us by climbing into a bottle. When you became a Christian, it felt as if you'd picked something—or someone—over me. As if you were cheating on me with . . . God. I know that's dumb, but I'm just trying to let you know how it felt to me. You keep telling me about this God of yours, this Father. Can't you see that I don't know what a father is supposed to be? I mean, all I got from my dad was pain and rejection."

"I hadn't thought about it that way," Mark said, his eyes wide. "Look, we don't have time to talk about this now, Mercy, but unlike our parents, God loves us perfectly. He *is* love, and He can heal all the hurt inside you. I can't do it. No human being can. Including you. Only one person can reach down into our messed-up souls. You don't have to believe that just because I said it. You just have to give Him a chance. Bruised, battered, scarred . . . He doesn't care. He's got the answer to all of it. Healing for everything that hurts us."

"Maybe," she whispered. "Maybe I'll try that . . . sometime. But for now I just needed you to know that I never really wanted to break up with you. Besides Tally, you're the only one who ever got past my—"

"Walls?" Mark finished for her.

She smiled. "I guess so."

Perhaps it was the pain in her head talking, but Mercy was

afraid. What if she didn't make it through this? What if she never got the chance to tell Mark how she felt? She took another deep breath. "Just in case we're not . . . or I'm not . . ."

"You'll be fine. I won't let anything happen to you."

She didn't respond to his attempt at reassurance. Did he understand what she was trying to tell him? Was he taking it seriously? If she died today, she wanted him to know that she loved him. As much as she could ever love anyone.

As she searched his face, she could think of only one way to let him know how she felt. She put her hands on either side of his face and pulled him down to her. At first his response to her kiss was tentative. Then he wrapped his good arm around her and pulled her tightly to him. The passion of that kiss melted into something else. A sweetness she'd never experienced before. Something that transcended a mere kiss. She realized that everything she'd wanted to say had just been said. He knew how she felt. When she gently pulled back from his embrace, she saw the love in his eyes. It was all she needed to know.

"We're not going to die, Mercy," he said, his expression solemn. "I know it. Trust me. We'll be okay."

She nodded, but she couldn't share his confidence. "I'm ready," she said, removing her gun from its holster, steeling herself for what was ahead, and fighting back the nausea rising inside her.

He smiled at her and nodded before turning to open the door. So much snow had blown up against it that he had a hard time pushing it open enough so they could slip through.

Once they were finally outside, they found themselves fighting through a chest-high snowbank. Even after they freed themselves from the pile of snow that had drifted against the house, they still had to wade through snow that was almost to their knees.

Mark pushed ahead of Mercy, trying to clear a path. They fought their way around the house until they reached the front.

"There's the snowmobile," Mark said. He reached into his pocket and pulled out a key. "Hold this. I'll try to pull it over here. Then we can start it up."

"You can't drag that thing by yourself," Mercy said. "Especially with one arm. You'll need my help."

"I don't want both of us out there. We have no idea if we're being watched."

"We have no choice, Mark. If we have any chance of getting that snowmobile, we'll have to work at it together. And I've been thinking. We should check the barn first before we try getting help somewhere else. If Tally's there, going the other direction doesn't make sense. I think it's the most logical move, don't you?"

"Maybe, but that isn't what we planned."

"I know. I'm just trying to get to Tally as quickly as possible."

"I understand. But once we get away from the house, we're liable to be seen."

Mercy nodded. "We could leave the snowmobile here and get to the barn on foot."

"So then we're slow-moving targets? Not sure that's a good idea either."

"We'd need to stay as low as possible, blend in with the snow."

Mark shook his head. "I say we get the snowmobile first, and then we'll decide what to do."

"Okay, okay. Should we just run out there and grab it?"

"Well, I could try calling it, but I'm not sure it would obey."

She slapped him lightly on the arm. When she did, she remembered his gunshot wound. "I'm worried about your arm."

"I'm fine."

"I don't believe you."

Mark's expression hardened. "We don't have many options, do we?"

"What if you hurt yourself even more?" Mercy asked. "If your wound opens up, it'll start bleeding again."

Mark grunted. "You let me worry about my arm. If I say I'm okay, I'm okay."

"All right," Mercy said. "Just don't try to be a hero. I'm taking the front—you push from the back." Mark started to say something else, but Mercy held up her hand to stop him. "No debate. That's it."

Mark frowned at her but didn't offer any further resistance.

Mercy peeked around the side of the house. Thankfully the wind was still blowing enough that it reduced the visibility somewhat. That should help them. Although the day was cloudy, the sun periodically came out from behind the clouds. When it did the snow glistened with so much brightness it hurt Mercy's eyes. It felt like someone stuck a knife in the side of her head. She closed her eyes for a moment and refocused. Her pain wasn't important right now. She had a job to do. She forced her eyes open and glanced around, ignoring the sharp twinge once again. She couldn't see any movement beyond the road.

"Are you ready?" she asked.

Mark nodded. "Let's go."

They both moved carefully around the front of the house, staying behind the snow-covered bushes on the side of the porch. When they were as close as they could get to the snowmobile, they got ready to run out from behind their hiding place, grab the snowmobile, and drag it to the side of the house. Just as Mercy began to move, Mark grabbed her.

"Wait a minute," he said. "Something's wrong."

"What do you mean?"

"Stay here," he ordered.

Crouching low to the ground, he stepped out from behind the bushes. After getting only a few feet away from the house, he paused for a moment. Then he quickly returned to where Mercy waited.

"What's going on?" she asked when he righted himself and leaned against the side of the house.

"We won't be using the snowmobile," Mark said.

"What? Why not?"

"Someone cut the fuel line. Gas leaked out all over the ground. We wouldn't get very far."

"Can we fix it?"

"Not without tools. I think our choices have been whittled down to two—the barn or the house. Either we go back inside the house, or we try to get to the barn without being killed or captured. Hopefully, Tally's there. We're taking a big chance, though, Mercy. He may not be anywhere nearby." Mark looked deeply into her eyes. "I know what your choice is, but I don't think our chances are good. I just—"

"I know," she said. "Maybe you should send up a few prayers."

"Believe me, I have," he said. He took her hands and bowed his head. "Father, we need your help. Please keep us safe and help us to rescue our friend." He looked up and saw Mercy watching him. "And please, God, will you show Mercy how much you love her? She needs to know." With that he lowered his head again, leaving Mercy stunned by a sensation that seemed to envelop her in a warm cocoon of love.

CHAPTER
TWENTY-FOUR

"Get up."

Tally's head snapped up at the loud command. How could he have fallen asleep? True, he hadn't slept for over thirty hours, but being held captive wasn't exactly relaxing. He shook his head to clear his mind and looked up into the angry face of Elias Vargas.

"Get up, I said." He kicked at Tally, his boot striking his thigh. More than anything, Tally wanted to put his fist through the face of the smug drug dealer. Annie wouldn't approve, though. She was always preaching forgiveness and love. Although he respected her sweet nature, being a police officer wasn't about love. It was about justice. And right now he'd like to dole out a little justice to the man who stood over him.

"Cool it," Tally said. "It's hard to stand up when you're handcuffed to a pole. Maybe if you took these off . . ."

Vargas bent over and slapped Tally across the face. "May I remind you that you're not in control, my friend? Do what I tell you, and do it now!"

Swallowing his anger, Tally pulled his feet up and shimmied himself into a standing position. The handcuffs caught several times on the pole as he pushed himself up. He had to shake them free to keep them from stopping his ascent. He felt the skin on his arms tear as warm blood oozed from the cuts. When he was finally on his feet, he glared at Vargas.

"I'm standing. Now what?"

A smile spread across Vargas's face as he pulled a gun from inside his jacket. He then walked around behind him. Tally was surprised when Vargas undid his handcuffs. Could he overpower the drug dealer and get away? Before he had a chance to make a move, Vargas pointed the gun at Tally's head. "Now take off your clothes," he said.

Mark had found a small shovel in a storage shed in the backyard. He would use it to help them get to the barn. Unfortunately, any previous tracks they could have followed had been covered by blowing snow.

For camouflage, he was wearing Angel's white jacket to blend in with the snow. Mercy's coat was blue, so she removed it and turned it inside out since the lining was a light beige color. The deep snow froze their legs, making them feel numb. Little by little they pushed their way closer and closer to the barn, wondering if at any minute bullets would start raining down on them.

Mark couldn't help but wonder if this effort to find Tally wasn't a suicide mission. Batterson wouldn't approve. He would have told them that stopping the cartel came first. Unless the cartel's plan was quashed, law enforcement across the nation would be under their thumb for quite some time.

Anyone with a family or a career to protect would feel over-whelming pressure to cave to the demands of the cartel. And law-enforcement officers' lives would be ruined if the doctored videos got out. There was no question about that. The only thing that would stop them was the video on Darius Johnson's flash drive. Proof that the doctored videos weren't real. Mark realized that in the end, Johnson could actually end up helping the police if they obtained and released the original footage. He would have been outraged to know he'd assisted the people he hated. But Johnson had already paid the ultimate price for his stupidity, and he wouldn't be around to see the results of his mistakes. He would only be a sad footnote of an even sadder story. He was already part of the past, and no one mourned him. Gangs preached loyalty, but the truth was their members had no friends.

Mark became aware of Mercy's grunts as she trudged through the snow. She was behind him so he couldn't see her, but he imagined she was beyond tired. Lack of sleep and the physical exertion it took to keep moving forward was exhaust-ing. His chest burned, not only from breathing the cold air but from clearing a path for Mercy. He had to rely on his good arm, since the other one was still hurting badly. The shovel helped, though not nearly as much as he'd hoped. Nonetheless, he was determined to keep going.

He wasn't so sure about Mercy, however. He wanted to offer her a chance to rest but was certain her pride wouldn't allow her to admit she needed it. Yet he had an overwhelming urge to protect her. He stopped and twisted around. "Do you want to stop and rest for a minute?" he asked.

She shook her head. Mark noticed her face was bright red.

He'd tried to get her to wear Angel's ski mask, but she'd refused. He certainly wasn't going to wear it and let her go without, so they'd left it at the house. He should have insisted she put it on. Then again, he thought they'd be riding the snowmobile. Mercy could have kept her head down and protected her face by leaning against him.

He stopped and turned around again. "Seriously, Mercy, it won't hurt us just to stop long enough to catch our breath."

She didn't answer, just shook her head. Mark was concerned about her labored breathing. She'd die trying to save Tally if that was what it took. He nodded at her and went back to shoveling his way through the layers of ice and snow.

As they fought their way toward the barn, once again Mark questioned the depth of his love for her. Why were his feelings so strong? They couldn't share the most important thing in his life. How could they work as a couple if she didn't believe in God? He'd even talked to his pastor about her.

"Instead of thinking about this woman romantically, as someone you want to be with, can't you just see her as a friend?" Pastor Andy had asked him. "I suspect she's in your life for a reason. Just love her because . . . you love her. Sure, sometimes we do need to walk away from people who want to keep us from our God-given destinies, but you know what? If we walk away from everyone who rejects God, what have we shown them? That they're not good enough for us? That they're not good enough for God? Is that the message we want to send?"

"But our relationship wasn't exactly . . ."

"Chaste?"

Mark had nodded, embarrassed.

"When I was in my twenties," Andy went on, "I was in a rock

band. And I got caught up in the lifestyle. You know, drugs, girls, rock-and-roll. Yet Jesus took me anyway. What I experienced back then was nothing like the closeness and passion my wife and I share today. Don't worry about what you've already done, Mark. That's gone and forgiven. It happened, but it doesn't shape who you are now."

"I don't think Mercy sees it that way."

"Of course she doesn't. But don't you see that when she realizes the past doesn't have to define us, she will want that too? Just live your life with God in a real way. Don't put on an act. It's the only way others will ever want what we have. They want to see real people who have been changed by the love of God."

Ever since that conversation, Mark had tried hard to release Mercy to God. He knew there was no chance they could be together unless she opened the door to accepting Him. Sometimes it seemed impossible, but he loved her so much he wouldn't give up hope. He couldn't see himself with anyone else.

As he shoveled the path to the barn, Mark forced his thoughts back to the present. He began to wonder whether backup was on its way. If Batterson hadn't discovered the mole, and no one was coming, it would take a miracle for them to escape with their lives. Angel said the address had been changed in the file. Had it been changed before or after Batterson saw it? There was no way for him to know.

The weather certainly wasn't helping. First the ice storm, then the snow that covered it.

Mark was fairly certain getting in and out of the area around them was nearly impossible. All he could do was count on Batterson's loyalty to his deputies. If there was a way, Batterson would find them. For now, the only thing they could do was to keep pressing forward—until someone or something stopped them.

It took almost an hour for them to get to the barn. Once there, Mark stopped and turned around. What he saw concerned him. Mercy's face was even redder, her eyes glassy. "I want you to stay here," he said. "I need to get a quick look inside first. We have to know what we're up against."

His words didn't come out quite the way he intended with his teeth chattering so violently, but she seemed to understand. Mark could only pray there was some way to warm her up inside the barn. He doubted if Mercy could make it back to the house.

He noticed for the first time that the wound in his arm was bleeding again. The blood dripped through his white coat and onto his glove. Great. All he needed was for Mercy to notice. Worrying about him wouldn't help anything. His arms and legs had gone past tired. Now they felt like pieces of wood, something not actually part of his body. He had to purposely move his limbs since he could no longer feel them.

Mark put his ear up against the side of the barn, trying to hear if anyone was inside. There was only silence, but at this point he couldn't trust his senses. Was it really quiet or were his ears frozen? He spotted a small window nearby, but it was frosted over. He struggled as he moved around the structure until he could see the large double doors at the front. The first thing he noticed was that the snow had been cleared, allowing the doors to open. Not far from the clearing he found tracks in the snow made from large tires. Some kind of all-terrain vehicle had been here—and then left. The tire tracks led away from the barn and the house. That was good news. But had everyone gone or was someone still inside? Someone dangerous?

Mark got out his gun and held it as tightly as he could. Honestly, he wasn't sure he could fire it. His fingers were so frozen, he could barely move them. He tried one of the doors and found it unlocked. Slowly he pulled it open. He stepped inside and swung his gun around in an arc, making sure no one was behind him or to his side. The building was deathly quiet. He began to walk in farther when he heard a noise behind him. He twirled around, his gun in front of him. He watched, horrified, as the gun went flying out of his numb hand. He looked toward the front of the building. Mercy stood there, staring at him.

"If that's supposed to instill confidence in your ability to protect me, you just failed miserably," she said through quivering lips.

Without saying anything he ran over and picked up his gun, which wasn't easy with frozen hands encased in thick gloves. Whatever made him think he could handle his weapon—especially with his left hand?

"Not funny," he said when he reached her.

"It kind of was."

He shook his head while looking around them. The barn appeared to be deserted. "I told you to wait for me," he said softly.

Mercy pulled her hood down. "What?"

"I said . . . Oh, never mind." Still holding his gun, he moved forward, making sure they were alone.

"No one's here," Mercy said.

"I guess not." In one way their discovery was bad news. Someone had been here, and now they were gone. They probably had Tally—if he was still alive. They had no way to know.

At the same time, they were inside, out of the cold. Mark found a space heater on a shelf and pulled it down. Thankfully it ran on batteries. After clearing away straw from the floor, he set it down and turned it on. He was grateful to find that it worked. It wasn't large, but a rush of warmth made him hopeful they could at least thaw out a little.

"Mark!"

Mercy's voice was almost a scream. Mark ran toward the back of the building and found Mercy standing next to a pole streaked with blood. And on the floor was a pile of clothes.

Tally's.

CHAPTER
TWENTY-FIVE

"I'm sorry, son, but I just can't afford to put a heater upstairs. Even if I could afford one, I couldn't pay to run it."

"But I'm so cold, Mama."

"I know, but you have to be a big boy for Mama, okay? Your sisters need the downstairs room. The only space left is the attic."

Even at eleven, Tally had understood the weariness in his mother's face. Hopelessness. In his neighborhood that expression was contagious. It was seen in the faces of those who sold everything they had for the drugs that made them feel better—even for an hour or so. He also saw it in the expressions of the mothers whose children ended up dead in the streets of north St. Louis. He'd seen it in his own mother's eyes when his older brother Paul died, shot in a gang fight. After that, his mother had become determined the same thing wouldn't happen to Tally. Whatever strength she had left, she used it to protect him, to keep him away from the gangs that roamed their neighborhood like sharks.

"It's okay, Mama," he'd told her. "The blankets keep me warm enough. I'll be fine."

But he wasn't fine. Some nights were so cold he shivered and shook all night long. His legs ached so badly he would lie in bed and cry. Oftentimes he would grab his blankets and bring them downstairs. His mother slept on the couch while his sisters shared the only real bedroom in the house. Snuggled on the floor, not far from his mom, he'd felt safe. Since his mother kept the thermostat set low, it was still chilly in the living room, but it was a lot better than the drafty attic. Later, when he was twelve, his mother told him he couldn't come downstairs at night anymore.

"I might have company," she said. "We'd keep you up. Best if you stay in your room, son. I'll go to the thrift store this week and look for another blanket."

Sometimes Mama's company was a woman everyone called Sister Lilly. Sister was a deacon in the church down the street and was always telling his mother how much she needed Jesus. Mama seemed more peaceful after her meetings with Sister. But other nights Tally heard a man's voice coming from downstairs. Mama wouldn't tell him who the man was, but the next morning that hopeless look was back. Yet after the man's visits, things seemed to go better for a while. There was enough food, and Mama even bought candy for him and his sisters. Even now, as an adult, Tally wouldn't allow himself to think about what his mother might have been doing to keep them eating. He wouldn't even discuss it with Annie. It was a closed subject.

"Son, you need to stay awake." His mother's voice shook him out of his brief visit to the past.

"I can't, Mama. I'm freezing," he whispered.

"I know, Tally. Everything will be okay. You just stay awake. It's not time to sleep yet."

Tally found his mother's last sentence slightly disturbing. The minister at Sister Lilly's church used similar words when he preached at the funerals of young men and women killed by violence in their community. He even said it when Paul died.

"They've earned their reward," he'd say. "Now it's time for them to sleep." As a young boy, there was a time when Tally refused to close his eyes at night—afraid he'd end up in a coffin with people crying and carrying on at his funeral. What kind of reward was that? It didn't make sense. Tally grew to loathe Reverend Timmons. And God too.

He and Annie had been married for a few years when she started going to church. After a while she'd asked him to go with her, and he'd refused. He told her he couldn't worship a God who might arbitrarily decide to take his life, or the lives of the people he loved. Annie had explained that people have free will. They can make decisions. Some of them will turn out for their good, while others lead to destruction. The kid who shot Tally's brother made a choice. It wasn't God's will. Annie believed the world was full of evil, and sometimes things just went wrong. Even for good people. Even for innocent people.

"But, Tally, if we live under the shadow of His wings, we can have His protection. I pray over our children and you every night, thanking God that His angels have charge over us, that they will keep us from harm. I believe that, and I'll keep believing it so long as I draw breath."

Little by little, Annie's view of God began to soften Tally's heart, and eventually he started going to church with his family. Pastor Arthur was totally different from Reverend Timmons.

What he said made sense, and Tally was beginning to see a different God from the one presented by the reverend. He was much more like the God Sister Lilly believed in.

His mind drifted to Paul's funeral, when Sister had pulled him aside. "Your mother tells me you want to become a police officer when you grow up," she'd said with a smile. "I believe the Lord wants you to know that He will give you the desire of your heart. That you will be an excellent policeman and protect and save many people." She'd tapped her bony finger on his chest. "You keep that dream alive, boy. It's your calling."

Had he made a difference? Sometimes he wondered. He tried so hard to warn the young people away from gangs. He'd held the hands of gang members as the life drained from their eyes, and he'd stared at the bodies of innocent people caught in the gangs' crossfire, lying dead in the street. So many of them were young men. A lot of them being raised by grandmothers because the parents were either caught up in drugs or were already dead. Killed by addiction or violence.

When he first joined the force, he'd hated gangbangers. Their stupidity and violence enraged him. It was difficult not to deal with them harshly when they were arrested. The pain and misery they spread throughout their community made them not much more than an evil that needed to be extinguished. But after listening to more than one brokenhearted mother or grandmother wonder what happened to that happy little boy who used to love life—and her—Tally's heart began to soften. Every single gang member had once been a child with hopes and dreams. Then the gangs lured them with promises of money, power, and family. The kind of family that would never let them down. Of course, that was a lie. Gangs only provided the kind of family that could get you killed. And the truth was, loyalty was a myth. One wrong move—one mistake—and you'd probably be found lying in the middle of a vacant lot. Just like Darius Johnson. Executed and alone.

His thoughts drifted back to his mother. Now she lived in a nice little house in a decent neighborhood. Tally and Annie bought it when the owner died. It needed a lot of work, so Tally spent almost every moment off duty remodeling the house and making it a home for his mother. She'd finally taken Sister Lilly's advice and joined a church. Even though Sister passed away years ago, her influence on Tally and his mom lived on. When things looked impossible, Tally remembered her words: *"You will be an excellent policeman and protect and save many people. You keep that dream alive, boy. It's your calling."*

More than anything he wanted to talk to Annie. Tell her how much he loved her. Beg her to ask those angels she told him about to help him now so he could get back to her and their children. Annie had been after him to "make Jesus his Lord and Savior" now for weeks. But he'd been putting off that decision. All in all, he did pretty well on his own.

"Son, I told you to stay awake. Now you wake up, Tally. Right now!"

"Okay, Mama, but I'm so cold. Can you bring me another blanket?" Tally's eyes popped open. It took a minute for him to remember where he was. Tied to a tree, clothed only in his underwear. Left to die in the cold without any hope of rescue. Even if Mercy and Mark could get away from Angel Vargas, they'd never find him in time. He could be miles away from the house. Elias had told him about Angel before leaving him alone out here. Tally was shocked. He'd swallowed Angel's story about being an LA detective hook, line, and sinker. He was angry with himself for not seeing through his charade. Now Mark and Mercy were in terrible danger. He loved Mercy as if she were his own sister. Knowing she was in trouble and that he had no way to help her grieved him to the very center of his soul.

The wind blew past him, driving the bitter cold deeper into his muscles and joints. He was going to die—in the worst way possible. He looked around, trying to figure out some way to save himself, but all he could see were trees, snow, and ice. There was something in the top of a tree not far from him, but he couldn't tell what it was. A piece of trash caught by tree limbs when the wind blew, he guessed. Nothing that could help him.

He'd lost all feeling in his extremities. He tried to figure out what his kidnappers had used to bind his hands. If he were to free himself, he'd have to tear up his hands, possibly even lose at least one of them. Could he do it? Would he do it for his family?

Tally closed his eyes. "Lord Jesus . . ." he whispered through frozen lips.

CHAPTER
TWENTY-SIX

"What does this mean?" Mercy asked. "Why would his clothes be here? And what about the blood?"

Had she lost Tally? Was he really dead? Mercy felt herself sway. She grabbed a nearby bale of hay. She was glad that Mark didn't seem to notice.

He was bent down, carefully examining the pole smeared with blood. "I think he was tied up here," he said. He turned to look up at Mercy. "There's not that much blood, Merce. I'm fairly sure he's okay."

"Okay? What about his clothes? How can he be okay without his clothes?"

Mark rose to his feet. "Do you remember what Angel said?"

"You mean that we can't save Tally without their help?"

"Yeah." He came over and put his hand on Mercy's shoulder. "I'm not sure, but I think he's out there somewhere. In the cold. Unless we give them what they want, he'll freeze to death."

"Tally hates the cold," she said quietly. "We can't let that happen."

"I know," Mark said, "but how do we find him?"

"We follow the tracks. They'll lead us right to him."

Mark looked away for several seconds, as if thinking about what she'd said. When he turned his attention back to her, she saw something in his face that gripped her heart with fear.

"What?" she asked.

"Do you really think they'd leave us such obvious clues as to where they took him? I mean, I realize no one counted on this weather, but if you wanted to hide something, would you leave clear tracks in the snow?"

She frowned at him. "But they couldn't help it. How would they . . . ?"

"They might be trying to lead us to them, not to Tally. They could be waiting for us somewhere along the way. If so, I seriously doubt Tally is with them." Mark shook his head. "Mercy, I hate to say it, but we might be too late to save Tally."

She moved back, pushing his hand away. "No. I don't believe that."

Mark's eyebrows arched. "You're not facing facts."

"Yes, I am. That's the point," she said sharply. "If Tally is dead, how could they use him to manipulate me? They're smart enough to know I'd never give them what they want if I thought Tally was already dead. They have to keep him alive if they want the flash drive."

"I hope you're right," he said. "But they could lie to you and tell you he's alive—even if he isn't."

"Then I'll demand proof that he's alive."

"That might work, but once we're captured they'll find the flash drive, Merce. You have it on you, right?"

She nodded. "We've got to hide it someplace where they'll never find it. I've got to have something to bargain with."

"Right." Mark began looking around the barn.

"I don't think this is a good place," Mercy said. "If they know we've been here, they'll tear this building apart trying to find it."

Mark stared at her. "Any ideas?"

"Yeah. One place they'd never think to look."

She pulled the hood of her parka down and removed her wool hat, careful not to touch the bump on the back of her head. She took the flash drive out of the bag in her pocket and worked it into her hair, which she'd swept up on the top of her head after her shower. It was secured with an elastic hair tie.

"Are you sure about that?"

Mercy nodded. "I don't know what else to do, Mark. They might pat me down and check my clothing, but most people never think to check someone's hair. Besides, with my hood, the flash drive will be protected from the elements. If you have a better idea, I'd be happy to hear it."

"Okay," he said slowly, obviously not convinced. "So now what?"

Mark wasn't going to like what she said next, but she couldn't think of anything else to do. "We let them capture us."

"You're joking."

"No. It's the only way we can save Tally. We need to negotiate for his release. They have him; we have the flash drive."

Mark shook his head. "And once they have the flash drive, they'll kill us all. You know that, right? They can't leave us alive, Mercy—we know too much."

"Not necessarily. We can't prove anything without the video. Once they have what they want, maybe they'll just let us go."

Mark's face twisted with exasperation. "Sure, because Mexican cartels are known for their humanity. Maybe they'll also give us massages and bathrobes as parting gifts." He snorted. "Trust me, they plan to kill us." He frowned at her. She was a well-trained agent who knew the risks. The idea that the cartel would let them go was not only naïve, it bordered on insanity. What was wrong with her?

"Then we'll have to find a way to keep ourselves alive."

"Maybe if we had an army behind us," he said sarcastically.

"But we do," Mercy insisted. "We just need to stall long enough to give Batterson a chance to reach us."

"If he can figure out where we are," Mark said. "If he can't, our goose is cooked."

"Quit saying that. Where is this faith of yours? I thought God was supposed to help you in times of trouble. Or is that just another fairy tale?"

Mark fell silent. Finally he smiled at her and said, "Sorry. Not sure why you're the one challenging me to trust God. If this isn't one of those times we need faith, I don't know what is."

"I'm not trying to bust your chops, Mark, but we need to have some positive energy here. Telling me what won't work doesn't help. Tell me what *will* work."

Mark walked over to a wooden chair sitting against the wall. "We need to talk about realities here. We're exhausted, and before long we're going to need to eat and sleep."

"We'll sleep after we find Tally."

Mark nodded. "I agree. That means we need to find him soon—without walking into a trap. So how do we locate him? Do you really want to follow those tracks outside and see where they lead us?"

Mercy walked over and stood in front of him. "No. You're right, we can't take the chance. All I know is that we need to get warm. This small heater isn't enough, and the batteries won't last long. Staying out in the cold too long could cost us our lives. We can't help Tally if we're dead. Let's go back to the house. Hopefully the cartel hasn't moved in. I'm thinking that if they can use Tally for leverage, we can use Ephraim Vargas's son the same way."

"It could work—so long as we find a way to contact them."

"They'll show up. Eventually. And so will our people. Our target should be the house . . . for everyone. We shouldn't be here in the barn. We have to go back." She shook her head. "We should have stayed in the house. We've given away the one place where we were safe."

Mark shrugged. "We had to find out if Tally was here, Mercy. I know you. I couldn't have talked you out of checking."

"I'm sorry. Hopefully I haven't put us in even more danger."

"I was right there with you. You have nothing to apologize for." He paused for a moment before saying, "We could still try to reach one of those farmhouses."

"They're miles away. Frankly I'm surprised we made it this far."

"What about the other direction? Away from the house?"

"We're out in the country," Mercy said impatiently. "There might not be another house for miles. We can't take the chance. If we're wrong . . ."

Mark didn't need to hear the end of that sentence. It was obvious. They might not be able to get back. They could die of exposure—and Tally would certainly be lost.

He checked his watch again. Though the face was still frosty, Mark was able to wipe it off and read the time. It was ten o'clock.

It had taken them much longer to reach the barn than he'd

first estimated. "Okay, let's go back. I think it's our best chance."
He looked around the large structure. "I was right about the
horses. They were never here."

"I hope the horses at the real house are all right," Mercy
said. "I mean, if the real Jess Medina is dead, who's taking
care of them?"

Mark sighed. Only Mercy would be worried about horses
when her own life was in danger. "I'm sure they'll be fine. As
soon as we're rescued we'll make sure someone goes there to
check on them. Okay?"

"Okay." Mercy took out her cellphone and tried it again.
"Still not working," she said with anger. "What's the point
of these things if you can't use them when the weather gets a
little rough?"

"A little rough? A major storm is more than 'a little rough.'"
Mark pulled out his own cellphone and tried it too, but then
shook his head when he couldn't get a signal. As he slid the
phone back in his pocket, a strange look came over his face.

"What are you thinking?" Mercy asked.

"The landline in the house . . . did you try it?"

"No. Did you?"

"No. Jess . . . I mean, Angel, told us it wasn't working,"
Mark said. "What if he was lying?"

Mercy considered the possibility. "We should have double-
checked that phone."

"At the time we thought Angel was a detective from LA. Why
would we doubt his word?"

"We've got to get back to the house," Mercy said. "Now."

The trip back was a lot easier than their original trek to the barn. Mark simply followed the path in the snow he'd dug earlier. He was worried, though. Was this really the best thing to do? Even though Mercy was prepared to be captured, the cartels were known for their cruelty. Shouldn't they be running away from Vargas and his minions? But no matter what scenario he played out in his head, he couldn't come up with a better solution. They wouldn't last much longer out here.

He was growing more and more concerned about Mercy. They were both cold and under stress, but he wondered if there was something else going on. He wavered between wanting to protect her and a commitment to treat her as his equal. Balancing his feelings was getting tougher because he was so desperately in love with her.

Mark found himself bargaining with God. Telling Him how hard he'd work at being a good Christian if He would just take care of the woman he loved. He'd lost Audrey, and it had taken him years to recover.

How could he lose Mercy now? But even though he was a new believer, he knew God wouldn't be moved by his manipulation. Really trusting God meant letting go and believing He was in control, that He had a plan. Mark also had to trust God with Mercy. It was hard for him to give up the management of his life, and he was ashamed of that. He recalled the story of a man in the Bible who had been in the same place Mark was now. "God, I believe," he prayed quietly. "Please help my unbelief."

The clouds had increased and grown darker, and the blowing snow had turned into a thick, frozen mist. After wiping it off, Mark checked his watch again. They'd been walking a little over an hour.

It would have been better to go in the dark, but Tally couldn't wait that long. Nor could they. Right now, Mark was grateful for the icy cover. It might not be as dark as night, but it would do. Anything that would help to hide them from the cartel was a blessing.

As he pushed ahead, he realized he hadn't heard a peep out of Mercy for quite some time. He turned around and was shocked when he didn't see her. He threw his shovel aside and made his way back through the snow until he found her lying motionless.

"Mercy?" He knelt down to check her. She was unconscious. He gently picked her up. Waves of pain shot through his right arm, but he ignored it. She was so pale. He put his face next to hers to make sure she was still breathing. He could feel her breath, but it was shallow. He had to get her inside, and soon. He started trudging again toward the house. What would he find when he got there? Was the cartel waiting for them? Would he and Mercy live through this day? And what about Tally?

As he pushed through the snow, he prayed, *God, please protect Mercy and Tally. Help me get them out of here alive. I can't save them by myself—I need your help. I'm putting my complete trust in you.* He glanced down at Mercy's still face. *And, Lord, please heal Mercy's broken heart. I love her. Why would I love her so much if we're not supposed to be together?* Mark blinked away tears. *Yet not my will, but yours . . .*

The last part was difficult to pray, but Mark knew real love meant he had to put what was best for Mercy ahead of his own desires. He gathered up all the strength he had while placing what he didn't possess in the hands of God. *Not my will, but yours be done*, he finished.

CHAPTER
TWENTY-SEVEN

Mercy found herself in a room where the walls were gleaming white, and there was a big picture window on one side. She looked for a way out, but there were no doors anywhere. What kind of room doesn't have an exit? Finally she peered out the window, even though for some reason she didn't want to.

She realized she was looking out onto the street where she'd lived as a child. How could that be? She was an adult now. A deputy U.S. Marshal. While everything in front of her seemed to be wrapped in some sort of fog, she began to see shapes moving slowly through the smoke. She saw her father. This was the day he left. As he walked toward his car, her mother followed him, holding Mercy's hand. Mom was begging him not to go, but her father acted as if he couldn't hear her, as if he didn't know she was even there.

Mercy stared intently through the window, squinting so she could see things more clearly. There was a woman in the car. Mercy had seen her before. She'd come to the house a couple of times when her mother was gone. The woman wouldn't look at her or her mother. She just stared straight ahead.

Her mother grasped her dad's coat sleeve, but he shook himself free. Before he got into the car, he looked back at Mercy.

"I'm sorry," he said. And then he was gone.

As her mother sank to the ground, sobbing, Mercy, the ten-year-old girl, walked up to the window where the adult Mercy watched the scene unfold before her. Tears flowed down the young girl's face. The child looked into the woman's eyes for a few moments, and then she turned and walked away.

"That was the last time I cried," Mercy whispered to herself.

The mist swirled and changed, as if blown by an invisible wind. Now it was her brother driving away from home, going off to college. Even though she'd worked so hard to get him to this day, Mercy had felt abandoned. Left alone to care for her troubled mother.

Scenes of other past events flashed in front of the window as if it were a giant movie screen. Her mother showing up at school, drunk, yelling at the teacher and falling down in front of her entire class. Christmases and birthdays forgotten because her mother was so hungover she couldn't get out of bed. Mercy trying to take care of herself and her little brother, praying no one would call social services. Her fear of being stuck in some strange family, separated from Jeremy, had forced her to work hard to keep up appearances. Mercy helped her brother with his homework, cleaned the house, did the laundry and the shopping. She enrolled in a local college so she could stay at home until Jeremy graduated high school. Even after he moved away, she stayed behind to care for her mother. There wasn't anyone else.

Once again the scenes disappeared as if the wind had whisked them away. She saw her father on the last day of his life. She heard him say, "*I also want you to know how proud I am of you. In spite of me, you grew up to be a fine young woman and a great law-enforcement officer. I know you won't believe this, but I love you, Mercy. I've loved you every day since you were born, even though I've done a terrible job of showing it.*"

She watched herself tell her father she hadn't forgiven him. The look on his face hurt her inside. She wished she'd told him she'd never stopped loving him. Never stopped wishing he'd come back. Why couldn't she have reached out to him? Anger? Bitterness? Revenge? Now it was too late. Her father disappeared, and two other faces appeared. Tally and Mark. She called out to them, but they didn't seem to hear her. They both looked frightened, and Mercy wanted to help them. She ran around the room once more, trying again to find an exit, but there wasn't one. She was trapped. She hurried back to the window and watched them fade away like smoke in the wind.

Now she was completely alone. Fear choked her, making her unable to move. It took all her strength to raise a hand and bang on the window, trying to find someone still out there, hoping to get their attention.

"I don't want to be alone!" she yelled. "Please don't leave me here!" First she called Tally's name. No one came. Then she called out to Mark. Over and over she called his name. "Get me out of here! Mark, please get me out of here!"

"I'm here, Mercy. I'm here. It's okay. You're okay."

She strained to see through the fog, searching for him. At last she forced her eyes open. Mark's worried face looked down at her.

"What happened? Where . . . where am I?"

He wiped her forehead with a washcloth. "We're back at the house. You collapsed outside, and I brought you here."

Mercy tried to sit up, but dizziness overtook her and she put her head back down. "I had the worst dream." She tried to look around. Again the room spun. "Where's Angel? Is everything all right?"

Mark stroked her face. "I'm sorry, Mercy. I really am. But I had no choice. I was afraid you were going to die."

"I don't understand. What do you mean?"

"He means you're in trouble, little lady."

Mercy turned her head again, ignoring the dizziness. A man she didn't know stood a few feet from the couch. "Who are you?" she asked.

"I am Elias Vargas."

Even though she felt sick and disconnected, she couldn't help but notice how ugly Elias Vargas was. His face was pitted with scars, and his pushed-in nose reminded her of a pig. Probably the result of getting it broken too many times.

"Where's Angel?"

"I'm here too," a voice said. "No thanks to you and your boyfriend."

Mercy squinted and was able to make out Angel as he came toward the couch. It was hard to see. Just like the dream, everything—and everyone—was fuzzy. Like figures made out of smoke.

"I think you have a concussion, Mercy," Mark said gently.

"You didn't tell him you hurt yourself when you fell down the stairs, did you?" Angel said. His tone was mixed with contempt . . . and something else. Something Mercy couldn't interpret.

"You should have let me know," Mark said, a twinge of accusation in his voice.

"You wouldn't have gone out to look for Tally," Mercy replied. She felt so weak that even talking was a strain.

"You still don't have Tally, and now you've been captured," Angel said.

Mercy didn't respond. Was it really over? Would they die here? And where was Tally?

"You know what I want," Elias said. "Give it to me and we will rescue your friend. Bring him here to . . . warm up."

Mercy struggled once more to sit up. "Where is he?" She wanted to sound strong and in control, but her voice shook.

Elias came over and sat down on the coffee table. Mark moved closer to her on the couch.

"He is still alive," Elias said, leaning so close to her the stench of cigarette smoke made her stomach turn. "Although I can't promise how much longer that will be the case."

He took a smartphone out of his pocket and tapped the screen several times. "As you can see, he still breathes. However, it doesn't look as if he has long. Better get him inside as quickly as you can. . . ."

He held the phone up to Mercy's face. It was Tally. He was tied to a tree, dressed only in his underwear. And he wasn't moving.

CHAPTER
TWENTY-EIGHT

Mercy held her breath as she stared at the video. Finally, Tally moved, shifted his body in an obvious attempt to get more comfortable. His breathing appeared to be labored, and his eyes were wild. He was probably in shock.

"This was recorded about thirty minutes ago," Elias said. "Your friend may last a couple more hours if he's lucky."

"You want the flash drive," Mercy said.

"Of course."

She nodded toward her coat that had been thrown over a nearby chair. "It's inside the lining."

Elias gestured to Angel. "Get it."

Angel went over to the coat and picked it up. The bruises on his face had darkened. Mercy was concerned he would seek revenge. That killing Mark would be one of the first things he did after the Vargas family got what they wanted. She had to keep that from happening.

Angel felt around on the coat's lining but didn't seem to find anything.

"Give it to me," Mercy said. "I'll get it."

Elias nodded at Angel, and he handed her the coat. She frowned as she pretended to search for the flash drive. Then she touched a tear near the bottom of the lining.

She looked up at Elias. "It fell out," she said. "I must have torn my coat on something. It's probably out in the snow somewhere."

Elias's already hostile expression darkened. "Do you think I am stupid?" His accent deepened, and his eyes flashed as he turned his gun on Mark. "I will kill him first, and then I will kill you. The policeman will die as well."

Mercy locked eyes with the incensed criminal. "I won't give in to threats. You need my help to find the flash drive. If you want it, you'll have to do things my way."

"Wrong," Elias spit out. "All we need to do is follow your tracks in the snow. It will not be hard to discover."

Mercy forced herself to ignore the ache in her head and glared at Vargas without flinching. "Unless I'm lying about losing it and purposely threw it out there somewhere. If I did, you'll never find it without me." She shook her head, refusing to concede to the pain slicing through her skull. "Why would I give up the only bargaining chip I might have? As soon as you get what you want, you plan on killing us. I'm not going to give you the flash drive unless we cut a deal. Until I can find a way to get us out of here alive." She paused, then added, "And threatening to kill my partner won't work. If Mark dies, or if Tally dies, you'll never see that flash drive. If you knew my father, then you know me. I won't break. Not for any reason."

For the first time a glint of insecurity flashed in Vargas's eyes. Mercy was certain her father hadn't broken under their torture. Would Vargas believe the same of her? She needed him to. The truth was, she'd never let him hurt Mark. But right now she needed to save Tally. Then she could concentrate on Mark . . . and herself.

"I'm not sure if the snow and the cold will affect the device," she said with a tight smile, "but if you want to make certain it will be okay, you'll do what I ask."

"So if I do things your way, you will tell me where the flash drive is?"

She nodded.

"And what is it you want?"

"You bring Tally here. I have to know he's all right. Once I'm sure of that, you let Tally and Mark leave. That's the only way you'll get what you want."

Elias looked confused, and Angel shook his head.

"You will stay behind?" Angel said.

"Yes."

"No, she won't," Mark said. He grabbed Mercy's shoulder and turned her toward him. "I won't allow it. They'll kill you."

"I'll take my chances," Mercy said.

Angel walked up to them and aimed his gun at Mark's face. "If you care about this man so much, then you will give us the flash drive now."

"But I won't," Mercy said. She took a deep breath and looked into Angel's eyes. "I'm not kidding. If you shoot him or harm him in any way, it's over. I mean it."

"But your friend is still out there."

She saw something in his eyes, maybe something she could use. "I know, but it's clear he's not in good shape. It may already be too late. It isn't logical for me to bet everything on him."

"Logical?" Elias said. "Everything is logic with you?"

"Of course. Do you want me to make decisions based on emotions? Feelings? Logic is the only thing I can trust."

Elias continued to stare at her, and Mercy directed all her energy to staying still, not showing fear or pain. She was playing a long shot, but she couldn't think of anything else to do. Right now she had to get Tally back to the house. She intended to get them all out alive. If she could just stall long enough, it would give Batterson time to find them. The one thing she couldn't do was give Elias the flash drive and hope he'd release them. It was too dangerous. She glanced over at Angel. If she was forced to stay behind, Angel might be the key to saving her life. She had a hard time believing he would just stand by and watch her die, but she could be wrong.

Angel turned away from Mercy and backed away from them. "Let's try it their way, Uncle."

After a long moment of silence, Elias sighed. "Go get their friend." He pointed a finger at the younger Vargas. "And he better get back here without any additional injuries, you hear me, *mi hijo?*"

"Yes, Uncle."

"I mean it, Angel. Bring him back here alive."

Mercy was certain a look of relief crossed Angel's face. "I will do as you say."

"Take Manuel and Deeray with you."

"More members of your cartel?" Mercy asked once Angel left the room.

Elias sniffed. "Manuel is a trusted friend. The other person is not. Unfortunately I've been forced to work with some of the gangs in St. Louis." He leaned forward and lowered his voice.

"Despicable thugs. I refuse to use their gang names. Childish."
He leaned back and shrugged. "But what can you do? The price
of business."

"They murdered my father," Mercy said through clenched
teeth.

"Yes, and I feel badly about that. Your father was a smart
man. I liked him, but he took something that didn't belong to
him."

"So you let Darius Johnson kill him."

Elias shook his head. "Mr. Johnson took that action on his
own. To cover his tracks. He was afraid we would deal harshly
with him once we discovered he'd disobeyed us."

"And you certainly did that." Another sharp pain cut through
Mercy's head, and she involuntarily touched her hand to her
forehead.

"Are you okay?" Mark asked.

"You're worried about me?" she said through gritted teeth.
"You got shot. I just got hit on the head."

"I'm fine."

Mercy lightly touched Mark's shoulder. He winced in pain.

"Look," she said to Elias, "I need to change his bandage, and
I could use some aspirin. Would you let us go to the bathroom?
Everything we need is in there."

Elias hesitated. He called out, and a young man came rush-
ing around the corner dressed in Bloods colors, a red bandanna
around his head. "Go check out the bathroom. Take out anything that could be a weapon."

"I'll need a pair of scissors for the bandages," Mercy said.
"Unless you want me tear them with my teeth."

"No scissors." He gestured to the teenager waiting for

instructions. Mercy didn't like the way the kid looked at her, his eyes running up and down her body. "If you find any, bring them to me along with anything else that is sharp."

After one more glance at Mercy, the young man left.

Elias pointed at Mark. "You wrap his arm. I'll cut the bandage. That's my best offer. Take it or leave it."

"We'll take it," Mercy said.

They waited a few minutes for the kid to return. When he came back he tossed several things on the coffee table, including a razor, scissors, fingernail clippers, and tweezers.

Mercy looked at Elias. "Too bad he found the tweezers," she said sarcastically. "Ruined my plan to tweeze you to death."

"I'm not allowing you around anything that could be used as a weapon."

"You don't trust me?"

"I don't trust you," Elias said. He turned back to the kid. "Walk them to the bathroom and then walk them back. Use your gun."

He nodded, pulled a Glock out of his waistband and pointed it at them.

Mercy started to stand up but wobbled as she got to her feet.

Mark gripped her arm, steadying her. He grunted from the pain. "Lean on me," he said.

"On your good side," she insisted.

Mark walked around her, and she leaned in to him while he supported her with his left arm.

Mercy hated showing weakness to Elias, but she couldn't help it. She was so dizzy she could barely walk. They made their way to the bathroom with the kid right behind them. When they got there, Mercy sat down on the edge of the bathtub.

Mark searched the medicine cabinet until he found some pain relievers. "Will this work?" he asked her.

Mercy nodded. "Anything would help, but I'd love to find my pain pills."

"I left them on the kitchen counter. Are they gone?"

"I have a feeling our friends found them. We can ask when we go back, but for now this will have to do."

Mark took a small paper cup from a nearby dispenser and filled it with water. Mercy took the pills.

"Thanks," she said. "The gauze and tape are below the sink."

"I know. I changed my bandage earlier."

Mercy shook her head. "Sorry, I forgot."

While he retrieved what he needed, she reached up into the cabinet behind her and got the hydrogen peroxide. After asking Mark to remove his shirt, she tended to his wound. Though they'd tried to keep it clean, the skin around the wound was red—a sign of infection. Mercy didn't say anything since there was nothing they could do about it. She decided telling Mark would only make him tentative. And right now she needed him to be as sharp as possible.

Her contingency plan was now the best chance they had to get out of this situation alive. She wanted to tell Mark what she was getting ready to do, but the kid stood in the doorway, watching their every move. Finally, Mercy leaned over just enough so she could partially hide behind Mark. Then she caught Mark's eye, winked, and ever so slightly nodded toward the gangbanger holding a gun on them. Thankfully, he didn't see her. Mark frowned but didn't say anything. It was the best she could hope for under the circumstances. At least he would be somewhat prepared when she made her move.

She quickly used the rest of the bandage on Mark's arm and taped it down. She wouldn't need Vargas's scissors after all. When she was done, Mark helped her up.

Mercy turned her attention to the kid, who gave her a look that made it clear she would have trouble with him if they were ever alone together. "Um, I need to . . ."

He looked clueless, so she tried again. "Could I have a minute alone? I need to use the bathroom."

He smiled slowly. "Go ahead. We won't look."

"Hey, jerk," Mark said, "unless you want me to call your boss over here, back up and let the lady have a little privacy."

Mercy wasn't sure the kid's boss would be that concerned about her need for privacy, but Mark's threat did the job. It was obvious he was afraid of Elias.

"You got two minutes," the kid said. "And we gonna stand right here and wait for you."

"How comforting," Mercy said.

The kid and Mark stepped back as Mercy closed the door. She quietly locked it and then went over, reached behind the toilet tank, and removed the loaded gun taped to its back. She hadn't watched *The Godfather* over and over for nothing.

Now things were about to change.

CHAPTER
TWENTY-NINE

Mark locked eyes with the punk standing outside the bathroom. The kid's expression was meant to intimidate him, but it didn't. He saw guys like this every day, brought up in poverty and filled with rage because they'd been told nothing was their fault or responsibility. They were convinced the world had it out for them. There was no way they could ever get ahead. Their victim mentality excused every robbery, every assault, and every crime they ever committed. The world owed them. Sadly, the kid didn't realize he had an expiration date. Vargas would never allow him to live after this was over. He couldn't take the risk of letting the kid brag to his friends about what had happened here.

The punk started banging on the bathroom door. "Time's up, lady. Get out here now or I'll come in."

"Okay. Take it easy."

The door opened slowly, and Mercy stepped out. She still looked pale and she was unsteady on her feet, but Mark noticed a look in her eyes. He'd seen it before—right before she took down a perp.

He stared at her questioningly. She smiled at the kid, who seemed to salivate every time he looked at her. She had some kind of plan, but Mark couldn't think of anything she could do that wouldn't put them in more danger. Yet in that moment he realized he'd learned to trust her. He gave her an imperceptible nod in return.

"Get goin'," the kid said, pushing Mercy with his gun.

"Give me just a minute," she said, slurring her words. "I . . . I don't feel so good." She kept her eyes on Mark as she collapsed back into the kid. Momentarily distracted, he tried to grab Mercy, moving the gun right toward Mark, who snatched it out of his hand. He quickly put the gun to the kid's head.

"Just give me a reason," Mark hissed, hoping the kid wouldn't figure out that one gun against Elias and his crew wouldn't give them much of an edge. He prayed Mercy really did have a plan. If she didn't, she might have just signed their death certificates.

Mercy reached behind her back, pulling out a pistol. Mark recognized it as her backup weapon.

"How in the world . . . ?"

She grinned at him. "*The Godfather*. This is the first time I actually got to use it."

If they weren't still in incredible danger, Mark would have laughed out loud. Instead he just smiled at her and shook his head. "Now what?" he asked.

"You take care of the guys in the kitchen. I'll handle Elias and Ace here." She scowled at the kid.

Manuel, Deeray, and Angel had gone to get Tally. There were three more left besides Elias. A gangbanger and two of the men from his cartel were in the kitchen. Mark wasn't worried about the punk, but he knew the other two guys were tough, well-trained. However, he was smart enough to know that this was their best shot. Mercy had given them a chance, and they had to take it.

Mark nodded at her and turned toward the kitchen. As he proceeded down the hallway, he prayed silently for God's help. They needed a miracle. He crept around the corner and saw the three people sitting at the kitchen table. He realized he needed to make his move before Mercy confronted Elias. He put the gun behind him and strolled into the kitchen, trying to look casual.

"Elias wants a cup of coffee," he said, catching them off guard. Before any one of them could react, he grabbed the nearest man and put his gun to his temple. He yanked the guy's gun from its holster and tossed it on the floor, then ordered the other two to place their weapons on the table. The second guy from the cartel appeared to realize that protecting the other two knuckleheads wasn't the most important thing at that moment. He hesitated a few seconds. It was too long for Mark. He slammed his gun into the side of the guy's head, knocking him out. Keeping his gun trained on the other two, Mark knelt down and removed the unconscious man's pistol. He put that gun with the other. Then he took the punk's gun and added it to the pile. He could tell that the punk was scared—and much less dangerous than Elias's men.

"Get up," he ordered.

"Sure, man. Don't shoot me, aight?"

"If you do what I tell you to, you might stay alive," Mark said.

"You got it," the kid said, his hands in the air.

"Take that guy's belt off," Mark said, gesturing toward the man who was unconscious.

"Sure." He slid off the man's belt and handed it to Mark, who then ordered him to sit down. He obeyed without argument.

Mark used the belt to tie up Elias's other henchman, who glared at him with murder in his eyes. It was important to secure this man first; he was clearly the most dangerous. Mark made temporary handcuffs by looping the belt through the buckle twice. It wasn't ideal but would hold until he could get a pair of real handcuffs. He held the gun in his right hand, ignoring the pain. He needed his left hand to bind up Vargas's men. If he couldn't do it, they were in real trouble.

After taking care of the first guy, Mark ordered the kid to put the unconscious thug in a chair while Mark removed the bound man's belt. Once again, Mark turned the belt into makeshift handcuffs and secured him to the chair. The man he'd hit was beginning to moan and would soon be conscious.

Mark stared at the kid for a moment, trying to decide how to keep him from messing things up. He wasn't wearing a belt, and Mark didn't want to remove his. He wasn't sure he could, as the pain in his arm was almost more than he could endure. Finally he ordered the kid into the bathroom, closed the door, and pulled a kitchen chair in front of it, tipping it until it was wedged up tight under the doorknob. With the kid contained, Mark leaned his head against the bathroom door. His arm felt as if it were on fire.

"You stay in there," Mark said. "If you try to come out, I'll blow you away. You got it?"

"Got it," the kid responded, his voice choked.

Was he crying? Mark couldn't be sure, but he decided to do

everything he could to get the kid out in one piece. Maybe he'd gotten sucked into this situation and didn't really want to be here. Maybe he had a mother who loved him. If Mark could bring him home unharmed, perhaps the kid could still turn his life around.

He shook his head. Was he getting soft? He had to keep his mind focused on Vargas and his pals, not worry about some young gangbanger.

Mark hugged the wall as he moved slowly toward the living room, hoping Mercy had everything under control. Sure enough, Vargas was seated on the couch. Mercy sat across from him, her gun pointed at his chest. Ace was lying on the floor, a nasty bump on his head. Obviously, Mercy had knocked him out. With his good arm, Mark dragged Ace over to a chair next to Vargas and dumped him there.

Mercy looked over at Mark. "Everything okay?" she asked.

"Everything's fine," Mark said, "But I need the rest of our cuffs from the tactical bag. Can you keep an eye on these guys while I get them?"

Mercy nodded. "Make it fast, okay?"

"You got it." He started to leave when Mercy called him back.

"Hey, I brought an extra pair of handcuffs. They're in my valise."

He grabbed handcuffs from the tactical bag and found the extra pair in Mercy's bag. He removed the ammo out of the guns he'd taken from the cartel and the gangbangers. He opened the window in his room and punched out the screen. Using his left arm he threw the guns outside, keeping the ammunition in case he and Mercy needed it. He couldn't risk having too many guns in the house. So long as he and Mercy had what they needed, it was best to keep any extra weapons out of reach.

It had started snowing again. He prayed that before long the guns would be buried beneath a blanket of white so they wouldn't be easy to recover. He hid the extra ammunition under the mattress. Mercy's reference to *The Godfather* jumped into his thoughts. He and Mercy were in a war with the Vargas cartel. They'd certainly *gone to the mattresses*. Hopefully it would turn out better for them than it had for the Corleones.

Once everything was secure, he hurried back to the kitchen. He added the real cuffs to the men from the cartel and removed the makeshift belts. They wouldn't escape from these.

Then he went back to the bathroom and let the kid out. "We're going to the kitchen. I'm going to tie you up. Just don't cause any trouble and I might be able to get you out of this in one piece."

The kid blinked away tears. "If they see I been cryin' . . ."

With his gun still trained on the kid, Mark grabbed some tissue from the bathroom and handed it to him. "Wipe your eyes and don't worry. They're too busy thinking about themselves to be concerned about you."

Wide-eyed, he took the tissue, mopped his face and tossed the tissue in a trash can. "Why you bein' nice to me?" he asked.

"Because it's just possible you're not as dumb as your friend in there. I'd like to see you get out of this alive if possible. Maybe you can redeem yourself." Mark shook his head as the waterworks started again. "Hey, you need to get it together. These are very dangerous men."

"I know, I know."

The kid's dark brown eyes were filled with pain. He was a good-looking kid—under the stupid gang costume.

"What's your name?" Mark asked. "Your real name, not your gang name."

"It's Troy. Troy Thomas."

"You gotta start thinking with your own brain, Troy," Mark said. "Don't believe everything these losers tell you. Can you do that?"

Troy studied Mark's face. "They'll kill me and my dad if I turn against them."

"If we get out of this alive, and if you'll help me put these guys away, I can promise you a new life. Ever hear of the witness protection program?"

"Yeah."

"Look," Mark said, "I don't have time to talk about this now, but I'm a U.S. Marshal. That's what we do."

Troy shook his head. "You don't understand. You can't help me."

"Yes, I can. You've got to trust me."

Troy nodded and said, "Just don't let them kill me, okay? I'll do what I can to help you, but you can't tell those guys I flipped on 'em."

Mark gestured with his gun, letting Troy know it was time to move. "You have my word, Troy. Now let's go."

The kid's sigh was probably one of relief. Mark just prayed he could keep his promise. He didn't make the rules, and he couldn't guarantee Batterson would approve the deal. This boy had touched something in him, and Mark intended to get him and his family out of the life—if humanly possible.

Mark kept his gun aimed at Troy until they reached the kitchen and then ordered him to sit down. He tied him up with a belt so he could keep any extra handcuffs for Vargas's men. Mark was careful to treat Troy roughly so no one would suspect he'd cut a deal. The kid was putting on a pretty good show for his friends.

"You idiots stay in here while we talk to your boss," Mark ordered. "If I catch any one of you trying to get out of your cuffs, I'll shoot you. Understand?"

There was no response. Just glares from the other two and a nod from Troy. Mark went back to the living room while keeping an eye on the kitchen.

"So now what?" Elias said as Mark came in. "I assume you have a plan?"

Mark smiled at him. "Actually we have a couple. In one of them, you live. In the others, it doesn't turn out so good for you."

Elias's harsh laugh was obviously intended to mock them. "You have no idea who you are dealing with."

While Elias was trying to come across with confidence, Mark could tell from the man's posture and lack of eye contact that he was worried. Good. That meant they were on the right track.

"I don't think you know who *you* are dealing with," Mercy said to the drug dealer.

Mark heard the determination in her voice, but he had to wonder if she was strong enough to see this operation through. She obviously had a concussion—or worse. He felt responsible for getting them all out. With his injury, Mercy's concussion, and Tally gone, his odds were pretty slim. But he had no intention of letting Vargas know he was anything but completely sure of himself.

He walked over to the shelf under the counter where he'd seen Angel put the phone. Mark wondered if he'd been keeping it out of sight so they'd forget about it. He pulled the phone out, put it on the counter, and picked up the receiver. When he heard the dial tone he looked at Mercy and nodded. "We took Angel's word that the landline wasn't working," he said. "We should have checked it out ourselves."

"We need to call for backup," Mercy said. Mark hesitated while he and Mercy exchanged a quick look. There was a mole in the Marshals' office. Who was it? Would this call give the mole the information he needed to contact Vargas's people? Mark wasn't sure what to do.

"You look a little confused, my friend," Elias said. His greasy smile meant he knew something, but what was it? Did he know that this call could bring about their downfall?

"I'm not confused," Mark shot back. "Just trying to figure out how to tell them where we are." He looked at Mercy. "Angel said we were two miles away from the original address, right?"

She nodded. "Tell Batterson to look for a large house with a barn within a two-mile radius of the address he has. It shouldn't be that hard."

"Too bad they can't pick up the GPS on our cellphones," Mark mumbled.

"They can find the car with GPS, but I have no idea how far away it is, or where we are in relation to its location."

"I know." A thought occurred to him, and he snapped his fingers. "The landline. If it shows up on caller ID . . ."

"It won't," Elias said. "Sorry. Private number."

Mercy grinned at him. "Sorry. Law enforcement. We can trace any number we need to."

Elias's smug expression slipped a little, but he quickly pulled it back up. "Good luck with that. Thousands of residents are most likely without phone service. How long will it take to get help? Angel will be back shortly with your friend. I doubt he'll be very happy to see what you've done."

"We're not worried about him and his friends," Mercy said. "Frankly your men aren't well-trained—we just took out three of them."

"You mean five of them," Mark interjected. "Including this idiot."

Vargas gave Mark a defiant stare while Ace, now conscious, just looked worried. Vargas wouldn't give up easily. Ace was probably weighing his options. Mark didn't trust him, but Vargas couldn't either. Ace was probably for sale. Could they turn him? Use him against the cartel? For now, Mark would just have to keep a close watch on him.

Mark caught Mercy's eye again. What should he do? Could he contact Batterson safely or would they play right into the mole's hands? Mercy shrugged. She seemed to be as unsure as he was about how best to proceed.

"I'm calling Batterson," he said finally, "but not through the office. I'll contact him on his cellphone."

She hesitated a moment before nodding her agreement.

Mark carried the phone into the kitchen to check on his prisoners before placing the call. They were all secure. He'd just started to dial the number when Troy spoke up. "I . . . I have to go to the bathroom."

"You can wait."

"No, I can't. I have to go . . . now. Please. I promise I won't take long."

Mark caught the guarded look on the young man's face. Was he trying to tell him something?

"Okay, but you make it fast, hear me?"

Troy nodded.

Mark came around the table and undid the belt. He helped him to his feet and followed him down the hall to the bathroom.

Once they were out of hearing distance from the men in the kitchen, Troy stopped and turned to look at Mark. "There's someone in your office you can't trust," he whispered. "I don't think you should make that call."

Mark frowned at him. Did Troy know who the mole was? Or was he just saying what Vargas told him to say? Though Mark wanted to believe the kid, there was no way to know what was real and what wasn't.

"Thanks," he said. "I appreciate the information. I'm not calling the office, just my boss's cellphone. I'm sure it's safe."

Troy's eyes widened. "Please be careful. It's dangerous . . . you've got to believe me."

"I want to believe you," Mark said, "but I don't really know you, Troy. You might be trying to cozy up to Vargas. Maybe you think your odds are better that way."

The kid's head dropped. "I understand why you think that, but please . . ." He looked up at Mark. "Just be careful," he said again.

"I will. Do you really need to use the bathroom?"

"Yeah."

"Go ahead. I'll wait out here. Let me know when you're done."

"Okay."

Troy slipped inside the bathroom while Mark stood in the hallway, thinking. Would his next move save them, or would it lead to their deaths?

CHAPTER
THIRTY

Batterson put down his cellphone and stared at the wall. He had to get his people to safety, but after finding out he couldn't trust Carol, he'd begun to wonder if this operation had been compromised through anyone else. Who could he trust?

He grabbed the phone again and called his friend, Colonel Brad Austin of the Missouri State Highway Patrol. Within a few minutes he'd arranged for a helicopter. It was the only way he could think of to get close to his team.

After he located them, of course. Mark had given him a description of the property where they were—within two miles of the address Batterson had been given.

LA hadn't heard from Detective Jess Medina since he'd arrived in Missouri. Batterson was pretty sure the detective was dead. After getting his team out safely, he'd send someone to check on Medina, hoping to find him alive and in need of being rescued.

Next, he called in three of his most experienced deputies: Shauna Sparlin, a twelve-year veteran with a tough exterior and a heart of gold; longtime friend Tom Monnier, a man Batterson would trust with his life; and Al Thomas, another seasoned deputy he'd worked with many times.

These were people he trusted without hesitation. Of course, he'd felt the same way about Carol. At that moment, Batterson wasn't sure about anything—except that time was running out for Mark, Mercy, and Lieutenant Williams. If he had any chance of getting them out alive—and capturing two important figures in the Vargas cartel—he had to move now and rely on his gut instinct.

Once he'd finished contacting the deputies, he waited in his office. Although he hadn't been to church since he was fifteen, he lowered his head and prayed for God's help.

"Batterson is sending us to find his deputies and the police officer who went with them."

There was only silence on the other end of the line.

"You promised to let Troy go and allow us to move away if I helped you. I expect you to keep your promise."

Ephraim Vargas sighed into the telephone. "I did not say what you would have to do to obtain your freedom. You will not dictate terms to me."

"Listen here. Either you let Troy and me out or I go to Batterson right now and tell him the truth."

"And then I will simply direct my son to shoot your son. It would be very easy."

Al Thomas's stomach clenched. "You mean Troy is out there? In the middle of this thing?"

"He is exactly where I want him to be."

Al took a deep breath. "Either you swear to protect Troy and bring him home safely or I promise I'll bring you down, Vargas."

After another long silence, Vargas made a clicking sound with his tongue. "Here is the deal. You will make sure Angel gets out safely. You must guarantee it. He will not be shot, nor will he be arrested. Is that clear?"

"I understand. And you will guarantee the same for Troy."

"You have my word."

"And you will let us go after this?"

"Yes," Vargas assured, "I will release you from our arrangement. But only if Angel is unharmed."

"Then we have a deal."

Al Thomas ended the call, cursing under his breath. He'd spent his life in law enforcement, an exemplary career. One mistake and Ephraim Vargas had moved in like a tornado, tearing everything apart. Al had stupidly pocketed some of the money from a drug bust so that Troy could go to a good school—one without gangs. Somehow Vargas had found out and threatened to expose him. Since Troy's mother was dead, Troy would have gone into foster care. In the end, the money hadn't helped anyway. Troy had been pulled into a gang, probably under the direction of Vargas himself. Now all Al could do was try to get them out of St. Louis so they could start over. Troy was smart, and he still had a soul—something most gang members seemed to lose somewhere along the way. Al would do anything for him, anything to save him. He felt guilty turning on Richard Batterson, but when choosing between a man he admired and the son he loved, there really wasn't any choice. He'd done the only thing he could do.

He tossed the burner phone he'd used to call Vargas in the

trash and covered it with refuse so no one would find it. Then he prepared himself for a mission that would either save him and his son . . . or destroy their lives forever.

More than once, Mercy felt herself slipping. Her body seemed to be shutting down. It had to be her head injury. She fought to stay focused, but it was a losing battle. She needed help. Keeping her gun trained on Vargas and Ace, she called for Mark. Within a few minutes he came into the room.

"I need to talk to you," she said. Though she didn't want to let Vargas know she was struggling physically, she had to alert Mark before she made a mistake and lost control of the situation.

Mark walked over and stood next to her. When he leaned down, she told him she was in trouble.

"I understand. Let me cuff these two and then I'll watch them while you get some rest."

Mercy didn't want to give into weakness. And even though she fought it with all her strength, she could tell it was a battle beyond her control. She could handle lack of sleep, even injury, but this concussion seemed to have a mind of its own.

Mark went into the kitchen and returned with two more pairs of handcuffs. "This is it," he said. "The cuffs you used on Angel are wrecked, and I used two sets in the kitchen. When Angel gets back, we'll have to find something else."

Mercy nodded. "It will be fine."

Mark gave her a tight smile. "Once the guys return with Tally, I'll tell them if they try to cause trouble, I'll shoot their boss. I doubt that will set well with them—or him." Mark looked over at Vargas. "Good thing you came along for the ride. You're giving us leverage. I'm sure your brother wants you alive."

Vargas didn't say anything, but Mercy noticed his jaw tighten. Good. It was exactly what they needed if they were to pull this off.

Mark grabbed a pillow from the couch and put it on the love seat nearby. "Lay your head down here. That way I can keep an eye on you, Vargas, and Ace at the same time."

Mercy felt like she was letting Mark down. He needed her beside him. It wasn't fair to ask him to guard Vargas and his men alone. Especially since he was injured.

"I'm going to sit up for now," she said through gritted teeth. "I'll try to stay awake. When Angel gets back, wake me up if I happen to nod off. I'm sorry about this, Mark."

"It's not your fault, Mercy. You have a concussion." He pointed at the pillow. "At least put that next to you in case you need to close your eyes. It will be hard for me to catch you if you pass out.

Mercy took his advice and put the pillow against the arm of the love seat. She turned sideways, drawing her knees up and leaning her head back. She struggled to keep her eyes open, but the room began to spin like some kind of crazy carnival ride. Just seconds later, she felt herself drift away.

Mark was growing increasingly worried about Mercy, and he wasn't sure how to help her. He hoped allowing her to get some rest was the answer, but in many cases people with head injuries were encouraged to stay awake.

Was he making a mistake? Would she be all right? He went over to check on her. He gently stroked her head, hoping Vargas would think he was just concerned. Trying to block Vargas's line of sight, he carefully ran his fingers through Mercy's hair, looking to find the flash drive. It wasn't there. She must have moved it, yet he had no idea where. Hopefully, Vargas was convinced it was out in the snow somewhere. Was he still willing to bargain with them for Tally's life? How long would it take Batterson to get here? If the timing was wrong, or if Vargas decided not to play along . . . There were so many things that could go wrong. One thing he knew for certain. Vargas would do whatever he could to leave before Batterson showed up. He had no illusions about being able to withstand an onslaught of trained Marshals.

The pain in Mark's arm was constant now. He had no choice but to bear it and concentrate on his job. He had to keep an eye on Vargas and his gang. Eight against one. He didn't like the odds. As he sat there he tried to come up with a plan to contain things once Angel arrived.

"You will never get out of here alive, you know," Vargas said. "Angel will be back any minute. You have no hope of overpowering all of my men."

Mark smiled at him, trying to look nonchalant. "Well, you're tied up and so are your men. And I have a gun pointed at your head. I don't think it will be a problem. Angel won't allow me to shoot his uncle."

Manuel snorted. "You do not understand us at all, do you? Ephraim runs things, and he has drummed one truth into all of us. The cartel comes first. Not the people. Not even his brother. He would certainly sacrifice him to save the cartel."

"Well, that's just sad," Mark said. "Money before family. What a terrible legacy. Does he feel the same way about his son?"

Mark saw Elias's eyes widen. He'd struck pay dirt. "How about this? If you give me trouble, I'll shoot Angel. Let's see how your brother likes that."

Elias shrugged. "It would not make a difference."

"You're lying."

"I am not. The Vargas cartel is powerful because we will not allow anyone to stop us. No matter the cost."

"You and your men are helpless, and I'm the only one with a gun. It seems you *have* been stopped."

At that moment the sound of a loud engine came from outside. Mark got up and touched Mercy's shoulder. Her eyes opened slowly.

"What's going on?" she asked, slurring her words a little.

"They're back."

Mercy struggled to sit up and grabbed her gun. Mark hated to wake her, but he needed backup, and Mercy wouldn't have understood if he'd left her sleeping.

Mark's gun remained trained on Vargas as he walked backward to the front of the house. Mercy stood and pointed her gun at him as well. Mark prayed she'd be able to cover him if something went wrong. A quick peek out the window revealed the vehicle that had left tracks by the barn. If Mark wasn't trying to appear cool and confident, his jaw would have dropped. It was an Avtoros Shaman 8x8 ATV, an eight-wheeled Russian monster that cost well over a hundred grand. Mark had heard of them, but he'd never seen one up close. No wonder Elias and his men could get around in all the snow and ice. He also noticed a smaller ATV parked next to the house.

The back door of the Avtoros opened, and two men got out. They helped Tally down and supported him so he could walk.

His feet were bare, and a blanket had been placed around his shoulders. Angel got out of the driver's-side door and followed them toward the house. As soon as they pushed the front door open, Mark stepped in front of them.

"Hold it right there," he said. He could only hope Mercy had his back.

Angel's eyes widened with surprise while the others just glared at him. Mark tried to get Tally to look at him, but he seemed disoriented. At least he was alive.

"Get him in that chair," Mark ordered, cocking his head toward a recliner in the corner of the living room.

At first the men just stared at him, but finally they helped Tally to the chair and lowered him into it.

"Now hand over your guns," Mark barked, trying to sound more confident than he felt.

"You're a fool," Angel said. "You have no chance of getting out of here alive."

"So your uncle has informed me. Still, I have a gun and he doesn't."

A large man with dark hair and even darker eyes held his gun out for Mark to take. As he reached for it, the man charged him. Mark fired, hitting him in the chest. At the same time, Angel lunged for Mark and knocked him to the floor. Mark's gun flew across the floor, and he found himself staring up into the barrel of Angel's weapon. He called out for Mercy, but got no response.

"Now let's see who's in charge, shall we?" Angel said, his lips twisted into a cruel smile.

CHAPTER
THIRTY-ONE

Tally awoke to someone calling his name. For a moment he thought it was his mother, but as he tried to force his eyes open, he realized it wasn't her voice he heard. At first everything was fuzzy, and then his vision cleared finally. He found himself looking up into Mercy's face. Her expression registered concern.

"Are you all right?" she asked.

"I . . . I'm fine." He licked his dry lips. "Just sleepy."

"You were out in the cold a long time."

Tally turned his head, even though the action made the room around him tilt. "Where am I?"

"You're back at the house. In one of the bedrooms."

Slowly, Tally remembered being tied up outside in the snow. He'd given up. Believed he was going to die out there. He pushed himself up, ignoring the overwhelming frailty that gripped his body. "Where's Mark? And Vargas?"

"Mark is in the living room with Elias."

"But . . . why are you here?"

"She's making sure you're okay. Once she's convinced you'll live, she'll hand over the flash drive."

Tally looked toward the door and saw Angel Vargas standing there with a gun.

Tally frowned at Mercy. "I don't understand. What . . . what happened?"

"Elias and his men were here when Mark and I got back from searching for you. We took over . . . for a while, but they're in control now. Once you and Mark are safe, I intend to give them the flash drive, Tally. I don't have a choice."

"You found it?"

Mercy nodded.

"You can't do that, Merce. If you do, you'll put law-enforce-ment officers at risk all over the country."

Mercy smiled at him, but Tally could see the resignation in her eyes. She'd made a decision, and she had no intention of being talked out of it.

"Time's up," Angel said. "We need to get out of here before your Marshal friends arrive. Time is running out. If you don't give my uncle that flash drive, he'll kill all of you. Please tell me where it is, Mercy. If you don't help me, I can't protect you."

"Protect me? You have no plans to protect me—or anyone else. First I want you to let Tally and Mark go. You've got two vehicles. Give them one. Once they're out of sight, I'll give you the flash drive."

"My uncle won't go for that. Your only hope is to give it to me. I'll use it to bargain for your life."

"I don't believe you. You don't care anything about me."

"You're wrong, and I think you know that."

Mercy snorted. "Oh, yeah. You showed what you thought of me when you pushed me down the stairs."

"That was an accident. I reached out for you, but I didn't push you. You fell because you pulled away from me."

For the first time, Tally noticed Mercy's drawn face and unfocused eyes. "What's wrong?" he asked.

"I may have a concussion," Mercy said. She shook her head slowly. "It's messing me up. I tried to back Mark up, but I spaced out, Tally. They took my gun."

"She fired at us, only she missed," Angel said. "She needs to be in a hospital. So do you."

"You caused this?" Tally asked, glaring at Angel. Even in his weakened condition, Tally felt anger rising inside him. If he ever got a chance, he'd make Angel Vargas pay for hurting Mercy.

"It really was an accident. I'm not a monster," Angel said. "To be honest, I'd like to see all of you get out of this thing alive. I just don't know if it's possible."

Mercy stood, and Tally could see she was shaky on her feet. "So if we die, you can live with that? That makes you a monster in my book."

Angel's look of compassion slipped as his eyes hardened. "I can live with whatever I have to. It doesn't mean it's what I want. When you're the son of Ephraim Vargas, you don't have a lot of choices in life."

"You told me you learned law-enforcement lingo from a cousin who was with the LAPD," Mercy said. "Seems he made different choices than you did."

"Yes, he did. Two years ago they found his body near the border of Mexico and Texas. His choices cost him his life. I didn't want to suffer the same fate."

"He died a hero. You're living as a coward."

Angel strode up to Mercy and raised his hand, his face tight with anger. Tally struggled to get up so he could protect her. However, instead of striking her, Angel slowly dropped his arm. "You said you wanted to check on Tally," he said, his voice low. "You've done that. Now I need you to go back to the living room before my uncle comes looking for us."

He pointed to a kid sitting in a nearby chair. Tally hadn't noticed him before. Dressed in typical gang clothes, the kid held a gun that was pointed right at him. Under normal circumstances, Tally could easily take him out, but at the moment he felt defenseless. He needed to get his strength back, and he didn't have a lot of time to do it.

Angel pointed his gun at Mercy. She leaned over and kissed Tally lightly on the cheek before turning and leaving the room. Now it was just Tally and the kid.

"I want to get dressed," Tally told him. He pointed to his suitcase sitting on the dresser. "Please. I won't try anything."

The boy nodded. "Just don't make any fast moves. I'll have to shoot you."

Tally could see the trepidation in his eyes. Vargas had probably threatened to kill him if he allowed Tally to escape. Fear was a great motivator, but it was also very dangerous. Reason flew out the window in its presence. Tally would have to be extra careful.

He rose slowly from the bed, gripping the edge of the nightstand to maintain his balance. Once he felt in control, he walked over to the suitcase and flipped it open. After removing clean underwear, jeans, socks, and a shirt, he quickly changed clothes. Almost immediately he felt more like his old self. He'd checked his suitcase for something he could use as a weapon, but there wasn't anything there that could help him. He thought about pocketing his razor or toothbrush, except such things were useless against guns. He pulled out a pair of sneakers he'd tucked into the suitcase's side pocket and sat down on the bed. As he tied the laces, he assessed his situation. He had to get close enough to the kid to overpower him and take his gun. But how? The first thing was to get the boy to trust him. When he finished with his shoes, he leaned back against the headboard and studied the young man. Vargas must not have considered Tally to be dangerous if he put this kid in charge of watching him.

"How many men does Vargas have?" he asked. "He can't have much help if he put you in here with me."

"Mark shot one of his guys. Now there are just seven of them including me."

"How many other gangbangers like you?"

"One. The guy Mark shot was Deeray. He was in the Rollin' 60s."

Tally was surprised the kid was so forthcoming with him. And something else. He'd called Mark by his name. What was up with that?

"You know he won't keep you and your friend around, right? Once he gets his hands on the flash drive, you're both dead."

"No. He knows my father—he won't let anything happen to me."

"Who's your father?"

The kid shook his head. "I can't tell you."

Tally shrugged. Probably some dope dealer the cartel dealt with. "Vargas isn't too good about keeping promises. He promised to protect Darius Johnson, and he's dead."

"Darius was stupid."

"You're right. Because he trusted Vargas."

"There's nothing I can do." The kid gulped and lowered his voice. "I tried to help Mark, but Vargas got him anyway."

Tally struggled to keep the surprise from his expression. What was he talking about? "How did you try to help Mark?"

The kid's lips thinned as if he regretted what he'd just said. "Look . . . What's your name?"

"Troy. Troy Thomas."

Interesting. No gang moniker. The kid gave his real name.

"Okay, Troy. Tell me how you tried to help Mark." Tally's patience was wearing thin, but he worked to keep his voice steady. He needed to gain Troy's confidence, and time was running out.

Troy glanced toward the door. He got up and opened it a few inches, peering through the crack to make sure it was safe to talk.

Tally could hardly believe his good fortune. A gang member who wanted to help the cops? Except for drug-addicted CIs who needed a break to stay out of jail, this was a first.

"I told him there was someone in his office who's hooked up with Vargas."

"And who is that?"

"I can't tell you," he said again.

"You realize our lives are at stake, right?"

Troy stared at him for several seconds. Tally stared back at him until finally Troy looked away. "I don't know what to do."

"I think you do. I can only see one chance here. If you give me the gun, I promise to keep you safe."

To Tally's surprise, tears slipped down Troy's face.

"Hey," Tally said, "I see you're not a punk. Let me help you."

"I . . . I don't want to die. And I don't want my father to die."

"Why would your father die? Does he work for Vargas?"

Troy shook his head. "No. Vargas makes him do things . . . because of me."

Tally frowned at the kid. "I'm sorry, Troy. I don't understand."

Troy wiped the tears from his face with his free hand, the one not holding the gun. "He uses people. Threatens their families. It's not right."

"So Vargas has threatened your dad?"

Troy nodded.

Tally took a deep breath. "Troy, the only way I can help you and your dad is if you give me that gun. My friends and I can take control of this situation so we can all get out of here. There's no other way. Unless we do that, we're all going to die. I'm sure of it."

"Will you keep my dad safe too?"

Tally nodded. "Sure. I'll do my best. What's his name?"

"You might know him," Troy said softly.

"Really?"

"He's a deputy U.S. Marshal. His name is Al Thomas."

Even though Tally had prepared himself to stay calm, he was left shocked. Al Thomas? He didn't know him personally, but he certainly knew who he was. So this was the mole? He had to let Mark and Mercy know as soon as possible. If Batterson had sent people on a rescue mission, Al would know about it. He was one of Batterson's top agents.

Troy's expression mirrored the panic he obviously felt. "My dad did everything he could to keep me safe, but I got involved in a gang anyway. Darius made me feel ashamed of my father. Said he hurt people for no reason. I know now he was lying.

Vargas wanted my father to do stuff for him. He told my father I'd get hurt unless he did everything he told him." Troy shook his head slowly. "I don't want something to happen to me or my dad before I tell him I'm sorry. I'm not ashamed of him. I'm proud of my dad, and I want him to know I love him. I just want another chance. For both of us."

Tally was moved by Troy's words. He could see his own son's fear in the boy's eyes, and he hated it. Hated that Josh worried every time he left the house, worried that he might not come back. Being in law enforcement wasn't a solo gig. Everyone who loved you was involved—even if they didn't want to be.

"I know who your dad is, Troy, and I'll do everything in my power to help him. Now you've got to give me the gun, okay? We're running out of time."

"He isn't going to be giving you no gun."

Tally looked over at the door. One of Vargas's men stood there, holding a weapon. Before Tally could respond, Troy pointed his gun at the man and fired.

CHAPTER
THIRTY-TWO

When they heard the shot, Mercy reacted first, leaping up from the love seat and slamming her body into one of Vargas's henchmen. Mark dropped and rolled on the floor, grasping for the gun that flew out of the man's hand. As soon as he had it, he flipped over on his back. Vargas's thug charged him. Mark fired, and the guy fell like a sack of potatoes. Then Mark jumped to his feet and trained his gun on Vargas.

"Drop it, Mark!" Angel yelled. Angel's gun was aimed at Mark's head.

"You know I can't do that," Mark said. "But if you put your gun down, I won't kill your uncle. It's your choice."

Angel swung his gun around until it was pointed at Mercy. "If you put *your* gun down, I won't shoot Mercy."

Mark checked out the one remaining thug Vargas had—and Ace. Neither one of them was armed. Mark had tossed out most of their weapons, so they were limited. But Mercy's gun lay on the coffee table, only a couple of feet away from Vargas's enforcer. If he moved quickly enough . . .

"Put the gun down, Angel."

Mark looked to his left, relieved to see Tally, his weapon pointed at the younger Vargas.

"I'll only ask once."

Angel slowly lowered his weapon.

"Hand it to Mercy."

Mercy went over to where Angel stood. She took the gun from his hand and then pointed it at his face. "You would have shot me?" she asked quietly.

Angel didn't answer, just looked away from her.

"All of you on the couch," Mark said. "I want you where I can keep an eye on you."

Ace and the remaining Vargas thug they'd called Manuel joined Angel and Elias on the couch.

Mercy ran over to Tally and hugged him. "I'm so glad you're okay."

Tally hugged her back, still keeping his gun aimed at Vargas. "How are you doing?" he asked her.

"A little better now, but I don't trust myself completely. You and Mark need to keep an eye on me. I still drift in and out."

"Who was shot?" Mark asked. "Is Troy all right?"

Tally shrugged. "He's alive, but he shot one of Vargas's men. Pretty tough thing for a kid to handle. I moved the body to another room and told Troy to stay in the bedroom for now. Until we're sure it's safe for him to come out."

"Good." Mark couldn't believe Troy had shot someone, but he couldn't deal with that now. He had to focus on the immediate threat.

"Mark, we need to talk," Tally said, his tone low and serious.

Mark nodded. "Mercy, can you hold them for just a minute?"

"Yeah. Just don't take too long."

"Don't worry," Mark said. "I'll stay where I can see you."

He and Tally walked a few feet away. Not far enough to lose sight of their enemies, but far enough that they wouldn't be overheard.

"I know who the mole is," Tally said softly when Mark indicated it was okay to speak.

"I do too. I talked to Batterson earlier. They're on their way here."

"How will they reach us?"

"I have no idea," Mark said, "but Batterson will figure it out. We just need to control these guys until he finds us."

"Where's the flash drive?"

Mark shook his head. "I honestly don't know. And I don't want to know. Mercy hid it somewhere. Better if we don't have information Vargas and his men want."

Tally sighed deeply. Mark could tell he was relieved. So long as they held off Vargas and his thugs, they would make it out of this alive.

"I never would have suspected Carol as the mole," Mark said.

Tally's expression changed. "Carol? Carol Marchand? You think she's the mole?"

"Yes. That came from Batterson himself. We got through to him on the landline and called for help."

Tally frowned at him. "That kid, Troy? He said he tried to help you."

"That's right. He got caught up in this, but I think he's a good kid. I'm hoping we can do something to help him and his dad."

Tally was silent for a moment. Finally he said, "Mark, do you know who Troy's dad is?"

"No. Who?"

"Troy is Al Thomas's son. His father has been working for Vargas. Under duress, but we can't trust him."

Mark couldn't believe his ears. He knew Al Thomas. A good man. A good Marshal. How could he be involved with Vargas? As soon as he asked himself the question, he knew the answer. The same way men like Vargas accomplished anything—through intimidation. He probably threatened him. Threatened Troy. Mark doubted money would have swayed Al, though Batterson had alluded to it being the reason for Carol's betrayal. Mark still had a hard time believing Carol had turned her back on Batterson. Now he had to face the fact that Vargas had turned a good Marshal. The knowledge made him feel sick to his stomach.

"We've got to let Batterson know. He might be bringing Al with him." Mark pulled his cellphone out of his pocket and checked it again. Still no signal.

"You said the landline is working?"

Mark nodded. "I'll try Batterson's cell again. If I can't get ahold of him, I'm not sure what to do next."

"Listen, Mark, just because Al can't be trusted doesn't mean the rest of the people who work in your office are traitors."

"I know that, but so far two of them have completely fooled me. I would have bet my life on Carol or Al. At this moment I'm not sure who I can count on."

"Then let me call my chief. He can get word to Batterson. He's smart, and he'll do it right."

Mark considered this. The St. Louis police chief was a man well-respected by those in law enforcement. If anyone could handle this situation besides Batterson, it was Chief Kennedy.

"Sounds like a good idea. Go ahead and call him."

Mark and Tally walked back over to where Vargas and his men waited. Mark sat down next to Mercy. "How are you feeling now?" he asked her.

"Better. Still tired and a little fuzzy, but I'll make it. Sorry I let you down earlier."

"Forget it. The important thing is that we're in control now and we have the guns. If we can just hold out long enough, we have a chance of going home alive."

"Mark."

Mark turned to see Tally standing at the edge of the kitchen. His expression made it clear something was wrong.

"What is it?" Mark asked.

"The phone. Looks like no one will be calling anyone on it."

Still keeping his gun pointed at the men, Mark hurried over to check the phone. It lay in pieces on the kitchen counter. He walked into the living room and glared at Elias. "What did you do?"

Elias shrugged and tossed Mark a self-righteous grin. "I contacted my people—who know where we are, by the way—and asked them to pull us out of here before your friends arrive. I'm sorry to tell you that you and your team will not be left alive. The phone was insurance against a situation . . . just like this one. You are certainly not the last honest law-enforcement officer in the world, but after today the number will decrease."

"I thought you wanted that flash drive."

"I know the flash drive is here somewhere," Elias said. "Even if Mercy Brennan dies, we will still find it."

"I don't believe you."

"That is not my problem. Your deaths are now more important to me than that video."

Mark was almost certain Vargas was lying, yet it was clear he intended to kill all of them. Whether it was right away or after he tortured them for information was the only question remaining. Their only hope was that Batterson would find and rescue them in time.

Mark turned to catch Tally's eye. His expression was grim. It was now a race. Who would get here first? Who would be left standing at the end of the day?

Batterson's frustration level rose with each sweep of the area. Where was his team?

"What do you want to do?" Sergeant Davis Bullock turned his head to stare at Batterson.

Not wanting to yell over the noise of the engine and the blades overhead, Batterson made a circular motion with his hand, meaning *go around again.*

While the sergeant didn't argue, Batterson could tell he was ready to quit. They'd flown over the same area four times and hadn't found anything that looked like the property Mark had described. He'd tried to call Mark back, but the phone number he had wasn't working. Neither was Mark's cellphone. In fact, he couldn't get through to anyone. A check with their phone carrier revealed that the ice storm had knocked out all the cell towers in the area. It would be a day or two at least before they were up and running again.

Out of irritation Batterson leaned forward and tapped the sergeant on the shoulder. "Add another mile to the search area. We've got to find them."

The sergeant nodded as he moved the cyclic stick, causing the helicopter to head out of the pattern they'd been in.

As Batterson and his team searched the land below, Bullock's partner manned the searchlight. They'd only been looking about fifteen minutes when Shauna yelled out. Batterson looked to find her pointing at something on the other side of the helicopter. Batterson tapped Bullock once again and gestured to the spot Shauna indicated. Bullock banked the helicopter and circled the area. The searchlight picked up a large house with a barn. The helicopter dropped lower, and Batterson spotted two all-terrain vehicles parked outside the house. This had to be the right place. He was getting ready to tell Bullock to find somewhere to land when the sergeant pointed at something to their right.

Batterson noticed another helicopter headed their way. Before he could tell Bullock to start evasive maneuvers, something struck the outside of their helicopter. They swayed violently in the air. Another blast punctured the window next to Bullock, and they began spinning wildly in a circle. Batterson could see that Bullock had been hit.

As the helicopter nose-dived toward the ground, Richard Batterson prayed for the second time that day.

CHAPTER
THIRTY-THREE

Mercy saw the flash of light outside before the loud blast that followed it. She grabbed her gun and ran to the front door.

"Keep your eye on them," she called to Mark and Tally. If Vargas and his people believed they were on the verge of rescue, it might give them the confidence to try something foolhardy and dangerous. At that moment, Mercy didn't trust herself or her reflexes.

She turned off the front porch light and stepped outside. In the distance she could see two helicopters. One was obviously in trouble. It turned in circles, getting closer and closer to the ground. It rose then, and the two copters seemed to confront each other. As they moved past the tree line across the road, Mercy could barely make them out. She heard another explosion, and one of the copters swung back and forth in a crazy arc before disappearing from sight. As she peered into the blackness, all of a sudden the ground shook and a huge ball of fire lit up the sky. It was obvious one of the copters had crashed.

Mercy prayed that their only way out hadn't just hit the

ground. If that were the case, they were in big trouble. She glanced up into the night sky.

"God, if you're there, and if you care anything about us, can you please help? Even if you just save Mark and Tally, that would be enough for me. But if you could find it in your heart to give me another chance too, I'd appreciate it. Uh, thank you." She had no idea if her prayer would do any good, or if anyone was really listening, but it was the best she could do right now. She went back into the house.

"What's going on?" Mark asked.

Not wanting Vargas to hear, she gestured for him to come to where she waited. When he drew near, she leaned in close and told him what she'd just seen. "I have no idea which helicopter was ours," she whispered, "but we need to prepare. Either we're going to be rescued, or they're coming to kill us."

"Remember, they still want the flash drive, no matter what Elias says. And we have it and Ephraim Vargas's son."

"Hard to bargain with someone when we can't communicate. They may come in here shooting first and asking questions later."

Mark nodded. "We've got to stop them from breaching the house. If they get in . . ."

"Our only hope is that they'll try to protect Elias and Angel. That might be just enough hesitation for us to take them down. Hopefully it'll be Batterson and not Vargas's men who come through that door."

"I can only pray you're right. But we have to prepare ourselves as if you're wrong. Even if it *is* Batterson, we still have a problem." He quickly told her about Al Thomas.

"I . . . I can't believe it." Mercy shook her head. "Does he know his son is here?"

"I have no idea. If he does, he'll try to protect him. But if he doesn't . . ."

"What's going on?" Tally asked. He looked nervous, as did the men sitting on the couch.

Mercy looked at Mark. What should they say in front of Elias Vargas? Mercy walked back toward the living room. "We need to be prepared, Tally," she said firmly. "No matter who shows up."

Tally frowned, but he didn't say anything. Mercy wondered if he understood what she was trying to tell him.

The only chance they had would come from Batterson, but with Al Thomas on the team, anything could happen. Mercy wished she knew what Al intended to do. Would he act on Vargas's behalf, or would he support the Marshals he was sworn to protect? "Let's get prepared," she said. "We need to watch both the front and back entrances. They might try to come up the stairs to the deck and through the kitchen."

Mark hesitated. "You saw the crash. Could anyone have walked away?"

She shook her head. "Doesn't mean someone didn't bail out first." She heard the doubt in her own voice. The truth was, there hadn't been much time. It was unlikely anyone had survived the awful crash.

Mark sighed as he went into the kitchen to turn on the back-yard lights.

"Now what?" Tally asked when he returned.

"We get ready for battle," Mark said. He motioned to Elias. "Get up."

Elias stayed put. "Why?" he asked.

"You're our insurance."

The man didn't move, so Mark went over and grabbed him by the arm. "I told you to get up."

"What are you thinking?" Mercy asked.

"We put this scum near the front door. His people won't shoot right away. Not if they run the risk of hitting him."

Elias snorted. "You are delusional. They will not care about me. They only want two things: you and the flash drive. I am simply collateral damage."

"Maybe," Mercy said, catching Mark's idea, "but Angel isn't. His father won't want anything to happen to him."

Mark nodded. "Move them both near the front door." He looked at Tally. "Put the other two by the back door. You watch that entrance."

After grabbing Elias and Angel, Mark and Mercy planted them in two chairs at the front entrance.

Tally secured Manuel and Ace near the door to the deck, tying them to kitchen chairs. "What about the basement door?" Tally asked.

"I'll check it," Mercy said. "So long as it's locked, it should hold. If they do try to come in that way, we'll hear them. We'll take them out before they reach us."

"I need to tell Troy what's going on," Tally said. "I'll be right back."

"Tell him to hide," Mercy said. "No matter what happens, he needs to stay safe. If our people come in, we'll have to secure his father immediately. There won't be time to—"

Before Mercy could finish her thought, Mark shouted. "Here they come!"

Mercy ran toward the front door, her gun drawn. Mark got down on one knee. He faced the door, his weapon ready. Mercy glanced at him once before the door shattered and men with automatic weapons entered the room. But their guns were pointing down, and their attitude was anything but combative.

Mercy immediately recognized Shauna Sparlin and Tom Monnier. The two Marshals were silent as they dropped their weapons to the floor and kicked them away. As they put their hands behind their heads, Mercy, Tally, and Mark kept their guns trained on them, not sure what to do next.

Then Batterson came through the door with his hands up. Al Thomas stood behind him, the barrel of his weapon pressed up against Batterson's back.

"Put your guns down," Al called out. "Now. I don't want to shoot the chief."

"Don't listen to him," Batterson said. "Do your job."

Batterson hit the floor, leaving Al exposed. It was the perfect time to take him out, but right before she took the shot, Mercy heard another voice.

"Dad!"

She spun around to see Troy standing on the other side of the room, staring at his father.

"Get up," Al yelled at Batterson. He grabbed him by the collar and jerked him to his feet, once again using Batterson as a shield.

Mercy had lost the moment. Had her hesitation cost them their lives? Had she just made another mistake—like the night she was shot?

Mark and Mercy looked at each other. What could they do? They didn't want to shoot Troy's father right in front of him, but they couldn't let Vargas go free. They were all dead if that happened.

"Troy, go back to the bedroom," Tally said, "and stay there until I come for you."

"Please, son, do what he says."

Even though Mercy was furious with Al Thomas's betrayal, she couldn't help but feel compassion for him. His tortured expression showed the conflict in his soul. She decided to use it to their advantage.

"Al," she said evenly, "we'll get you and Troy out of St. Louis. Give you a fresh start. You know we can do it. Just step away from the chief. You don't want to do this."

Al shook his head. "It's too late for that. I'll go to prison. I can't let that happen. I'm all Troy has."

"We can make a deal, Al," Batterson said. "We can keep you out of prison. If you help us take down Vargas, I guarantee the state will work with you. Ending the Vargas cartel is huge. You know that."

"Please, Dad," Troy said. "I'm sorry for getting you in trouble. Please take the deal."

"If you betray me, your son will pay the price," Elias said, his words spoken with staccato precision. "We have long arms. Even if you manage to take us in, the Vargas cartel will survive. However, you and your son will not."

"Shut up," Tally said. "Troy, please go back to the bedroom."

Tally was trying to get the kid to safety just in case something went wrong. For the first time, Mercy noticed Shauna's rifle lying just a few feet from where Troy stood. Obviously, Tally had seen it too and wanted Troy as far away from it as he could get. Troy had just taken a step back as if he were going to the bedroom when Angel jumped up and grabbed the gun out of Al's holster. Somehow he'd managed to free himself of his bindings. As if in slow motion, Mercy saw Troy pick up Shauna's rifle and point it at Angel. Before she could stop him, Troy pulled the trigger. His shot went wild, over Angel's head. Angel fired back, his reaction automatic. As soon as the bullet hit Troy, Angel cried out. He threw his gun down and ran over to the teen, who was lying on the floor.

"I didn't mean to shoot him," Angel kept saying, over and over.

Tally ran past Mercy and dropped to his knees next to Troy. He started administering CPR, but Mercy could tell that it was too late. Nothing could help Troy now.

"I'm sorry," Angel said. "I just reacted. I didn't mean . . ."

Those were the last words Angel Vargas ever said. Al Thomas began firing into Angel's body, his face a contorted mask of grief.

Tally stood slowly. He was covered with Troy's and Angel's blood. He forcibly took the gun from Al's hands. Then he slumped back down on the floor and began to cry.

CHAPTER
THIRTY-FOUR

"I want to commend you both for your exemplary work in this situation," Batterson said.

Two weeks had passed since the confrontation in Piedmont. Mercy had spent six days in the hospital being treated for a concussion. Afterward, Batterson sent her home to rest and recover while insisting she see Dr. Abbot and complete her sessions. Surprisingly, Dr. Abbot seemed to be helping her. Mark teased her that it only took being captured by a dangerous cartel and suffering a concussion to get her to open up. Even though he wasn't serious, there was more truth to his statement than he realized. Facing the possibility of losing the people she loved had broken something open inside her. Mercy felt she'd lost enough already. She wasn't ready to lose anything else.

Hearing God speak to her in the middle of a blinding snowstorm had changed her. Though she might be tempted to chalk it up to her imagination, she knew deep in her heart that God had reached out and touched her. There was no more doubt in her mind that He was real and that He'd heard her desperate prayer for help. Mercy could feel healing happening inside her—in the deepest, darkest places of pain. It was as if God held the key to everything that had kept her in bondage since she was a child. The little girl was healing—as was the woman.

Mark had spent a week and a half in the hospital after infection set into his gunshot wound, but when he got out, he and Mercy spent a lot of time talking. Mark had to tell her something that was difficult for her to hear. Batterson had worried that she might be the mole because Nick had kept some of the money given to him by Darius Johnson. He'd set up a bank account in Mercy's name. While it was the wrong thing to do, Mark believed Nick's love for his daughter was so strong that he'd convinced himself it was okay. It was Nick's desperate last attempt to let Mercy know he cared for her, a way to take care of the daughter he'd abandoned.

At first Mercy was angry when she found out what Nick had done. How could he do something so stupid? But with Mark's help, even though she couldn't respect Nick's actions, she realized that her father was human. Imperfect. With time she knew she would come to forgive him.

She realized too that Batterson was talking and so forced herself to concentrate on what he was saying. She would have plenty of time to sort out her feelings about Nick later.

". . . back to full-time duty." He frowned. "Is that all right with you?"

Mercy wasn't really certain what he'd just said, but she nodded anyway. "Yes, sir."

Batterson leaned back in his chair and sighed. "We lost a good man in Al Thomas. We need to keep a closer watch over our people. Vargas used Carol and Al against us. That can never happen again."

"What about the cartel?" Mark asked. "I know charges are being filed against Elias. What about Ephraim? Is there enough evidence against him to end his activities?"

Batterson grinned. "There is now. You remember Manuel? The Vargas thug you almost shot?"

Mark nodded.

"Well, his real name is Mario Cortez. He's the undercover fed who's been embedded in the Vargas cartel for the past three years. He's got the goods on them. Everything. The cartel has imploded."

Mercy's mouth dropped open. "So he's the guy who was deep undercover? Why didn't he tell us who he was? Wow . . . what if we'd taken him out?" As soon as she asked why they hadn't been informed, she knew the answer. He couldn't risk blowing his cover. Not until he was confident Ephraim Vargas couldn't wiggle out of a conviction.

"We appreciate your not shooting him," Batterson said dryly. "Mario worked hard to stay out of the line of fire. And he was able to keep his undercover identity intact throughout the entire operation. But in the end, with the video you turned over to the feds, it was obvious the time had come to step forward. He has detailed records of Vargas's activities and drug pals. It's over for Ephraim. The feds also cut a deal with Elias, and he's turned on his brother. We don't have to worry about the Vargas cartel anymore." He shook his head. "Of course, another one will jump in and take its place. So long as there are gangs, illegal drugs, and cartels, we'll be fighting to keep their influence out of our cities. Too often it's a losing battle. I'm happy we won for once."

"What will happen to Al and Carol?"

Batterson shrugged. "Not sure. We'll do what we can to help Al, but I'm not inclined to speak up for Carol. Al was trying to protect his son. Carol betrayed us for the money."

"She said it was for Marlon," Mercy said.

"I don't buy it," Batterson said. "She could have come to me for help. Down through the years, I've worked with her when she needed it. She might have tried to convince herself it was for Marlon, but I think Carol was in it for herself."

"What about Marlon?" Mark asked.

"He's staying with us for now. We applied to be foster parents and were accepted. When Carol is finally free, maybe she can mend things with her son." Batterson stood, a sign that they were dismissed.

Mark rose from his chair and held out his hand. Batterson shook it. "Thanks, Chief.

"Thank you both." He shook hands with Mercy as well. "I'm proud of you. Sorry you ended up in that situation. I never thought things would go so wrong. You two—and Lieutenant Tally—deserve the credit for our excellent results."

"I wish Troy hadn't died," Mercy said. "Or the real Detective Jess Medina. They both deserved better."

"I agree," Batterson said. "But their deaths weren't your fault. If anyone is to blame, it's me. If I'd just gotten a team to the correct address a little sooner, Troy might still be alive."

"There's plenty of blame to go around," Mark said, "and it doesn't rest with you." He raised a hand when Batterson tried to protest. "I know, I know. The buck stops here. But it wasn't your fault Carol turned on us. Nor was it your fault Al made the choices he did. Let's put the blame where it belongs—on the cartel."

"Sounds good to me," Mercy said. "Dr. Abbot says I need to give myself a break. How about we all give ourselves a break? We did the best we could under the circumstances. No one can do more than that."

Mark laughed lightly. "Did you just say that? Who are you, and what have you done with Mercy Brennan?"

Mercy smiled. "I'm not sure. It may take us a while to answer those questions."

Mark looked into her eyes. "I have all the time in the world."

Tally watched the front door of the café, waiting for Mercy. Even though it had been only a couple of weeks since they were rescued from the house near Piedmont, it felt like a lifetime ago. He was still trying to deal with Troy's death. At first, he blamed himself, but Annie had finally convinced him he wasn't responsible. Still, he wished he could have saved the kid.

He'd come home determined to open up the lines of communication between Josh and him. They'd had several good conversations. Josh was still worried about him, but Tally did his best to explain how important protecting the public was. He told Josh that there were other kids out there who also wanted their fathers to come home, and the police were there to make sure that happened. Josh seemed to understand. A promise that Tally would do everything he could to stay safe helped too.

He'd kept in touch with Al. He felt that by being supportive of Troy's father, it was helping Troy in the only way he could. Al was in a dark place and would face charges for killing Angel, and it would take time for him to recover from losing his son. But with a lot of help, Tally believed, Al would make it.

The front door opened, and Mercy walked in with Mark behind her. Tally couldn't help but smile when he saw her. She had changed since Piedmont, and it made him happy to see her so free. It had been a long time coming.

"Hey," he said as they approached the table. "Been a while, Mark. You look much better."

Mark smiled as he sat down. "I slept for twenty hours straight after they put me in the hospital. That probably helped me more than anything else."

Mercy laughed. "I think cleaning the infection out of your system was an important part of your recovery too."

"Maybe so, but sleep felt a lot better than that did."

"Are you both back on active duty?" Tally asked.

"Starting tomorrow," Mark replied. "Today's our last day to be lazy."

"We're going to the zoo after lunch," Mercy said. "Do you want to join us?"

Tally shook his head. "Too cold. For some reason, spending the day outside in freezing weather doesn't really appeal to me."

Mercy grinned. "That experience didn't help much with your phobia, did it?"

"Actually, you might be surprised."

"What do you mean?"

"I found that in the worst of circumstances, God is faithful. He took care of me. Did you know that when I was out in the snow, Annie knew something was wrong? God told her to pray for my safety. It must have worked because here I am."

"Does this mean you're going back to church?" Mercy asked.

"Yep. Now that I don't have to keep an eye on you, I want to be a good example to my kids. I don't want to just go to church. I want them to have a dad who lives for God—who's a good example of what a father should be."

Mercy smiled at him. "I'll be going to church with Mark in a couple of weeks."

Tally chuckled, surprised by Mercy's announcement. "*You're* going to church?"

"Very funny. Here's something that will really shock you— Friday night I'm going to church with my mom. And I'm going to check out that recovery group she's in." She shrugged. "Seems I do have a few . . . issues to deal with."

Tally leaned back in his chair. "I'm proud of you, Merce. That's wonderful." He looked back and forth between her and Mark. "And you guys?"

"Well, we're taking it one day at a time," Mark said, "trying to figure out what God wants us to do. But I'm hopeful."

"So with all these changes, are you finally ready to let Pippin move in?" Tally asked, grinning at her.

Mercy sighed. "If he doesn't, I'm not sure what I'll do with all the dog toys waiting for him at my place."

Tally shook his head. "Wow, you really have changed."

"And what about you, Tally?" Mercy asked. "What have you decided about the force?"

"When Troy died, I felt so . . . hopeless. Another kid lost to criminals. I decided that if anything good could come from his death, I would have to help other kids stay out of trouble. Save all the Troys I can. Let them know they're important to the world—and to God. I can't do that if I walk away. So I'm staying."

Mercy nodded and stared down at the table. "I'm so glad to hear that."

Tally studied her for a moment. Finally he said, "Merce, look at me."

When she raised her head, he was shocked to see tears on her cheeks. "Merce, you're crying. I can't believe it!"

Mark reached over and took her hand. "Frosty the Snow Cop is dead," he said softly. "Long live Mercy Brennan."

Tally smiled as he gazed at his friends. "Amen," he said. "Amen."

ACKNOWLEDGMENTS

Writing this book took me down a new path in my writing career. Yet it is a familiar path because it's the realization of a desire in my heart for many, many years. Writing stories about law enforcement is a joy and a privilege, but it is also a challenge. There are a few people to thank, without whom I could never have made it past page one.

First of all, my heartfelt thanks and lifelong gratitude goes to retired U.S. Deputy Marshal Paul Anderson. After agreeing to help this clueless but passionate author, he began to bring life to my characters and my story. He is without a doubt one of those treasures authors pray for. I absolutely couldn't have written this book without him. He has given me a glimpse into the lives of the U.S. Marshals, and I will never be able to repay him.

Thank you, Paul, for your incredible responses to my simple questions. Working with you has been like taking a crash course in law enforcement. I hope we will work together for a long time to come. God bless you.

I also want to thank Officer Darin Hickey with the Training and Community Affairs Division in Cape Girardeau, Missouri. He has been an invaluable resource and has given me a glimpse into the lives of police officers in Missouri. I will never forget his heartfelt and poignant description of an officer's funeral. Since the officer was also his friend, I know it cost him something to share it with me. I am so grateful. May we never forget those in law enforcement who are gone. They will always twinkle like stars in the heavens, still watching us, still on guard.

Thank you, Carol Halbert, for introducing me to Darin. You're a doll, Carol!

My love to my wonderful daughter-in-law, Shaen Mehl, for her touching poem. She is such a great writer. One day I hope to help introduce her first book to readers.

I am blessed to work with one of the best editors in the business. Raela Schoenherr has been a bright light in my life for many years now. Thank you for reining in my unbridled passion and reminding me how to keep my story first and my opinions second. A great editor has the ability to tell you what you don't want to hear—and make you grateful for the lesson. I'm so thankful God brought you into my life.

As always, my deep appreciation to my Inner Circle. You all keep me enthused and encouraged. Love you guys!

My thanks to two people who helped to spark my passion for law enforcement. Trish Dennison and her husband, Doug, are my heroes. They have dedicated themselves to letting those in law enforcement know how valuable they are to us. I pray more and more people will stand up and support the men and women who put their lives on the line to protect us. Thanks, Trish and Doug.

In *Fatal Frost*, I mention a ministry that is touching the lives of those who are dealing with pain from the past or who may be battling addictions. The name of this ministry is Celebrate

Recovery. Please check them out. If you need help, you can find out more at www.celebraterecovery.com.

Most of all, I want to offer praise to my Best Friend for never giving up on me. Though I sometimes stumble, you've always held out your hand and helped me up. I pray I will stumble less and less and that you will be glorified more and more. It's still all about *you*.

ABOUT THE AUTHOR

Nancy Mehl is the author of more than twenty books, including the ROAD TO KINGDOM and FINDING SANCTUARY series. She received the ACFW Mystery Book of the Year Award in 2009. She has a background in social work and is a member of ACFW and RWA. Nancy writes from her home in Missouri, where she lives with her husband, Norman, and their puggle, Watson. To learn more, visit NancyMehl.com.

Sign up for Nancy's newsletter!

Keep up to date with news on Nancy's upcoming book releases and events by signing up for her email list at nancymehl.com

More From Nancy Mehl

The small, primarily Mennonite town of Sanctuary, Missouri, is something of a refuge. In this private community, many secrets dwell undetected. As three young women investigate mysteries centered here, each will unknowingly put her life—and her heart—in jeopardy.

FINDING SANCTUARY: *Gathering Shadows, Deadly Echoes, Rising Darkness*

⬦ BETHANYHOUSE

You May Also Enjoy . . .

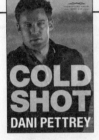